THE DISTANT CHASE

Also by Cap Daniels

THE
DISTANT CHASE

CHASE FULTON NOVEL #5

CAP DANIELS

ANCHOR WATCH
PUBLISHING
** USA **

The Distant Chase
Chase Fulton Novel #5
Cap Daniels

This is a work of fiction. Names, characters, places, historical events, and incidents are the product of the author's imagination or have been used fictitiously. Although many locations such as marinas, airports, hotels, restaurants, etc. used in this work actually exist, they are used fictitiously and may have been relocated, exaggerated, or otherwise modified by creative license for the purpose of this work. Although many characters are based on personalities, physical attributes, skills, or intellect of actual individuals, all of the characters in this work are products of the author's imagination.

Published by:

** USA **

13 Digit ISBN: 978-1-7323024-7-1
Library of Congress Control Number: 2019935279
Copyright © 2019 Cap Daniels—All Rights Reserved

Cover Design: German Creative

Printed in the United States of America

Dedication

This book is dedicated to…

My brother, Dennis, upon whom, Dennis Crowe, a character in this novel is based.

Dennis and I are products of a well-respected, mannerly family whose expectations we didn't always meet. It is safe to say that Dennis and I have, over the years, taken turns being the black sheep, and have occasionally provided our family with dual, simultaneous black sheep. From Dennis, I learned that life isn't always about meeting the expectations of others; sometimes it's about making the absolute most of the moment and savoring the rewards thereof, with disregard for the consequences. I'll always be indebted to him for teaching me this lesson, for adherence to that idea has resulted in some of the most unforgettable moments of my life, many of which appear in these novels. Well-mannered, well-behaved boys rarely have great stories at the ends of their lives. Thank you, Dennis, for inspiring me to reach the fifth decade of my life with a headful of magnificent stories…some of which are far too spectacular to be fiction.

Special Thanks To:

My Astonishing Editor:
Sarah Flores—Write Down the Line, LLC
www.WriteDowntheLine.com

Sarah has become far more than a hired editor for me. She has devoted countless hours teaching me why and how our language works,
inspiring me to hone my craft, and forcing me to expect nothing
short of excellence in everything I write. She is brilliant, stubborn,
dedicated, emotionally invested, and an integral part of the creation
of this series. Without her, my work would be unreadable.

Table of Contents

The Distant Chase

CAP DANIELS

Chapter 1
First Fight

November 2, 1944. RAF Bodney, Norfolk, England.

I don't think I've ever been so scared in my life. I wonder if it'll get easier next time. It wasn't dying that scared me. It was more like fear of the unknown. What was down there in those frozen woods other than hundreds of thousands of Germans?

I got here three days ago. It was Halloween, so I guess it stands to rights that I should be scared. I checked in, and they assigned me an airplane—the prettiest plane I've ever seen. At first, I thought I'd be flying the P-40, but I did well enough to qualify in the Mustang, and I guess they needed pilots for it, so here I am. I couldn't believe my eyes when they showed me that big, beautiful P-51 Mustang, shiny silver all over except for the dark-blue nose. That's why they call us the Blue Nosed Bastards of Bodney. There's no mistaking one of our Mustangs.

We took off this morning before daylight. The range on these Mustangs is unbelievable—we can stay in the air over eight hours. No other fighter in the world can do that. We flew a penetration into Germany to pick up a squadron of B-24

Liberators, and we were supposed to escort them to Merseburg to blow an airfield off the map and then fly back home. But we never made that rendezvous with our bombers.

I was Chalk Four in a four-plane formation led by Captain Donny Burnes. There were sixteen of us altogether, and Donny was the flight commander. He likes to keep the new guys close to him for the first couple of missions. At least that's what they told me. That's how I got to be in formation with him.

About two hours into the penetration, before we ever saw the bombers, we came upon a huge flight of ME-109 Messerschmitt fighters. There must have been fifty or more of those things. Captain Burnes gave the order to go balls to the wall and dive on the 109s, and that's what we did. I shoved everything forward and nosed over into the first real dogfight of my life.

The krauts never saw us coming, and we never slowed down until we were in gun range. I saw Donny's tracers streak through the sky when he started firing. Nobody ever gave the order to shoot, but we didn't need an order. As soon as we saw Donny light up that first kraut, there was no keeping our fingers off those triggers. I singled out a Messerschmitt, pulled a little lead on him, and squeezed the trigger. The cannons thundered in my wings, and I watched my tracers tear into the German's fuselage. White smoke poured out of the engine, and he started spiraling for the ground. I shot down my first German on my first try on my first mission, and I was over-the-moon happy—until I remembered that I wasn't supposed to be shooting. I was supposed to be covering my wingman, Marvin Russell.

Marv had been in the squadron almost a month and already had eight kills in eleven missions. I was assigned to be his wingman and cover his tail when the shooting started. I guess I just got too excited when I saw those four dozen 109s out the window. I strained to peer over my right shoulder, hoping to see Marv's Mustang, but he wasn't out there. He was gone, and I was alone.

I wasn't really alone. Messerschmitts were everywhere like a swarm of angry bees. Germans were everywhere, but there were darned few American Mustangs. There'd been sixteen of us when we took off from Bodney, and I couldn't see more than five or six. I had to either go hunting for my squadron mates or Germans. The numbers alone made my chances a lot better hunting for krauts, so that's what I did.

I shoved the throttle to its stops and pulled the nose of the Mustang through the horizon, trying to trade some airspeed for altitude. I made it to almost ten thousand feet before I ran out of airspeed and had to nose over. Below me were 109s and Mustangs going at each other like wild animals. I tried to count the P-51s, but it was like counting gnats in a swarm, so I picked out a 109 and dived in on him. We have the K-14 lead-computing gunsight that's supposed to give us the lead we need to shoot down the 109s without wasting too much ammo, but my hands were shaking too bad to program the thing.

I rolled in behind the 109 I'd picked out and immediately realized I was carrying way too much speed into the turn. I slid right past him at over three hundred miles per hour and saw flashes in my mirrors. They were his cannons blasting tracer rounds into the air. I yanked the stick to the left and pulled hard. I knew I could outturn the 109 if I could get inside his stream of bullets. My Mustang roared and bit into the sky, driving my butt harder and harder into the seat. I was determined not to get shot down on my first mission.

I kept pulling as hard as I could. If I could keep turning inside the German long enough, I'd end up behind him, and I could throw a couple hundred pounds of lead his way.

I strained to look over my shoulder, hoping to see the German getting farther and farther away, but what I saw was even better than that. Donny was a quarter mile behind the 109 that was chasing me, and his cannons were belching orange fire. My flight leader caught the German who was intent on catching me, and he paid with his life.

When I saw the 109 burst into flames, I rolled my wings level and pitched up again, trying to stay out of the cloud layer below me. I'd planned to join up on Donny's wing and get back in the fight, but by the time I could get my bearings, he was gone.

I caught my breath and headed back into the firestorm. Determined not to overshoot my next target, I set the throttle and pulled what I thought was a good lead on a single 109 who was outside the fray. I don't know if the kraut lost his nerve or if he was just lost. Either way, I was going to bring the fight to him. I squeezed the trigger and watched my tracers sail harmlessly across his nose. He chopped the power and dived hard right. I gave chase and followed him into the clouds with my guns on the verge of melting out of the wings. I must have shot at that guy for half a minute and never got close.

When the windscreen turned white and I couldn't see the propeller anymore, I knew I was in trouble. I tried to focus on my instruments and get out of the clouds, but my eyes were telling me one thing and my gut was telling me something different. My stomach thought I was diving, but my instruments said I was dead level. I knew I had to trust the panel, but the urge to pull up was irresistible. I popped out of the top of that cloud, and my windscreen filled with the belly of a Messerschmitt not fifty feet away. I was going to hit him, and there was nothing I could do about it. I cut the throttle and shoved the stick full forward just as the German rolled hard right. His unexpected roll saved my life, and we missed by inches, but I was instantly back in that damned cloud. Disoriented and scared, I forced my hands and feet to fly the airplane by the panel. I added enough power to climb out of the clouds again and break free of the tops. The melee I saw above was far more frightening than what was beneath me. There were still two dozen 109s battling it out with my squadron.

I checked my six and was happy to see nobody back there. I poured on the coals and headed back for the fight. My fingers finally stopped shaking enough to program the gunsight, and I smoked another 109 with a three-second burst. The tip of the German's right wing tore off, and the plane started snap rolling to the right. I watched him disappear into the cloud and wondered if he'd get out before the plane pranged into the German countryside.

I was still celebrating my second kill when I heard the worst sound a fighter pilot can ever hear: twenty-millimeter German bullets tearing through the skin of my airplane. I watched a line of bullet holes form in the top of my right wing. He put more than a dozen rounds into me, but my Mustang was still flying.

I rolled left to repeat the escape I'd made earlier by out turning the German, and hoped another of my squadron mates would show up to get this one off my tail. It didn't work. Nobody showed up, and the German pilot was darned good. No matter how hard I turned, he turned with me. He couldn't get his guns through me, but he was staying with me, turn for turn. I tried to outclimb him, hoping he'd stall before I did, but that didn't work either. I was getting desperate when I finally remembered a maneuver one of my instructors tried to describe back in the States, but I wasn't sure I could do it in the Mustang. I was tired of seeing German tracer rounds rip past my canopy, and I wasn't sure how much longer my wounded right wing would hold together, so I went for it.

I closed the throttle, yanked the stick into my gut, and stomped the left rudder pedal as hard as I could. I wasn't sure if I remembered what the maneuver was supposed to make the airplane do, but my head slammed into the canopy almost hard enough to knock me out, and the Mustang started plummeting. I stalled and spun my P-51. Then, I was falling like a rock. I watched the German fly past me overhead, and I shoved the stick forward, hoping to get the plane flying again. The nose came down, and the airspeed came up. I felt the plane responding to the controls, and just like that, the old girl was flying again. I turned tail and ran like the scared pup I was, not wanting anything more to do with that German pilot, whoever he was.

I made it to the rally point and learned that we'd lost four of sixteen Mustangs, and downed thirty of fifty 109s. We were shot up, low on gas, and exhausted with more than two hours of flying ahead of us to make it back to Bodney.

Lt. Robert D. Richter

Chapter 2
What Happened Today?

"I'm worried about you, Chase. Are you okay?"

I raised my head from the tattered, sixty-year-old journal that had been Dr. Robert "Rocket" Richter's while he was in Europe from 1944 to 1945. He'd been my mentor, the closest thing I had to a father after my parents were murdered, and the man who'd recruited me into the world of American covert operations.

The beautiful, ocean-blue eyes of Penny Thomas watched me with an expression of loving concern. I'd been silent for several hours, lost in self-pity, and mentally, thousands of miles away. I tried to speak, but words wouldn't come.

Penny forced a smile and handed me a tumbler of honey-colored whiskey over cubes of crystal-clear ice. Her finger traced the scars across the back of my right hand. "What happened today?"

I wanted to answer her. She was the one person in my life who never thought she knew what was best for me, or if she did think so, she never voiced those opinions. She just loved me in spite of my flaws—or perhaps because of them. She deserved an answer, and I owed her far more than any single response. I owed her the absolute truth.

"I don't know," I whispered.

I reached inside my jacket and pulled out a neatly folded document bound inside a heavy blue cardstock cover. Penny took it and slowly unfolded it, and I watched her lips move as her eyes traced across the page.

"In the Probate Court of Clarke County, Georgia. Having no living heirs, the estate of Robert Douglas Richter…"

I stopped listening. I'd committed the document to memory, but none of it mattered because the very foundation of it was an absolute lie.

"Did you know he had this much money?"

I shook my head.

"Did you know *any* of this?"

I continued the slow, back-and-forth movement of my head.

"Did you really know *anything* about him?"

"I know I love him," I heard myself whisper.

Penny laced her hand behind my neck and pulled me against her. I made no effort to resist. My face came to rest against her hair, and I thought of the thousands of hours I'd spent with Dr. "Rocket" Richter. I thought of all he'd taught me, and most of all, I thought of all the conversations we'd never have.

"Why would an old psychology professor leave you practically everything he owned?"

"He wasn't just a psych professor," I said as I tried to string together the myriad thoughts, memories, and emotions that were… *are*…Dr. Richter.

I couldn't fathom the idea of him being gone, of never talking with him again, of never listening as he revealed some universal truth about the world with one of his mysterious, cryptic word games.

I stared off into the horizon. "He was the single most influential person in my adult life."

"He was CIA or something like you, wasn't he?"

I closed my eyes and swallowed the lump in my throat. "No. He was nothing like me. No one word can describe what he was. He was a World War II fighter pilot, a Cold War intelligence operative, a brilliant psych professor, and my mentor."

She placed her hand on my thigh. "Intelligence operative means spy, doesn't it?"

"He knew my father and mother. And he's the one who recruited me into the work I do."

"Why don't you ever talk about your parents?"

"They died when I was fourteen."

She covered her mouth and gasped. "Oh my God, Chase. What happened?"

The things I'd learned over the past several weeks about how my parents and sister had died were daggers that would never leave my skull.

"There's no way I can tell you everything, but first, we have to do something we agreed *not* to do."

She furrowed her brow and lowered her chin, but didn't say a word.

"First," I said, "I want you here. With me. There's a magic about you—about us—that feels like home. I don't have to pretend to be anything I'm not with you. I get to be who and what I am, even though I haven't been able to tell you what those things are."

The corners of her lips curled upward in the dawning of a warm, beautiful smile. "You don't have to do this, Chase. I'm not going anywhere. I'm here as long as you want. I won't ask, and I won't expect."

"That's exactly why I have to do this." I took her hands in mine. "Look at me."

She bit at her bottom lip.

"I'm not a spy," I began. "Spies work for the CIA, NSA, DIA, or a handful of other government agencies. They gather information, theoretically, without being detected, and report that information back to analysts. That's not what I do."

Her smile was gone, replaced with a blank expression, as if she couldn't believe the discussion I'd just begun.

"I'm a covert operative, and I don't work directly for any of those alphabet-soup agencies. I don't gather intel, and I don't report back to any analysts. I get assignments from Dominic, Clark's father, then I go somewhere and do things my country needs done but can't have government employees getting caught doing."

"Killing people?" she whispered.

"No, not always. But sometimes that becomes necessary."

The conversation was easier than I'd feared, but it had only just begun.

"Chase, you really don't have to—"

"Yes, I do, Penny. For you to understand why Dr. Richter is so important to me, you have to know the truth about who and what I am."

"But if you're not ready to tell me, it's okay. Really, it is. Like I told you, I'm here because I want to be here. I love the time we spend together, and I feel safe with you."

I chuckled. "I'm not sure feeling safe is a rational thought process. People tend to get hurt around me."

She offered up that sultry little smile of hers. "Yeah, well, something tells me you're not going to let anything happen to me."

I leaned forward and kissed her forehead. "I'll do my best."

"It's really none of my business, but he left you a lot of money." She held up the court documents from Dr. Richter's estate.

I felt the lump in my throat again, but I held back the tears. "Yeah, but it's just money. It can't bring him back."

"But it's almost three million dollars, Chase. What does a person do with that kind of money? You'll never have to work again. You can do whatever you want."

"I already do whatever I want." I looked at *Aegis*, my beautiful, fifty-foot, custom sailing catamaran, and then back at her. "I have everything I want right here. I have *Aegis*, and I have you."

She laid her head on my shoulder and sighed. "But now you have more money than most people make in their whole lives."

"What I do pays extremely well. The money that Dr. Richter left me will be a very nice safety net, but it won't change my lifestyle—our lifestyle—and we aren't going to run out of money. Besides, that money isn't really mine."

"But you work for the government," she protested.

"No, I don't. I'm a contractor. I work for Dominic…sort of. Each assignment has a price attached to it. If I accomplish the mission, I get paid. If I fail…Well, I don't fail."

"See," she said, "that's why I feel safe with you. You don't fail."

"It's not always that simple," I confessed. "Sometimes people get hurt. Sometimes I get hurt. And even worse, sometimes people die."

She looked at me with a waxing look of concern. "You're not going to stop, are you?"

"No, I'm not going to stop. It's what I do, and it's what I am."

"And Clark?" she asked. "Is he one, too? A covert operative or whatever?"

"He is."

"And Elizabeth?" she said with animated disbelief in her tone.

"No, Skipper's not an operative, but she once thought she wanted to be. I think she's settled on being an analyst now. She's off with Ginger and learning the tricks of the trade."

"An analyst like the ones you said spies bring intel to?"

"No, not exactly. A different kind of analyst. Ginger's going to teach Skipper to oversee operations and provide support to operators like Clark and me in the field. Those kinds of analysts are masters of information, and they have computer skills that most people could never fathom. They can process massive amounts of data and feed the operators the information they need to accomplish their missions and stay alive."

Elizabeth, who I'd called Skipper for years, was the daughter of my college baseball coach. She'd made a few bad decisions and wound up in the hands of some nasty guys in the world of porn production on the slimy side of Miami. With the help of Clark Johnson and Anya Burinkova, I'd rescued her from that world. Clark was a former Green Beret turned covert operative, and Anya …well, Anya was impossible to explain.

"Now's your chance to stop me," I said.

"Stop you?"

"I mean, if this is all too much for you, I'll stop, and I won't tell you any more than I already have. Most Americans don't want to know people like me exist, and most women aren't interested in the bullshit that comes along with a man like me."

Penny had a knack for talking too much, but occasionally, she cut right to the point. "I'm not most women."

For the first time in weeks, I genuinely smiled. "No, you certainly are not."

"I'll be right back," she said. "I'm pretty sure I'm going to need a drink for the rest of this conversation." She returned moments later with a tumbler a lot like mine. "Okay, tell me about Anya."

I reached for my glass and tried to decide where to start. "What do you want to know?"

She smirked. "So, that's how this is going to work, huh? You're not going to volunteer anything. I have to drag it out of you."

"No, I'll tell you every detail. I have no reason to hide anything from you anymore."

She sat back in her chair and crossed her legs. "Okay, so let's hear it. I want to start with Anya. Tell me what made her so perfect."

"She was beautiful," I began.

Penny's eyes widened. "*Was* beautiful or *is* beautiful?"

"She *was* beautiful when I met her."

"Come on, Chase. Even *you're* not that shallow. There has to be more to it than the fact that she was beautiful. The world is full of beautiful women."

I thought of Anya's long blonde hair falling across her shoulders and her haunting blue-gray eyes. I remembered how it felt when she'd pressed her body against mine and whispered in my ear.

Penny snapped her fingers. "Hello? Wherever you went...come back."

"I'm sorry. I was just thinking about your question."

"Bullshit," she shot back. "You were thinking about her, and that's okay. Really, it is. But I want you to tell me what makes her so unforgettable."

"She was willing to die for me," I said, unable to make eye contact.

"Are you sure?"

The response came as if Penny had been saving the question for the right moment.

What did I really know about Anya? Was anything she ever told me the truth? Was anything about her real?

"Why are you so willing to put up with me?" I asked.

"*YA lyublyu tebya,*" she said, straining to form the words through her Texas drawl.

I couldn't resist smiling. "That was terrible, but I love you, too."

She leaned forward and gently kissed me. "I'm beautiful, too, you know."

"Yes, you certainly are, but not just on the outside."

We sat in silence, looking at each other differently than we had before.

"She was Dr. Richter's daughter," I said.

Penny shook her head. "What? I thought she was Russian."

"Her mother was a Russian KGB officer named Katerina Burinkova. Dr. Richter fell in love with her in the seventies while he was overseas. It's a long story, but Katerina was killed before Dr. Richter knew about Anya. She's his only living heir, so that money belongs to her, not me."

"So, what are you saying?"

"I have to find Anya," I said.

She closed her eyes and sighed.

Chapter 3
Hail Mary

I didn't recognize the number, but I stuck the phone to my ear anyway. "This is Chase."

"Mr. Fulton, this is Sister Mary Robicheaux. I trust you remember me."

"Of course, Sister. I've been expecting your call," I lied.

The truth was that the mission in Central America and Dr. Richter's death had all but overshadowed everything else in my life. I'd let Sister Robicheaux and her situation get lost somewhere in the mix.

"Are you still willing to help me, Mr. Fulton?"

Clark's admonition came flooding into my mind. *That's not what we do.*

I'd intervened, perhaps unwisely, in a confrontation between Sister Mary Robicheaux and a man she claimed was a pedophile stalking children at the school. I roughed him up a little after he pulled a knife on the nun, and in the aftermath, I promised to help Sister Robicheaux when I could.

"Of course I'm still willing to help, but first, you'll need to exhaust all efforts to get the local law enforcement involved. If this guy really is a threat to the children at your school, the local police will have no choice but to investigate and arrest him."

"You don't understand, Mr. Fulton. It's not that simple. This man's mother is Congresswoman Gail D'Angelo."

I'd just stepped into a pit I'd believed was only a puddle.

Trying to reassure her, I said, "It doesn't matter who his parents are. If he's—"

"You're being naïve, Mr. Fulton. I know you're some sort of federal agent, and that probably makes all of this even more difficult for you, but you saw what that man was willing to do to me. If you hadn't stopped him, he would've killed me, and he'd have gotten away with it, too."

"I don't think he was going to kill you, Sister. I think he just wanted to frighten you."

She scoffed. "Ha. I'm not afraid of him, and I'm not afraid of dying. I'm afraid of what he'll do to those innocent children if he gets the chance, and I'm not going to let that happen."

"I understand," I said. "Let me do some digging, and I'll see what I can do. Call me in a couple of days, and I'll let you know what I've learned."

Without another word, she hung up.

"I take it that was your nun," Penny said.

"You take it correctly. I want to help her, but I'm just not sure what I can do."

Penny squinted, trying to look as diabolical as possible for a woman as beautiful as her. "You could kill him."

I squinted back. "*You* could kill him."

She clasped her hands around my neck. "I could kill *you* if you don't help that woman. She's desperate."

"The world's full of desperate people."

"But most of them aren't nuns trying to protect innocent children."

I was beginning to believe that I'd never win an argument with her and hoped we'd never have a real disagreement.

"I'm *probably* not going to kill him," I told her, "but I am going to find a way to help her."

Penny let go of my neck and hugged me. "I knew you would. You're a valiant knight, eight hundred years too late."

"I'm no knight," I insisted. "I'm just not smart enough to keep my nose out of things that don't involve me."

"It's not your nose that makes you my knight in shining armor. I love you for your big white steed."

"Oh, so you only want me for my boat, huh?"

She smiled. "Yeah, well, maybe there are a few other perks, but mostly it's your boat."

I reached for her hand. "Let's go for a walk."

"Where?"

"To find Officer O'Malley."

We left the boat and headed across Avenida de Menendez into Old St. Augustine. Finding O'Malley turned out to be far easier than I'd expected. He was in the Plaza de la Constitución, talking with a group of tourists and teaching yo-yo tricks to a duo of young boys.

I was encouraged that he was the man I needed for what I was about to do. Penny and I sat on a bench and waited for him to finish the lessons.

O'Malley saw us and flashed a broad, knowing smile. He finished his conversation with the tourist family and then spoke into the microphone mounted on his epaulette. For such a big man, he moved with the agility of youth and the confidence of an athlete.

I stood to greet him. "Good afternoon, Officer O'Malley. Do you remember us?"

He glanced at Penny then looked me up and down. "Of course not. I've never seen either of you before, especially not at the scene of an attempted assault on a nun."

I was right. He was my man.

"Do you have a few minutes to talk about that situation you never saw?"

He checked his watch. "Sure. I've got ten minutes or so. What's on your mind, Special Agent?"

I frowned. "I'm not really—"

"I know," he said. "It's none of my business what you are. I'm just glad you stopped that scumbag from hurting Sister Robicheaux."

"That scumbag is what I'm here to talk about. What do you know about him?"

O'Malley cleared his throat. "I know he's a low-life piece of trash whose mother got herself elected to Congress."

"That's what I heard," I said. "Sister Robicheaux seems to believe he's potentially dangerous to the children at the school where she teaches. What do you know about that?"

"I'm just a beat cop, but if I weren't, I'd be thinking the same things that are going around in your head. That guy's trouble, and he needs to be stopped."

"Why haven't you arrested him?"

"We have, but it never seems to stick. Between the judges afraid of the Congresswoman, and D'Angelo's slimy lawyer, he never spends more than a single night in lockup."

"Does he make a habit of messing with kids?" I asked.

"We're off the record here, huh?"

"Absolutely," I said, leaning in.

"If I ever catch that son of a bitch by himself at night, I'll do more than just break his arm like you did."

"So," I said, "the nun's right?"

"Yeah, she's right about him, and that's not all. I think you know she's a grade-school teacher over at Saint Francis."

"Yeah, she told me that much."

"Well," O'Malley continued, "Congresswoman D'Angelo is trying to have the school shut down."

"This is sounding more and more like it isn't going to be easy to resolve."

Penny spoke up. "When was the last time you shied away from anything because it wasn't going to be easy?"

O'Malley glanced at her and then focused on me. "I don't know what you're thinking of doing, and I don't want to know. I'm a cop, for God's sake. I can't condone anything illegal even if I happen to agree with it. But what I can do is answer your questions as long as you don't tell me what you're up to."

"What's his name?" I asked.

"It's Salvatore D'Angelo."

"Let's say I had something I needed to deliver to Salvatore D'Angelo," I said. "You know, something that he really needed and was rightfully his. Where would I find young Sal?"

O'Malley smiled. "Oh, so you have this thing that belongs to him, and you just want to make sure he gets what he's earned, eh?"

"Exactly. It's only right that the man gets what he deserves."

"Ah, so you're a humanitarian." He pulled a sheet of paper from a notepad he kept in his shirt pocket. "In that case, Sal lives on the beach. Here's his address. I hear he likes to run by the ocean at sunrise."

I tucked the address into my pocket.

"Oh yeah, and if he's not there, it's pretty easy to find him at the Tidewater most nights. He fancies one of the bartenders out there, and he seems to like what they keep on tap."

"Do you happen to know if he carries more than that switchblade he likes to threaten nuns with?"

O'Malley shrugged. "He's never had a gun on him during an arrest, if that's what you mean."

"Thank you, Officer O'Malley. You've been more than helpful."

"Ken," he said. "Kendrick O'Malley's my Christian name, but my friends call me Ken."

"Thank you, Ken. You'll have to join us for a cocktail sometime when you're not in uniform."

"I'd like that. You're on that white catamaran. *Aegis*, right?"

"You don't miss much, do you, Ken?"

"Not much, Special Agent Fulton."

Penny and I shook Ken's hand and headed back, and we sat on the upper deck watching boats come and go for almost an hour.

"I like when you do that," I finally said.

She smiled. "You like when I do what?"

"Let me think when I need to."

"I could see the wheels turning. You've got a lot on your mind, and I thought maybe you could use some quiet time."

"You were right. I have a lot of things to figure out, not the least of which is what to do about Salvatore D'Angelo."

"Do you have a plan?" she asked with rare timidity in her tone.

"I decided we need some Russian lemonade."

"Some what?" she said.

"It's a long story, but it means we're going to take ol' Sal for a little sailing trip. First, we need to help him relax." I pulled my phone from my pocket and called Dr. Fred at The Ranch.

"Hello, Chase! How are you?"

"Hello, Fred. I'm doing great. How are things at the funny farm?"

He laughed. "Same as it ever was. To what do I owe the pleasure of a call from you?"

"It's not a social call," I confessed. "I need a concoction to help someone sleep. Preferably an injection that'll give the recipient three or four hours of quality time in the spirit world."

"I have just the thing," he said. "Are you in St. Augustine?"

"I am."

"Great. I'll have someone stop by this afternoon with a little care package for you."

"You're the best, Fred. I knew I could count on you."

"It's always great to hear from you, Chase. How's Penny?"

"She's spectacular, as always."

"Good, good. Please tell her again how much I enjoyed her nearly killing Gunny."

Gunny was the senior tactical training officer at The Ranch, the covert operations training facility where I'd become an operator. He was one of the most intimidating and deadly men on the planet, and Penny had knocked him out cold with a winch handle in the main salon of my boat. There are probably less than three humans who could claim to have knocked out Gunny and still survived.

"Will do. Thanks, Fred."

"Anytime."

I slid the phone back into my pocket. "Fred wants me to remind you how much he loves the fact that you laid Gunny out."

"I've got skills," she said from behind a brilliant smile.

"Indeed, you do."

"Are you going to kill Salvatore D'Angelo?"

"No, I'm not going to kill him, but don't tell him that. I want him to believe I'm willing and capable of ending him without remorse."

She inhaled a long, full breath. "I know you're capable of that, but I hope you're not willing."

Chapter 4
Apothecarial Delivery

"Mr. Fulton?"

A voice from the dock rang out, and I peered over the rail to see a man dressed like a copier repairman with a clip-on tie and short-sleeved shirt. He could've been Fred's nerdy little brother.

"Yes, I'm Chase," I yelled down.

"I have a delivery for you. Would you like for me to come up?"

"Sure," I said. "Come on up."

When he'd made his way awkwardly up the ladder, I pointed to a settee. "What have you brought me?"

"It's ketamine," the man said. "How much does your patient weigh, Mr. Fulton?"

"He's about one-ninety," I said, glancing at Penny for confirmation.

She nodded.

"Okay, in that case, ten to twelve milligrams injected in a large muscle will result in unconsciousness in twenty to thirty seconds. A tenth of a milligram per minute IV push will keep him quiet, but more than half a milligram per minute may stop his breathing."

I took the black leather bag from the man. "Thank you. Would you care for a cocktail before you go?"

His eyes darted back and forth between me and the leather bag. "Uh, no, thank you. I fear cocktails with you might not be such a great idea."

Penny involuntarily chuckled, and our pharmacist scampered back down the ladder.

She laughed and pointed at the bag. "I don't think I'll ever get used to being with a man who can just order up tranquilizers at will and then set about using them on unsuspecting victims."

"He's no victim," I said. "He's a pedophile. That means he volunteered for everything I'm going to do to him."

"I know," she said, "but it feels a little vigilante to me."

"That's how it *should* feel because that's precisely what it is," I admitted. "I don't expect you to be involved if you don't want to be. There's a great bed-and-breakfast—"

She placed her finger against my lips. "Shhh. In for a Penny, in for a pound...of ketamine. I wouldn't miss this for the world."

I kissed her. "In that case, let's go house hunting."

"Can we have lunch at Cap's while we're out?"

"Great idea," I said. "Bring your camera."

We hailed a cab on Avenida de Menendez, headed north, and crossed the Usina Bridge onto A1A. The address O'Malley had given us for Salvatore D'Angelo put his house among the lavish beachfront homes lining the eastern side of A1A.

We watched the numbers on the mailboxes until we were approaching the address.

"Can you slow down a little?" Penny said. "We're trying to spot the house our friends are planning to buy."

The driver obediently slowed the car.

"There it is," I said.

Penny started snapping pictures and then sat back in her seat. "Thank you. That was it."

"Sure. No problem, ma'am."

We pulled into the parking lot of Cap's on the Water, my favorite waterfront restaurant in St. Augustine, and possibly my favorite in the world. Lunch was perfect with only one minor exception—there were no pear ravioli.

Back at the marina, I stopped by to see one of my favorite people, Earl from the end.

"Hey there, Stud Muffin. I see Little Miss Hottie-Pants is still hanging on your arm."

"Hey, Sexy Momma," I said. "She knows I can't be trusted alone with you."

Earline laughed. "Piffle! Who *could* be trusted with all this sexy in one place?"

Earl from the End was actually Earline, a sixty-something woman who looked more like a weeble—as in *weebles wobble, but they don't fall down*—than a real person. She was about five feet tall and two hundred pounds, but she was the best diesel mechanic I'd ever met.

"I need a boat, Earl."

"You've already got a boat, baby boy."

"Yeah, but I need a rigid hull inflatable boat to use as a dinghy. Do you know anyone who might have one for sale?"

"Yeah, as a matter of fact, I do. There's a sixteen-footer with a seventy horsepower Yamaha for sale, and I know the motor inside and out. I went through it and changed the impeller and fuel pump. It's in great shape. I think the guy wants seventy-five hundred for it, but you could probably get it for closer to six if you haggle with him a little."

"I'll make a deal with you, Earl," I said. "I'll give you seven grand, and you go get that RHIB for me. You can keep the difference between the seven thousand and whatever price you can haggle. Deal?"

"You've got a deal, Stud Muffin. But there's one little caveat."

"What's that?" I asked, almost afraid to hear the answer.

"I get a hug and a kiss, too," she growled.

I turned to Penny for permission.

She said, "Fine, but no tongue. And keep your hands off his butt."

Earl didn't hear a word after "fine." I was both tongued and groped, but she showed up two hours later in my new boat. It looked practically brand-new.

I lowered my dinghy from the davits and tied the painter line to *Aegis*'s stern cleat. The new RHIB was significantly heavier than my previous dinghy, but the electric davit winches made short work of hauling her out of the water.

"Hey, Earl," I said. "See if you can find someone who needs my old dinghy. There's nothing wrong with it. I've just recently fallen in love with the rigid hull design. You can keep half of whatever you sell it for."

Earl eyed the dinghy and bit at her lip hesitantly.

"What is it?" I asked. It was rare to see Earl uncomfortable.

"It's just that I could really use that dinghy. Mine has more patches than original tubes. But I can't afford it, even at half price."

Penny jumped in. "Give her the boat, Chase. Surely she deserves it after that dose of lovin' she gave you."

"No!" demanded Earl. "I ain't no charity case."

"No way," I said. "Those supermodel looks of yours don't work on me, Earl, but you know I can't resist those greasy fingernails."

Both Penny and Earl glared at me as if I were speaking in tongues.

I said, "I'll trade you the boat for twenty-five hours of mechanic work. How's that sound?"

Once again, I was tongued and groped, and Earl led her new dinghy away by its painter.

Penny laughed. "That's one strange woman."

"She's a jewel, and she's one hell of a mechanic."

Penny stared at Earl's old boat. "What's her story? Where'd she learn to work on engines?"

"I have no idea," I admitted. "I don't know anything about her other than she's a genius on diesels and absolutely insane."

"I definitely agree with the insane diagnosis. That was sweet of you to barter with her for the dinghy."

"She's been good to me. I would've given it to her if I thought she would've let me, but I knew she'd pitch a fit if I tried."

"You're a good man, Mr. Fulton."

I smiled. "How do you feel about a dinghy ride, Ms. Thomas?"

"I'd love that," she said. "Are we doing a little recon mission, as you and Clark would call it?"

"We are." I was pleased she was catching on.

We lowered my new RHIB back into the water and Penny jumped behind the wheel.

"Hey, Earl got to grab your butt and stick her tongue down your throat, so the least you can do is let me drive the new dinghy first."

I offered no argument and settled into the passenger seat. We motored from the marina at idle speed, abiding by the no-wake policy, but when we were clear of the marina, Penny wasted no time. She shoved the throttle to the stop, and the Yamaha engine purred, quickly lifting the boat out of the water and accelerating to fifty knots. Penny handled the RHIB just as expertly as she sailed *Aegis*. I was running out of reasons to believe she wasn't perfect.

I wonder if she can shoot.

We turned east just south of the Usina Bridge and headed through the pass into the Atlantic. The tide was coming in, and the wind was from the west, so the pass was a little rough, but that didn't seem to faze Penny. She kept us at the perfect speed to stay on top of the chop, and I was impressed.

Turning north, we ran parallel to the beach until Sal's house came into sight. Penny slowed in front of the house about a quarter mile offshore.

"What's the depth?" I asked.

She checked the small LED screen. "Eighteen feet."

"That's perfect. Set a waypoint in the GPS, and head for the beach."

She did as I instructed, and we let the waves carry us toward the beach with just enough power from the engine to maintain steerage, and I watched the depth gauge count down. The bottom sloped gently and consistently toward the beach.

"Keep taking us in until we're in four feet of water, and then turn back to the north," I said.

She followed instructions and added power as we turned. "What now?"

"There are two vacant lots side by side about a mile up the beach. Let's practice a beaching up there."

"That sounds like fun!"

She quickly had us doing forty knots. We found the vacant lots, and she turned to me for directions.

"Hit the beach between seven and ten knots. Keep the engine running, but trim it up as far as you can to keep it out of the sand, and still have it in the water."

We hit the sand a little faster than I liked, but I leapt from the bow just before the boat stopped. I stumbled the first three strides, trying to compensate for the additional speed we'd carried into the beach, but I soon found my pace and ran to the dunes. I turned back to see Penny holding the boat almost motionless in the surf. I liked my new getaway driver.

I ran back for the boat at a sprint and jumped aboard, simultaneously shoving the bow around and into the surf. Penny added power and lowered the motor as we picked up speed. In less than ten seconds after I'd leapt aboard, we were cutting across the tops of the waves and approaching thirty knots.

"Let's do it again," I yelled over the noise of the wind, waves, and outboard engine.

We practiced our drill three more times until our timing and execution were perfect.

"This is going to be fun," she said after the final attempt.

"Yes, it is," I agreed, "but we'll have some added dead weight next time. The boat won't accelerate as quickly, and the bow will submarine if we hit the surf before I can get him to the center of the boat."

"I think we can manage."

I kissed her forehead. "I'm starting to believe there isn't much we can't handle together, but it's my turn to drive my new boat."

Chapter 5
The Real Thing

"Clark doesn't know you're doing this, does he?" With hands on hips, Penny watched me pore over the chart plotter.

"No, but this doesn't have anything to do with him. I got myself into this one, and you volunteered."

She frowned. "But he's your partner. And what if something goes wrong? Don't you think he needs to know what's going on?"

I sighed. "I've been thinking about that, and you're right, but I don't want to listen to his sermon on how wrong I am for getting involved."

"What if he did something like this without telling you?"

I smiled, thankful to have Penny as my anchor to sanity, and pulled out my phone and dialed Clark.

"Hey," he said.

"Listen, I need to tell you what's going on, and I know what you're going to say, but please just listen, okay?"

"I knew it," Clark said. "You're going after the guy who accosted the nun, aren't you?"

"Yeah, I am."

"I knew you would. Do you want my help?"

That wasn't the reaction I'd expected, and I immediately felt bad for thinking he was going to berate me with a speech on how stupid it would be to go after Salvatore.

"No, we're going to grab him off the beach at daybreak and run out into the Gulf Stream to get his attention."

"Sounds like fun, but who is *we*?"

"Penny's going to drive the boat, and I'll handle the rest."

"I can be there in three hours."

"Thanks, but we'll be fine. It's just a simple snatch-and-scare."

"Nothing is simple," he said. "Keep me posted, and let me know you're all right. When's this going down?"

"In about eleven hours."

He sighed. "Okay. Just call me before and after, will you?"

"Done," I said, and hung up.

Penny wound her arms around my neck and settled gently onto my lap. "See, that wasn't so hard, now was it?"

I kissed her. "I'd really like for you to stop being right all the time."

She smirked. "That's probably not going to happen. Now pour us some wine, and let's eat. The mahi-mahi is perfect, and the grilled vegetables are going to melt in your mouth."

* * *

I expected to toss and turn, but sleep came quickly. At ten 'til five a.m., we motored out of the Municipal Marina and under the Bridge of Lions. Making the turn into the pass that would take us into the Atlantic, I was pleased to see the surf was light, and a gentle breeze caressed the coast from the southwest. That meant the Gulf Stream would be calm. When the wind blows from the north, the four-knot flow of the Gulf Stream from the southwest churns into a torrent of violent seas that no mariner wants to battle.

About a quarter mile offshore from Salvatore D'Angelo's beach house, we anchored *Aegis* at the coordinates we'd saved the day before and dropped the RHIB into the water just as the sun was peeking over the horizon. Penny and I scanned the beach with our binoculars, and I was pleased to see it almost empty. I didn't want or need witnesses to what we were about to do. Kidnapping, after all, is a federal crime, and I suspected kidnapping and then leaving the country was even worse.

"Got him!" she said, pointing toward the beach. "Right there, running south."

I trained my binoculars on the spot. "Yep! That's him. Let's go."

We climbed into the RHIB and headed for the beach. I had prepared two syringes with adequate doses of ketamine to guarantee Sal would gladly accept my invitation to go sailing.

"If a dozen bullets will do, take two dozen," had been the philosophy of every instructor at The Ranch; thus, the two syringes.

Penny angled our boat to the north so we could turn and approach Sal from behind, and I took my position in the bow.

The engine RPMs decreased, and the tilt motor whirred, raising the foot of the outboard engine away from the sandy bottom as the beach grew ever closer. Sal never turned to see us approaching, and finally, Penny passed him and turned immediately for the shore. I felt the hull brush the sand, and I leapt from the bow just as we'd practiced.

I judged the speed perfectly as my boots hit the wet sand, and two strides later, I planted my shoulder solidly in the center of Salvatore D'Angelo's chest. A breath left his body as he collided with the hard-packed sand and my weight came to a crashing stop on top of him. Wasting no time, I sank the needle into his thigh and forced the plunger home. As he gasped to regain the breath I'd shouldered from his lungs, a look of recognition came across his face. "You…" Then his eyelids resembled wet dishrags, and the muscles of his clenched jaw relaxed.

I pressed two fingers to the side of his neck, making sure I hadn't killed him, and felt a steady but weak pulse. I capped and pocketed the syringe and then hefted Sal over my shoulder. Accelerating through lengthening strides, I sprinted for the bow of the boat. I saw Penny's hand ease the throttle into reverse just as my foot left the ground.

Jumping into the boat the previous day without an unconscious man on my shoulder had been a piece of cake, but practice doesn't always make perfect. The timing we'd worked out dictated that Penny would start adding power the instant I leapt, resulting in the movement of the boat simultaneously with my landing in the bow. But my leap was weak, and her hand was quick.

Instead of landing *in* the bow and letting Sal's body tumble forward into the center of the boat, I landed *on* the bow with my head and shoulders barely inside and my boots dragging in the surf. The weight of Sal's body over my shoulder sent my head crashing to the deck.

The extra weight on the bow made the small RHIB ungainly, even in the light surf. I kicked at the water, trying to find purchase so I could thrust our bodies completely into the boat, but there was nothing solid to be found. We hit the first small wave with the bow still burdened under the extra weight, and took a wall of salt water into the boat. Realizing that either Sal or I was going into the water, I decided to let it be me. I shoved at his dead weight with all of my strength, getting as much of him inside the boat as possible while I slid off the bow.

I'd expected to be in ten feet of water, but my expectation wasn't even close. Instead of sinking, I landed on my knees with a thud and my chin barely above the surface. Fearing Penny might run over me and chop me into fish food with the propeller as I'd done to Suslik—the Russian assassin in Havana—I looked up to gauge the position of the RHIB. To my surprise, Penny was kneeling beside the console with her right arm extended over the starboard tube in a perfect hook. I locked arms with her, and the forward motion lifted me from the water and deposited me like a sandbag on the deck of the RHIB.

I spat out a mouthful of salt water and caught my breath. "Where did you learn to do that?"

She shoved the throttle to the stops. "I watch a lot of movies, and that's how the Navy SEALs always do it."

Our guest was sleeping soundly on the deck, and we were on our way back to my beloved *Aegis*. The snatch portion of the operation hadn't gone as we'd planned and practiced, but phase one had worked.

Penny brought us astern of *Aegis*, alongside the boarding stairs, and I tied us off. She climbed aboard first, and I hefted Sal out of the RHIB. We dragged him through the cockpit and into the main salon where we'd hung an IV bag and built a nice, comfortable nest for our passenger. Penny disappeared back into the cockpit while I started the IV that would keep Sal in the clouds for a few hours while we put some distance between ourselves and the east coast of Florida.

By the time I'd finished, Penny had the anchor on deck, and *Aegis* was making fourteen knots toward Red Snapper Sink, a hole with no apparent bottom, about thirty miles offshore.

"Well, that was interesting," I said when I'd finished my Florence Nightingale work and made my way to the cockpit.

"I'm so sorry," Penny said. "I took off way too early."

"Relax," I insisted. "It wasn't your fault. I failed to consider how much more challenging the jump would be with Sal's weight."

"No, I shouldn't have been in such a hurry."

"No battle plan survives first contact with the enemy," I said. "Something always goes wrong. It was a minor hiccup, and you were amazing."

She smiled. "Thank you for letting me come along. I like working with you."

"I couldn't have done it without you," I admitted. "You just keep us heading for the Sink, and I'm going to find some dry clothes."

Two and a half hours later, Penny announced, "We'll be over the Sink in ten minutes."

I stopped the ketamine drip and hog-tied Sal with his arms and legs behind his back. It took all my strength to wrestle him onto the starboard deck where I'd rigged a hoist from the boom. After connecting the hoist to Sal's bindings, I gave the line a pull, lifting Sal's body from the deck and suspending him in midair. I swung the boom over the side, leaving Sal hanging over the water and above the bottomless Red Snapper Sink. It was time to sit back and wait for the ketamine to wear off.

It didn't take long.

He groggily opened his eyes and tried to make sense of his predicament. His eyes darted wildly and finally came to rest on me as I sat nonchalantly with my legs dangling over the side.

Rage overtook confusion, and he growled like a cornered animal. "You're a dead man! You have no idea who you're messing with!"

I smiled. "Look around, Sal. You're dangling from my boom, over a pit in the ocean, where no one's been able to locate the bottom. All I have to do is release this line, and no one will ever find your body. Ah, but that's not really a concern. The sharks would make short work of you anyway, so there wouldn't be anything left of you for anyone to find."

His defiance was not diminished. "You've started something you can't finish, asshole!"

I chuckled. "Do you really think you're in any position to be making threats?"

He was unfazed. "You're not going to kill me. You're a cop, and no cop is going to mess with my family. You obviously have no idea who I am."

I pulled a bag of grapes from the deck beside me and popped them into my mouth one at a time, occasionally throwing one at Sal's head. "Oh, I know exactly who you are, Salvatore D'Angelo, son of Congresswoman Gail D'Angelo. But I'm no cop."

"Bullshit," he roared. "I saw you badge that cop, O'Malley."

I laughed. "You have no idea what I showed Officer O'Malley, and I assure you, I'm no peace officer. I'm more what you might call an *anti*-peace officer. I make people like you—people who prey on little kids—regret the day they drew their first breath. I'm not afraid of you, your mother, or anyone else you think you have in your pocket. Now, it's time for you to do some listening before I let you go for a little swim."

A look of desperation replaced the mask of futile rage he'd been wearing. "Okay. Look, man. If it's money you want—"

In feigned excitement, I asked, "How much?"

Realizing I was willing to negotiate, Sal's eyes lit up. "A hundred grand."

I bounced a grape off his head. "I've got a hundred grand in the safe downstairs. You'll have to do better than that."

He squirmed and strained against his restraints. "Okay, okay. Half a million, then. Five hundred grand. Just get me down."

"Really? You've got half a million…in cash?" He didn't appear to be catching on to my sarcasm.

"Yeah, yeah! Just get me down, and the money's yours, man."

"I don't want your money," I said, and released the line.

Salvatore D'Angelo fell and splashed face-first into the Atlantic Ocean.

Penny gasped.

"Don't worry," I said. "I'm not going to let him drown."

I wound the line around an electric winch and pressed the button. Sal, dripping wet and screaming, rose from the water.

Believing I had Sal's full attention, I swung the boom back toward the hull and stared into the man's terrified eyes. I whispered, "How 'bout a million, Sal? Have you got a million bucks? How much is your putrid little life worth to you?"

Through trembling lips, he whimpered, "I don't have that kinda cash, but I can get it. Forty-eight hours."

I pressed my knuckles into the bridge of his nose, right between his eyes, hard enough to make him cringe. "You listen to me, and you listen very closely. You have forty-eight hours to put one million dollars in the bank account of Saint Francis Catholic School, and then you disappear from the state of Florida forever. Do you understand?"

"Yes, whatever you say."

"Oh, and here are a couple more things for you to keep in mind. I have a handy little sample of your DNA that's going into the National Crime Information Center database at the FBI. My highly placed friends and I will be watching your every move, and we'll know where you go every day for the rest of your miserable life. If you ever have so much as a fleeting dirty thought about touching anyone under the age of thirty, I will fall down on you from a great height, and you'll beg me to put you back in this hole in the ocean."

I raked my knuckles down his nose, leaving a bloody trail as I went. "Don't make me fall on you, Sal."

I plunged the second syringe into his butt cheek and watched him drift off.

Two hours later, just as the hull of the RHIB came to rest on the beach in front of his house, I woke Sal from his slumber.

"Remember what I told you. You now have forty-six hours to put one million dollars into Saint Francis's bank account and Florida in your rearview. Capiche?"

Free of his bindings, and groggy but aware, he said, "Yeah, I got it."

I placed the heel of my boot against his hip, and then rolled him off the RHIB and into the shallow surf right in front of his ocean-front palace.

Chapter 6
Cause of Death

Penny was uncharacteristically quiet, and that concerned me.

"Are you okay?"

"I think so," she said. "It's just that I've never seen anything like that before. Is that what you do when you're gone?"

I knew it would happen, but I hadn't prepared myself for the inevitable conversation. "Yes, that's what I do. I don't always kill people. Sometimes I just let them think I'm going to kill them. The psychology of believing you're about to die is primordial. No greater instinct is hardwired into our psyche than the will and desire to stay alive."

She wouldn't make eye contact. "It's kind of scary."

"It's supposed to be scary. That's why it works. It all happens in the brain's hippocampus and amygdala. When a person believes he's about to die—"

She placed her hand on my arm. "Chase, I don't want a biology lesson. I want to know how you do it. Doesn't it bother you at all?"

I brushed her hair back with the tips of my fingers and held her perfect face in my hands. "Remember those two kids you want? A boy and a girl?"

She nodded.

"Imagine Salvatore D'Angelo taking our beautiful little daughter by the hand and leading her to his car."

Her face lost its color, and she shivered in my hands.

"That's how I do it. Everything I do is to stop evil from prevailing. I'm not a soulless killer. What I do saves lives and protects countless people from facing unthinkable evils lurking in the shadows."

"Is Clark like you?"

I closed my eyes and tried to come up with the right words. "No. Clark is very different. He's a freight train on Main Street."

She furrowed her brow. "Huh?"

"Those are his words, not mine. He says I'm a surgeon, cutting out cancer with a very sharp scalpel, and he's a freight train on Main Street killing everyone in his way. Our operational styles are quite different, but both are crucial. What we do makes it possible for routine life to go on every day without most people knowing we exist. Everything we do is behind the scenes. We don't get medals or keys to the city. You'll never see us on the news or read about us in the newspaper, but we get to go to sleep at night knowing we've made a difference in the world."

The look on her face said she wasn't buying it. "Would you have killed him if he hadn't agreed to your terms?"

I considered her question. "I never had any intention of killing him. I held the position of power throughout the operation. I was in total control from start to finish. I would've kept pushing him until he believed I was going to kill him and he gave me what I wanted."

"The money. Do you think he'll really give it to the school?"

"The money wasn't part of the plan. I was just going to scare him out of Florida. He put the money in play, so I took advantage of what he offered. You heard what O'Malley said about the congresswoman trying to shut down the school. That kind of money will make closing the school nearly impossible. It was an unexpected collateral benefit. Sometimes those things happen. We score a piece of intelligence we didn't expect, or a scumbag pukes up a million bucks for a school."

"I'm sorry," she said. "I knew what you did was dangerous, but I never imagined what it was really like."

"Don't be sorry. This isn't easy for anyone to swallow."

"Did you kill anyone in Panama?"

The dramatic shift in her line of questioning took me by surprise, and I remembered the promise I'd made to her.

I will never lie to you.

"Yes," I admitted.

"Would they have killed you if you hadn't killed them?"

"Yes, without question. In fact, everyone I killed was actively trying to kill me."

"Then I'm glad you did it," she said, pulling me into her arms.

I wondered if the conversation was over, but I was smart enough not to ask.

"Get a room, you two!" Earl's shrill voice pierced the sincerity of our moment.

"This *is* our room," I said.

"Yeah, well, that might be your room, but them engines in there are mine. How long's it been since the oil's been changed?"

"I have no idea, Earl, but you can bet your buns that nobody's touched them except you."

"That better be the truth, and I'll know if it ain't as soon as I get my hands on 'em. I've got the oil and filters, so I figured I oughta go ahead and get that done before you run off again to God knows where."

I grinned. "Thanks, Earl. We've had a long day, so we're going to have a little siesta while you work your magic in the engine rooms."

"Fine by me," she said, "but I'm gonna service the generator and water maker while I'm down there, so I can't promise you I'll be none too quiet."

"Don't you worry, Earl," Penny said. "If you wake us up, I'm sure I can find some way to keep Stud Muffin here occupied."

"Ha! You go on and have your fun, Little Miss Sugar-Britches, but remember, I've been on the planet twice as long as you. My belly may not be flat like yours, but old girls like me know tricks you young chicks can't even spell yet."

Recognizing that as my cue to make an exit, I stood from the settee and headed for my bunk. I was looking forward to Penny keeping me occupied, but exhaustion had other plans for us. We were asleep within minutes, and we never heard Earl make a sound.

I opened my eyes, and Penny was sitting beside me with her legs crossed and the paperwork from the probate court on her lap. Her hair fell across her shoulders, and the light through the hatch above her head made her look like an angel.

"You're beautiful," I whispered as I laid my hand on her knee.

She tried to smile, but it was tempered with an emotion I couldn't define.

Is it doubt?

She placed her hand atop mine. "Is she dangerous?"

"Is who dangerous?" I asked, still not fully awake.

"Anya."

I couldn't remember if I'd ever heard Penny say her name before then. I opened my mouth, but the voice in my head screamed, "You promised not to lie to her!"

"Yes," I said. "She's the most dangerous person I know."

"Then why do you love her?"

The question made me feel like I'd been hit by a truck. I took Penny's hand in mine and pulled her toward me. Her body came to rest against mine.

"I love you, Penny Thomas."

She ran her fingers through my hair. "I know, but—"

"But nothing," I said. "You're the woman I love, and there's no one else. There was a time when I thought I loved her, but it was before I knew the truth. It was when my feelings were based on a lie…on a whole collection of lies. But none of it was real."

"It was real for you at the time."

Perhaps Penny was a better psychologist than I'd ever be, but I needed her to understand how I could compartmentalize the feelings I'd once had for Anya against the reality that it had all been a cruel ruse.

"Think of it like Sal hanging over the water this morning. He was in no real danger, and I was never going to kill him. I wasn't even going to hurt him, but he didn't know that. He believed I was seconds away from taking his life, but just because he believed that doesn't mean it was true. The truth doesn't change because of our perception. Water is wet. Fire is hot. No matter what we believe, the truth remains. I believed Anya was in love with me. I believed she was defecting. I believed all sorts of things, none of which were true, and none of which changed the truth. She never loved me, and she never stopped working for the Russians."

She held up the court paperwork. "So, even after all that, you're still going to risk your life to find her and give her this money?"

"It's rightfully hers," I said.

Penny squinted and swallowed hard.

I took her hand. "Say what you're thinking."

She inhaled deeply as if carefully considering what she was about to say. "It's just that…"

Silence filled the air, and I waited…and waited.

The corners of her mouth turned downward.

"It's okay," I tried to reassure her. "Just say it."

"It's just that she did those horrible things to you, and you still think she deserves the money." She blurted out the words as if they'd been boiling inside her.

"It's not that she deserves the money. It's just what's right. She's Dr. Richter's daughter, and—"

"Oh, bullshit! I don't care if she's the pope's daughter. She hurt you, and I love you, and that money isn't going to change that." She clenched her jaw. "Besides, she's beautiful and dangerous, and you're going after her, and what if she does it again? What if you can't tell her no? What if you can't resist and then I lose you? And then what? Huh? Am I supposed to just sit here on this boat waiting for you to come back, or maybe not come back at all? Maybe you'll decide to stay with her because she's beautiful and—"

I reached for her, intending to take her in my arms, but she slapped at my hands. "No, Chase! No! That's not going to fix this. I love you, and I don't want to lose you to her." Her shoulders drooped, and she pushed her palms into her eyes in a useless attempt to quell the tears.

"Penny," I said softly. "Listen to me."

"No! You listen to me." She cleared her throat and wiped her face. "It's not your responsibility. If you want her to have the money, that's fine, but what about the other stuff?"

"What other stuff?" I asked, knowing I was walking a tightrope between logic and emotion.

"The airplane and the house and all the personal effects? How about that diary or whatever it is you were reading about the war? What about all that stuff? Are you giving all of that to her, as well?"

I had no idea what to say.

What would Anya—or Norikova, or whatever her name is—do with a retired professor's house in Athens, Georgia? What would she do with a P-51 Mustang? Is it even possible for a Russian national, living illegally in the country, to own a house and an airplane?

"That's what I thought," she huffed. "You don't plan on giving her the rest of the stuff, do you? You just plan on giving her the money."

"I don't have a plan," I admitted. "I don't know what to do. I just don't think it's right—"

She cut me off. "You're right. It's not right! It's not right that she should get away with doing what she did to you, and besides…" Indecision was obvious on her face. She closed her eyes and whispered, "Who was the last person to see him alive?"

"What?"

"God forgive me, Chase, but I can't stop thinking that she was the last person to see Dr. Richter alive."

"No!" I said, refusing to follow her down the path she was taking.

"I'm not saying she killed him, Chase. I'm just saying…"

The thought of Anya killing her father was more than I wanted to let myself believe, but I had to accept her for what she was at her core: one of the world's deadliest assassins.

"Okay, I get it," I said. "You're right."

"About what?"

I sighed. "When Anya Burinkova is the last person to see someone alive, there's no question about the cause of death."

Chapter 7
Playboy Mush

"She killed him," I said into the phone.

"Penny killed D'Angelo?" questioned Clark.

"No, Penny didn't kill anyone. I think Anya killed Dr. Richter."

My phone became a bottomless pit of utter silence for several seconds, or perhaps minutes. I couldn't tell the difference.

"I'll be there in four hours," he said, and the line went dead.

* * *

I felt *Aegis* move slightly under Clark's boot when he stepped aboard.

"Okay, let's hear it," he said.

I didn't expect "Hi, honey, I'm home," but I also didn't think he'd instantly jump to the point.

"Remember the morning in Birmingham?" I began. "We were in the rental car on that bizarre quest for scotch, and you were asleep in the back seat."

"Yeah, yeah, I remember. Penny scored a bottle from a restaurant bar while the sun was still coming up."

"Exactly," I said. "When we made it back to the hospital and parked, we saw Anya through the window in Dr. Richter's hospital room, but by the time we could get to the room, she was gone, and he was dead."

Clark settled onto the settee without a word, and Penny put a tumbler of whiskey in each of our hands.

He studied the honey-colored liquid. "Why would she kill him? I mean, what does she have to gain by him being dead?"

Penny beat me to the punch. "Over two million dollars."

Clark wrinkled his brow and stared at me.

"Richter had over two million bucks, and he left it all to me."

"I'm not following," he said. "What does that have to do with Anya?"

"She's his only heir," I said.

Clark dropped his chin and swirled his drink. "I'm not buying it. What would she do with that much money? Run back home to Mother Russia and live a life of luxury?"

"No, I don't think so," I said. "I don't think she wants to go back to Russia. I think she wants to live here in America or maybe the Caribbean. With that kind of money, she could vanish from everyone's radar and live out the rest of her life almost anywhere she wanted."

He shook his head. "Nope. I'm still not buying it. You tried to give her that option, and she didn't take it. What's changed?"

"A lot has changed. First, she's underground now, living on the run. She has no support, no home, no income. She's completely rogue."

"How do you know?" said Penny. "How do you know she's not getting paid? Maybe she's still on somebody's payroll. Maybe she's not rogue at all. If you go at this thing with the wrong assumptions up front, and if she's as dangerous as you say, this could turn into—as you like to say—a train wreck in a swamp."

Penny had a knack for seeing through bullshit, and I was learning to listen when her BS alarm started going off.

"What *do* we know?" I said. "Let's list the things we're sure of."

Clark began. "We know she escaped a CIA safe house in Virginia after killing her highly trained team of babysitters, and we know she killed Michael Anderson on Cumberland Island."

Penny said, "It's starting to sound like killing people is all she does. I think the two of you are pretty lucky to have escaped her web unscathed."

"We didn't," said Clark. "She cut your boyfriend's tongue in half, and she would've cut his hand off if it hadn't been for the spare parts in his wrist that aren't so easy to slice with a fighting knife."

Penny glared at me and pursed her lips. I couldn't tell if she was angry because I hadn't told her, or if she was just thankful I was alive.

"It wasn't as dramatic as he makes it sound," I said in a poorly executed attempt to change the subject. "I'm not so sure you're right about what happened in Virginia. We believe that was her, but we don't know for sure. All we know for sure is that there was a pile of dead bodies in the attic and a missing chopper."

Clark nodded. "Yeah, you're right, but the thing on Cumberland Island had to be her."

"I think so, too. Skipper got a good look at her, and there's no question that was Anya's knife sticking out of Michael Anderson's back."

"We also know she was in Birmingham and that she was the last person to see Dr. Richter alive," said Penny. "And how did she end up in a CIA safe house? I didn't even know they were real. I thought they were only in movies."

Once again, I was impressed. Penny was asking all the right questions.

I said, "That's a giant piece of the puzzle we don't have. We have no idea how or why she ended up in that safe house...if that was actually her. Oh, and safe houses are very real, by the way."

"I have so much to learn," she said, "but don't you think that might be a pretty important piece of the puzzle?"

I locked eyes with Clark. "If anybody knows, it's Michael Pennant."

Clark scoffed and shook his head. "I don't think they'll be rolling out the red carpet for you at Langley after your last visit with DDO Pennant."

I had made an ass of myself at a security checkpoint in CIA headquarters to get in to see Michael Pennant, the Deputy Director of Operations. Pennant had worked his way up through the ranks at the CIA, starting as an operative in the clandestine services. He'd been legendary as a field agent, but as a deputy director, I believed he'd become little more than a bureaucrat. Regardless, he was a bureaucrat with vaults full of secrets, and I needed to peek inside.

"Maybe I should take him flowers and chocolates this time," I said.

Penny slugged my arm. "Hey, I like chocolates and flowers."

"I'm sure you do," I laughed, "but you're not part of the CIA hierarchy."

"Are you sure?" she hissed.

"At this point, nothing about you could surprise me."

I sipped my cocktail and started devising a plan. Plans are important, but in my experience, the ability to make decisions on the fly and adapt to ever-changing environments was more important. Pennant would never tell me the truth about Anya. He wasn't in the truth business. Even though he wore a suit and tie and sat behind a mahogany desk, he was still a clandestine services operative when it came to divulging secrets. I had to come up with a way to get the information I needed out of him.

As the ice in my glass rattled with the whiskey long gone, my phone chirped.

"Hello, this is Chase."

"Mr. Fulton, what have you done?"

"I'm sorry?" I said. "Who is this?"

"This is Sister Mary Robicheaux, and I don't know what you did or how you did it, but thank you, thank you, thank you and God bless you."

"Sister Mary, I wouldn't know what you're talking about."

"Mr. Fulton, Congresswoman D'Angelo delivered a check for one million dollars from the D'Angelo Family Foundation to Saint Francis School today. Whatever you did, you're an angel!"

"I'm no angel, Sister."

"Well, whatever you are, you're a godsend, Mr. Fulton. The million-dollar donation isn't the best part. That demon son of hers is gone, too."

"What are you saying, Sister?"

"When the Congresswoman made the announcement about donating to my school, she also stated that her son would be going to work for the family foundation in Italy. I'll never be able to thank you enough, Mr. Fulton. I want to know what you did, but you'll never tell me, will you?"

"I'm just a sailboat bum, Sister. I live on my boat and stay out of people's business. I'm glad your situation has worked itself out."

"You're an angel," she said as I hung up the phone.

"What was that about?" asked Penny.

"That was some nun from Saint Francis going on about a million-dollar donation and some congresswoman announcing that her son was going to work for the family foundation in Italy. It must've been a wrong number."

The first things I ever found beautiful about Penny were her infectious smile and enthusiasm for everything. Both came flooding back, yanking her from the drudgery of our conversation. She sprang to her feet and leapt onto my lap. I could feel the excitement and energy in her body as she flung her arms around me and pressed her lips to mine. Her innocence and joy were irresistible.

"Is this how it always feels for you?" she squealed.

"What do you mean?"

"Is it always this exciting when you finish a mission and you know the good guys have won?"

I glanced at Clark. He was shaking his head again.

"No," I said. "It's almost never like this. We go in, do a job, and get out. No one ever really knows what we've done. The world just continues to turn, and people are none the wiser."

"But what you do is important. I mean, you're like saving the world and stuff, right?"

"No," I said, "we just do our job and move on to the next one."

"So, this must feel great to you then—getting to see how you've made such a difference."

"Actually, it makes me a little nervous. I'd rather be anonymous."

"Me, too," echoed Clark. "In our business, publicity is a bad thing."

Penny furrowed her brow. "But it has to feel good knowing you've done so much good for so many people."

"It does feel good," I admitted, "but the things we do aren't the kinds of things that should end up on the evening news."

"I get that, but I'm really proud of you for this one."

I smiled. "I couldn't have done it without you."

"I just drove the boat. That's all."

"Oh, you did far more than just drive the boat, but as I'm sure you already know, we can't talk about what we did with anyone other than the three of us."

"Of course, I know that," she said.

Clark cleared his throat. "I hate to break up this little *Spies Like Us* party, but we need to get back on track."

Penny sighed. "Oh, yeah. Her."

"Yes, her," I said. "If we can get in to see Pennant, maybe we'll be able to get some answers out of him."

"Before we go running off to Washington to stir the pot, I think it would be a good idea to get my dad in the loop, don't you?"

Clark's father, Dominic Fontana, was my handler. My mission assignments came through him, and I was supposed to coordinate almost everything I did with him, but I'd never been good at asking permission.

"Yeah, you're right, but I don't think he'll be too supportive of what I have in mind."

Clark lifted his eyebrows. "You might be surprised."

"Don't you think a face-to-face would be better than a phone call?"

"Definitely."

"Can I come?" asked Penny.

The thought of inviting her further into my professional world terrified me. Everyone inside the circle eventually gets hurt...or worse. Penny was quickly becoming more than just the girl I was sharing a bunk with. I still wasn't sold on the whole two-kids-and-a-black-lab idea, but the initial desire and fascination I had for her had morphed into respect, and I couldn't deny the fact that I had fallen completely in love with her.

"Sure, you can come, but you'll have to spend the day on the beach or shopping in Miami while Clark and I meet with Dominic. Are you okay with that?"

She pressed the back of her hand to her forehead and sighed. "Oh, my. How's a girl ever supposed to cope with the horrible prospect of sunning on South Beach and shopping on the Miracle Mile? When do we leave?"

Clark and I simultaneously said, "Ten minutes."

Penny vanished into the interior and soon emerged with her hair in a ponytail and a duffle bag across her shoulder.

"How do you do that?" I asked.

"Do what?"

"Get ready to go so quickly?"

"South Beach, shopping, trip with two hot guys. How could I *not* be ready lickety-split?"

"That reminds me," Clark said. "Do you remember Lieutenant Joanna Grayson from D.C.?"

A former army captain for whom Clark had worked while he was on active duty had hooked us up with a pair of photo analysts while we were on a mission in the Shenandoah Valley of Virginia. One of the analysts was a stunning beauty who had left Clark stumbling over his tongue.

I laughed. "Yeah, I remember Duchess. She's the only woman I've ever seen turn you into a blabbering teenager."

He blushed. "Yeah, whatever. I see what Penny does to you, Romeo, so don't go making fun of me."

"Penny's never made me forget my name."

Before Clark could defend himself further, Penny whispered, "I'll make you forget more than just your name next time I get you alone."

It was my turn to blush.

"Anyway," he said. "She came down to Virginia Beach for a couple of days while I was home, and I sort of may have invited her to come down to St. Augustine and hang out on the boat. I hope that's okay."

"Of course it's okay," I said. "That's great."

"Ooh"—Penny pinched Clark's cheeks—"I look forward to meeting the girl who can turn the great playboy Clark Johnson into mush."

Chapter 8
Did You Hit a Bus?

We ran through the preflight inspection and soon had my Cessna 182 headed south along the eastern coast of Florida. Penny asked if she could ride up front, and Clark quickly agreed.

"I'll catch a nap in the back seat on the way down," he said. "I stayed up all night worrying about what kind of trouble you two had gotten into."

I'd come to think of Clark as part cat. He rarely missed an opportunity to enjoy a nap, even though he liked to brag about how little sleep Green Berets needed.

It turned out that I'd been wrong when I'd made the statement that nothing more about Penny could surprise me.

"Can I fly?" she asked somewhere south of Daytona.

"Sure," I said. "Just hold the yoke with one hand, and keep your eyes on the horizon. Turn left to go left and right to go right. If the horizon appears to be falling, that means you're pulling on the yoke. Simply push it back forward to lower the nose. Okay?"

She smiled and placed a gentle hand on the yoke. I kept my feet on the rudder pedals to help coordinate any turns she might make, but as it turned out, that wasn't necessary. She handled the plane like an old pro.

"You've done this before," I said.

She moved the microphone boom away from her lips, leaned toward me, and kissed me on the cheek. "I love surprising you."

"When did you learn to fly?"

"In high school," she said. "I told you my dad was a salesman for a liquor distributor. He and I took flying lessons together, and then he bought a Mooney. His sales territory was huge, so the plane made it easier for him to get to his customers without driving all over Texas every week. He got his instrument rating, but I just got my private license and only flew a couple hundred hours."

"How long has it been since you've flown?"

"Oh, maybe ten years. It's been so long, I don't even know where my logbook is anymore."

"Well, you clearly haven't lost your touch."

She shrugged. "Maybe it's like riding a bike."

I motioned toward the back seat. "You know, Sleeping Beauty back there is an instructor, so he can get you current again. It'll be nice to have another pilot in the family."

Her radiant smile reappeared. "I like that."

"What? Getting back in the air?"

"No, silly. I like that you think of me as part of the family."

* * *

Just over three hours after taking off from St. Augustine, we put the gear down and turned onto the final approach leg into the airport. Clark slept almost the entire time, but Penny bounced her landing just enough to get his attention.

Clark sprang from his fetal position on the back seat. "Did you hit a bus?"

"No, it was just a little bounce," I said. "That was her first landing in ten years or so."

He wiped the sleep from his eyes. "Hey, this is Key Largo. I thought we were going to Miami."

"We are," I said, "but it's been a while since I've seen my car. I'd like to take it back to St. Augustine with us."

"Good idea."

Penny taxied us to the parking apron, and my old friend, Hank, came strolling onto the ramp in his typical laid-back style.

"Chase! How's it goin', young man? It's been too long!"

I shook Hank's hand and introduced him to Penny. His eyes met mine with inquisition.

"It's a long story," I said.

Hank had adored Anya…and every other beautiful Eastern European woman he'd ever seen.

"I've come to pick up my car, if it's still here."

"Sure, sure. It's right where you left it. I crank it every couple of weeks to make sure the battery isn't going dead. It should be ready to go."

"Is there a bathroom inside?" Penny asked.

"Yeah." Hank pointed the way. "Just right in there on the left. Make yourself at home."

As Penny walked away, Hank said, "What happened to Anya? You didn't run her off, did you?"

"No, nothing like that. She wasn't who I thought she was, so she moved on."

Hank raised his eyebrows. "They're all more than they appear on the surface, son."

"Yeah, well, in Anya's case, the surface pretended to be red, white, and blue, but there was still a pretty big emphasis on the red, if you know what I mean."

"Ah, she still had some love for the motherland."

"To put it mildly," I said.

"Well, in that case, I'd say you've upgraded. That one going there sounds as Southern as grits and gravy. I doubt you'll have to worry about her waving a hammer and sickle."

"I think you're right, Hank. She's quite a catch."

He patted me on the back. "You go check on your car, and I'll get the fuel truck. You want me to top her off?"

"You don't fool me, old man," I said. "You're going in there to flirt with my girl. You keep your hands to yourself."

He raised his hands in mock innocence. "Why, I never!"

My car was just as I had left it beneath two enormous palm trees. I pulled off the fitted cover as Clark and Penny showed up.

"Is this your car?" Penny snatched the keys from my hand. "A boat, a plane, and a BMW. I've hit the boyfriend trifecta!"

I huffed and stuck out my bottom lip. "It looks like I'm the passenger…again."

Clark said, "I'll take the plane and meet you guys at Miami Executive so we won't have to drive back here after meeting with my dad."

"Perfect," I said. "We'll meet you there in an hour."

The flight would take less than fifteen minutes, but the drive across Card Sound Road and through Homestead would probably take an hour, unless Penny drove like Anya. If that were the case, we might beat Clark.

As we crossed the bridge over Jewfish Creek, I told Penny how I'd spent my first weeks aboard my first boat anchored less than a mile from there.

"What happened to your first boat?" she asked.

You promised you wouldn't lie to her.

"Anya set it on fire and sank it with an incendiary grenade."

"I guess it was never boring having her around, huh?"

I laughed. "No, boring would not be how I'd describe those days."

"You miss her, don't you?"

Women ask some of the most unexpected questions at some of the most bizarre times.

"I used to miss her," I confessed, "but not anymore. That part of my life is over. I have you now, and I've never been happier."

"That's a good answer, but I'm not convinced it's the truth."

I paid for a spot on the ramp at Executive to leave my airplane, and we collected Clark.

An hour later, we arrived at the marina, and I handed the key fob and a credit card to Penny. "I'll get us a place on South Beach and call you in a couple of hours. Have fun."

Clark and I walked past where the young Cuban receptionist should've been, and into Dominic's office.

"What a surprise!" Dominic embraced Clark in an overdue fatherly hug and shook my hand welcomingly. "Come in, come in. I get the feeling you two weren't just in the neighborhood and decided to drop in."

"No," I admitted. "We need to have a talk."

"Sure. Would you like a drink?"

He headed for a small bar in the corner of his office.

"Scotch would be great."

He poured three glasses and returned to his seat. "Okay, so let's hear it."

I wasted no time. "I have to find Anya."

Dominic took a long swig of his cocktail. "Well, that's quite the icebreaker."

"I don't see any sense in beating around the bush."

"Nope, there's rarely any bush beating with you, and I like that. So, why the urgency to find her?"

"I originally wanted to find her to give her two million dollars, but—"

"Whoa!" he said. "What do you mean, give her two million dollars?"

"Dr. Richter left me almost everything he owned, including over two million dollars because he had no living heirs. But she *is* his daughter."

"I'm obviously a little behind the power curve here, but you said you originally wanted to find her for that reason. What's the reason now?"

I took a long, slow breath. "I think she may have killed him."

"Killed who?" he said.

"Dr. Richter. I think she may have killed him. I saw her through the window of his hospital room only minutes before he died. By the time I got there, she was gone, and he was dead."

He pulled off his glasses and stuck the stem into the corner of his mouth. "That's some theory you have there, Chase. Why are you telling me all of this?"

"Because you're my handler, and I need your help."

"Okay," he said, placing his glasses on his desk. "What do you need?"

"I need to talk with Michael Pennant and find out what he knows about her. I need to know if she's still alive."

"Still alive?" He poured himself another drink.

"Yeah, I need to know if she's still alive. I can't be certain of—"

Dominic held up his hand. "Just hold on a minute, Chase." He walked to the window, gazed out over the water, and slowly swirled his drink.

I wordlessly asked Clark what was going on. He shrugged and joined me in watching his father stare into the distance.

"You won't be talking with Pennant," Dominic finally said.

"But he's our only—"

"Shut up and listen," he scolded. "She's still alive as far as we know, but she won't be for long."

I leaned toward the desk as Dominic turned from the window and bore holes through my eyes. I'd never heard him raise his voice before then, and I wasn't sure what was going on, but whatever it was, it had the man more upset than I'd ever seen him.

"I don't know what brought you two here with this idea about Anya killing Richter, but it wasn't her."

"But I saw her in the hospital in Birmingham the day Dr. Richter died."

"No, you didn't. You saw who you *thought* was her. You saw someone who you were *supposed* to believe was her. It wasn't Anya. It was Norikova."

When I'd learned Anya wasn't who she'd claimed to be, I was told by the CIA that her real name was Ekaterina Norikova, a Russian SVR captain. So much deception had occurred that it was impossible to sort out reality from the tangled web of lies.

I wanted to ask a thousand questions, but Dominic stopped me before I could begin.

"Just wait, okay? Sit there and wait a minute."

He stomped toward the corner of his office, and after pressing several numbered keys on a cipher lock, he pulled a door open. I watched him step inside the space and spin the dial of an old iron safe. He returned to his desk with three thick folders bound with twine and tossed the first one onto my lap.

"How's your Cyrillic?" he asked.

"Poor at best," I admitted as I opened the file. It was clearly a Russian case file written entirely in Cyrillic, but that wasn't the disturbing part. Paper-clipped inside the front cover were photocopies of two black-and-white pictures. One was Dr. Richter, and the other was me.

I scanned the first two pages. "I can't make out more than ten percent of this, Dominic. I'm going to need some help."

He shoved the two remaining files toward the edge of his desk and spun his chair to face the window.

I closed the file and placed it on his desk, and then took the first of the two remaining files. The same photocopies clung to the inside cover, and the documents inside were translated copies of the original Russian file.

Having a white-hot steel shank driven through my chest would've felt better than reading the documents. Details of my life, my training, and my weaknesses and strengths were spread out in front of me like a roadmap to my psyche. A similar dossier on Dr. Richter followed mine. His portion represented over five decades, while mine was less than two dozen pages. At the end of Richter's section were several more photocopies. I recognized the woman in the pictures immediately. It was Katerina Burinkova, the same beautiful woman whose image adorned the nose of Dr. Richter's P-51 Mustang. Burinkova was Anya's mother, and the woman he'd loved.

I closed the file and exchanged it for the remaining one on the desk. It could only contain one thing—the SVR's operational plan to infiltrate American covert ops. I imagined I was about to experience the Earthly equivalent of standing before Saint Peter as he reads off my list of sins at the Pearly Gates. My mouth felt like the Sahara Desert, and my heart pounded like thunder.

Chapter 9
Gang Aft A-gley

Sometime in the seventeen hundreds, poet Robert Burns wrote "To a Mouse" as an apology to a family of mice whose nest he'd destroyed while plowing a field. Little did he know when he wrote the line, "The best-laid schemes o' mice an' men gang aft a-gley," that three hundred years later we'd still be quoting him. Well, sort of quoting him.

The file resting in my lap, each page burning the very depths of my mind, contained one of the most diabolical and best-laid plans ever devised by mouse or man.

The world around me dissolved into melting blurs of reality as I digested every word of Colonel Viktor Tornovich's plan to train Corporal Anastasia Burinkova, a *sirota*—an orphan—to find, seduce, and recruit America's newest rising star in covert ops, namely, one Chase Fulton.

The plan was perfectly designed, right down to the most intricate detail. Reading the script for my own seduction was like watching hidden-camera video of my most private moments. The words, phrases, and sounds Anya made that left me utterly defenseless against her seduction were scripted, practiced, and perfected months before she ever whispered in my ear or let me brush her long, blonde hair. The tone and pace of her voice when she said, "*YA lyublyu tebya*," had been rehearsed a thousand times before I ever heard her confess her love for me. Every intimate moment she and I spent was predestined, scheduled, practiced, and perfected long before the love I had for her was born.

The file went on to detail the long-term extent of the scheme. Anya was to marry "the American" and bear his children, all the while routinely reporting every detail she could glean back to Moscow. She had been ordered to spend the remainder of her life pretending to be in love with me, solely for the purpose of gathering intelligence on our operations. I could never fathom dedication of that magnitude.

If she hadn't been shot, would I have ever learned the truth?

As devastating as phase one of the plan had been, the second phase felt like my heart had been ripped from my chest and crushed to a bloody pulp. Phase two detailed the platonic, paternal seduction of Dr. Robert Richter. The Russians had known all along that Anya was Richter's daughter, but she believed otherwise. The physical resemblance was undeniable, but the strategists in the Kremlin used that morsel of genealogy to further convince Anya that she was destined for this duty to the Rodina.

She would continuously bait the trap to lead me into sharing details about her with my mentor, Dr. Richter, until he was convinced that she was, in fact, his daughter. That the lie was actually the truth made the grift immeasurably easier to sell. Richter would believe every word because he wanted to believe it, and Anya would play her role as the good soldier, never knowing the lie she was selling was the God's honest truth.

Colonel Tornovich's ruthlessness seemed to have no limits. He would destroy the heart and soul of a great American and implant his agent so deeply inside American covert ops that Richter himself would succumb to Anya's scheme. Reading how Tornovich wanted to destroy Dr. Richter made me hate the Russian Colonel even more. I'd put a bullet in his forehead in the mountains of Virginia, but after seeing the exhaustive strategies he'd planned to destroy Dr. Richter, I wanted to have him resurrected so I could kill him again.

I replayed the interrogation I'd put the colonel through and tried to recall his answers. He'd lied even at the moment of his death. He had clung to the lie that Anya had actually been Norikova, but that hadn't been true. Tornovich had been so bound by his determination and duty to the Kremlin that he kept planting disinformation in my head even as I pulled the trigger and ended his life. Without the file, I would've never known the truth. I would've never been able to decipher the insanely intricate web of deception Tornovich had woven.

The next section of the file answered the myriad questions surrounding the identity of Anya and Norikova. I'd believed they were one and the same, but just like everyone else who thought that, I'd been sorely mistaken.

The file detailed the second agent, Captain Ekaterina Norikova, the half sister of Anastasia Burinkova. Norikova had been the result of an affair with a senior official of the Communist Party. Anya's mother gave birth in a hospital in Moscow, and the baby was immediately whisked away into state custody, raised in the home of the communist bureaucrat, and later served as a foreign intelligence officer in the SVR. The nearly identical appearance of Anya and her half sister was precisely the ace in the hole the Kremlin needed to keep Tornovich's plan in place, even after the original plan had "gang aft a-gley."

Just when I thought I could never despise anyone more than I detested Tornovich, Dominic turned from the window and reached for the file. "There's more."

I handed him the file and glanced into my empty glass. Clark appeared and wordlessly refilled my tumbler. I poured the contents into my mouth and felt it burn its way down my throat, past where my heart had once been.

"Chase," began Dominic, "today is the day you lose what is left of your innocence. Some things are done in the name of preservation of freedom that are, under normal circumstances, neither palatable nor fathomable, but when done for the purpose of liberty, are absolutely necessary."

I didn't know where he was leading me, but I believed his speech was designed to prepare me for information even more devastating than what I'd read in the files.

"You'll never read what I'm about to tell you in any file. No one other than me will ever brief you on this information. The theory you came in here with, as crazy as it sounds, is solid. What you think you saw in Birmingham makes sense."

"Wait a minute. You said what I *thought* I saw in Birmingham. I know what I saw."

"No, Chase, you don't. Just like almost everything else in our world, almost nothing is as it appears. What you saw was a thin, beautiful blonde through a second-story hospital window. Your mind identified that woman as Anya, but it was not. We know that with certainty."

"How can you possibly know that?" I demanded.

"We know it wasn't her because Anastasia Burinkova is in the Black Dolphin Prison, just south of Orenburg near the Kazakhstan border. The woman you saw was Ekaterina Norikova, and you did, in fact, witness her kill Robert Richter."

I drove my fist into the top of his desk. "Why hasn't she been arrested?"

"We don't arrest foreign intelligence officers, Chase. It's not how things work. But she has been detained and is being held overseas by some friends of ours."

"Friends?"

"Yes, friends. Friends who are very good at detaining people who don't necessarily want to be detained."

"You're not going to tell me who has her, are you?"

He shook his head. "No, I'm afraid not. At least not yet."

I took a long breath, trying to digest what I was learning. I glanced at Clark, and for the first time since I'd met him, he wouldn't look me in the eye.

Did he know this information, and has he been keeping it from me? Did he bring me here under the guise of it being my idea? Is he a coconspirator?

Dominic witnessed the silent exchange. "Clark, if you don't wish to be here for this, that's perfectly understandable, and I don't want you to feel any obligation—"

Clark didn't let his father finish. "How long have you known?"

Dominic cast his eyes to the floor. "Days."

"How *many* days?" he growled.

"Clark," Dominic said. "This sort of thing is very sensitive and can't be widely disseminated. These are matters that must be handled with the utmost secrecy."

Clark stood and placed his hand on my shoulder. "Look at this man, Dad. He has done every damned thing you've ever asked, and a thousand more. He's never once shied away from any mission, regardless of the dangers or the cost. He's given you his life to throw in front of any enemy you can find, and you've let bureaucratic bullshit stop you from telling him the truth. I've been in this game for seventeen years, and I've worked with and against some of the best operators on Earth—from countless countries—and I've never soldiered beside another man who had the courage and valor of Chase Fulton. He deserves the truth from you and from the people you work for, regardless of how devastating it may be."

I felt bad for thinking Clark may have been manipulating me. He would always be the most solidly loyal and dependable force in my life. His inability to look me in the eye wasn't a result of something he was hiding from me; it was anger and disgust with the heartless system sticking in his craw.

Dominic tried to defend his position. "It's not that simple."

"Yes, it is," Clark said, having regained his composure. "You've got good people working for you who are getting torn apart, inside and out, over bullshit that's being kept from them. You say you've known this information for days. How many days? And when were you planning to brief him on any of it?"

I was flattered Clark would stand up for me, but the conversation was getting out of hand. "Okay. Enough," I said. "The point is you're briefing us now, so let's hear the rest. But no more lies, and don't you dare hold anything back."

Dominic wore a look of embarrassment coupled with suppressed anger. His face was red, but his clenched jaw had turned the edges of his lips white. His nostrils flared as he took long, slow breaths, an exercise I'd used many times to calm my mind when things were on the verge of chaos.

My phone chirped, but I ignored it.

Dominic didn't. "Why don't we take a break and you answer your phone?"

I didn't move. "Why don't you tell me the rest? The phone can wait."

He pushed back away from his desk and crossed his legs. "The Israelis have Norikova. After Anya got shot, Tornovich's plan went all to hell."

"Stop there," I said. "Tell me what happened in the hospital. Anya was alive and breathing when I dropped her at the door exactly as *you* arranged. *You* told me she was dead, and that was a lie. Why?"

He sighed in resolution. "You're right. I lied to you, but I had no choice. By that point, the CIA discovered what was happening, and they took over. It was out of my control. Anya was stabilized and moved to another hospital where she recovered from her injuries. She was an extremely high-value asset in the hands of the CIA, and she started talking."

"Bullshit. Anya wouldn't just start talking. She's not that weak. What did they do to her?"

"It's not what they did to her that made her talk, Chase. It's what they threatened to do to you."

"To me? What could they possibly do to me?"

"They told her you would be tried for treason and most likely convicted and sentenced to death for colluding with her. And she cut a deal."

"What kind of deal?"

"In return for the U.S. Attorney's agreement not to prosecute you for treason, she agreed to not only tell us everything she knew, but also to work with and for us."

"Why would she do that? If her whole purpose was to dig her claws into me so she could infiltrate American covert ops, why would she turn her back on the Kremlin to protect me?"

"By all indications, her well-practiced act of loving you had stopped being an act and had become reality. She was willing to give up everything she believed in and everything she held dear to protect you, Chase. To save you from your own country."

Unable to form any other coherent words, I mumbled, "You were never going to prosecute me."

Dominic shook his head. "No, the U.S. Attorney was never going to prosecute you. The thought never entered anyone's head except the Agency interrogators. It didn't have to be true. They just had to make Anya believe it."

Stunned silence pinned me to my seat and left me bewildered.

Why would she do that? Why would she sacrifice herself to save me?

"If she was in CIA custody, how did she end up in a Siberian prison?"

"This is the part you're not going to like," Dominic said.

"I don't like any of it. Why would what comes next be any different?"

"Your little unsanctioned raid on the safe house in Virginia opened the door for a Russian snatch team to grab their girl back and whisk her away, leaving Captain Norikova in her place to wreak havoc while pretending to be Anya."

The thought of my actions being the reason Anya was dying in a frozen hell in some godforsaken prison was enough to send my mind cascading into a pit so deep I feared I'd never see the light again.

"So, what happens now?"

Dominic cleared his throat. "That's not up to us. It's up to the geeks and bureaucrats at the State Department. The Russians want Norikova back for many reasons, not the least of which is she's the daughter of an old-school Communist Party official. The fact that she's an SVR officer falls somewhere way down the list of reasons, but it's safe to say they're willing to make a deal to get her back."

"So, it's simple," I said. "We give them Norikova, and they give us Anya."

Clark grunted. "That'll never happen. State doesn't give a damn about Anya. They already have what they need from her."

No truer words had ever been spoken, and they tore at my soul. I would have to live the rest of my life knowing she'd thrown her life away to save mine, and all I'd done in return was get her thrown in the gulag.

Chapter 10
Not Exactly

Penny pirouetted in front of me with the tags still dangling from a dress that looked custom-made for her stunning body. "How about this one?"

I mumbled, "Yeah, that one's nice, too."

"Chase, what's going on with you? You didn't say a dozen words at dinner, and now I can't even get your attention in the sexiest dress in South Beach." She knocked on my head as if she wanted in. "What's happening inside there?"

"It wasn't Anya," I said.

"What wasn't Anya?"

"In the hospital. It wasn't her. It was somebody else."

She tucked her hair behind her ear and knelt between my feet. "Who was it, then?"

I couldn't make eye contact with her. "It was an SVR captain named Ekaterina Norikova, Anya's half sister."

Penny squinted her eyes and tilted her head in a gesture of disbelief.

"It's a long and convoluted story, but it definitely wasn't Anya in Birmingham."

"So, is she…"

"Dead?" I asked. "Probably. If she isn't dead now, she soon will be."

"What do you mean?" She seemed genuinely concerned.

"She's in a prison called the Black Dolphin in southwestern Russia, near the border of Kazakhstan. She's being held for treason, a capital offense in Russia."

I couldn't identify the look on her face. It may have been relief, but I couldn't be sure.

"So, there's nothing you can do, right?"

I didn't answer.

"Chase, what are you thinking? You're not going to Russia. You can't."

Again, I didn't answer, and the look on her face morphed from relief to utter despair.

"You're going, aren't you?"

I closed my eyes. "She went to prison because she spilled her guts to the CIA when they threatened to prosecute me for treason. She did it to save my life."

"No, that's not what happened. You know that's not the truth. Someone's trying to manipulate you."

"I don't think so," I said softly. "I think she believed they were going to convict me of treason and sentence me to death, so she did everything in her power to save me."

"Chase, you're being a fool. She's a spy. You said it yourself. She never did anything other than what she was trained and ordered to do."

I walked out onto the balcony. The Atlantic Ocean lapped at the sand of South Beach as tourists and locals drank, laughed, and misbehaved on the street below separating the hotel from the pristine beach. The late October sun had long since hidden itself beyond the horizon behind me, but the night air was still warm and humid. The horde beneath me danced and lived out their hedonistic debauchery, oblivious to the chaos of atrocities happening in the world around them.

I thought about Anya's flawless Eastern European skin, and how the subtropical sun turned it caramel. She'd face the sky with her arms spread, relishing the taste and smell of the salt air and the warmth of the sun. The rays would dance on the strands of her golden hair as if she'd been made for the Caribbean. As if she were part of the trade winds. She'd never feel that heat on her face again. She'd die in the bowels of that frozen prison, with her beautiful hair knotted and filthy, and her angelic skin returning to pale.

Penny's hands slid around my waist, and she pressed her body against my back. Her hair danced on the evening breeze, and her breath fell across the skin of my neck. She squeezed me against her and whispered, "It's impossible for me to know what you're feeling, but watching your heart break hurts me to my core. I love you, Chase. No matter how distant you are, either inside your head or on the far side of the world, I'll not stop loving you. And as long as you want, I'll be waiting for you to come home to me."

I pulled her in front of me and placed my hands on her waist, lifting her onto the railing of the balcony. Her eyes never left mine, and she didn't flinch, even though she was sitting on a narrow railing high above the street. The faith she had in me was unwavering, and I knew I could never let her fall.

"I'm sorry," I said. "I wish I could turn it off."

She pressed her finger to my lips and then laid her hands gently on my forearms. "I'm glad you can't. If you could, you wouldn't be the kind of man I could ever love."

"I'm not the man I want to be...not the man I should be."

"You're a man of extremes," she said. "A man who is dark enough to dangle another human being over a bottomless pit, all because the goodness inside you can't bear the thought of innocent little children being hurt. You're dangerous and terrifying to those who would harm defenseless people, but you're selfless and generous at the same time. How is that possible?"

I stroked her face with the back of my hand and tried to think of the right thing to say, but words wouldn't come. A crack of thunder roared through the air, and an explosion of light filled the southern sky. Penny leapt from the railing and into my arms with a startled, subdued scream, and then giggled like a delighted child. Ribbons of red, white, and blue fireworks painted the night sky, and the intensity grew until it was full of explosions of light. I stood with my arms wrapped tightly around her, and we laughed.

When the show was over, we made our way back into the suite, and the fashion show continued. Penny had bought some of the most beautiful dresses I'd ever seen. Every time she emerged from the bedroom, she looked more breathtaking than the time before. With every return, she left the door a little more ajar and rewarded me with a show even more dazzling than the fireworks.

We made love in the luxurious bed and finally found ourselves thoroughly lost in euphoric, wordless appreciation.

I excused myself then returned to the bed a few minutes later with a bottle of sparkling water and a few pieces of decadent, dark chocolate that had been left for us. Her new dresses were laid neatly across the arms and back of a chair, and I tried to decide which one I wanted to see her wear again.

"I can take them back if they're too much," she said, sounding almost like a timid child.

I placed a piece of chocolate on her tongue and kissed her nose. "Don't you dare take any of them back. You're astonishing in every single one of them. I don't care how much you spent."

"Are you sure?"

I lay down beside her and pulled her close to me. "I'm very good at what I do."

She motioned toward the nest of covers we'd created during the previous hour. "Oh, yes, you are."

"That's not what I meant," I said, "but, thank you. And you are more than any man deserves. Especially this man."

She snatched a piece of chocolate from my hand, unwrapped it, and slid it seductively into my mouth.

I licked my lips. "As I was saying before you tried to re-seduce me, I'm very good at what I do, and I'm paid exceptionally well for doing it. You don't need to worry about having the things you want. The card I gave you this afternoon is yours."

Her eyes widened, and she playfully slapped at my shoulder. "Yeah, I kinda noticed that. It had my name on it. When did you do that?"

"I figured you were getting tired of asking for an allowance like a bratty teenager—which I'm sure you were ten years ago—so I had the bank send a card for you last week. Don't start buying real estate or Rolls-Royces, but I want you to have the things you want and need."

She grinned. "You slept with Earl, and now you're trying to buy your way out of trouble. I knew it!"

I raised my hands. "You caught me. But in my defense, she's much hotter than you."

She doused me with the remaining contents of the water bottle, and we fell asleep in each other's arms, trying to avoid the wet spot.

I awoke to the smell of coffee, bacon, eggs, and hash browns. Penny was placing a tray on the bed in front of me and wearing nothing except one of my button-down shirts hanging loosely around her shoulders.

"Good morning, Sleepy Head," she said.

I yawned. "Good morning. I see you made breakfast."

She smiled. "I ordered breakfast. But if you want to believe I made it, that's perfectly fine with me. I thought you'd need some nourishment after the night we had."

We ate in relative silence until Penny looked up from her orange juice. "You're going to get her, aren't you?"

I closed my eyes, inhaled deeply through my nose, and tried to form the most honest answer possible. "Not exactly, but I am going to Moscow by way of Tel-Aviv."

"Tel-Aviv?" she questioned through a mouthful of eggs.

I dabbed at the corner of her mouth with my napkin. "Yes. We have to pick up a package in Israel and deliver it to Moscow."

She finished wiping her mouth. "Is Clark going with you?"

"Yes, he's coming. I wouldn't consider this mission without him. We learned a lot of information at yesterday's meeting with Dominic, and we have to take action now."

"So, you're leaving soon?"

"Probably tomorrow."

She cast her eyes away. "It's always going to be like this, isn't it?"

"Be like what?"

She took a long drink of coffee. "You disappearing at the drop of a hat and me not knowing when or if you're coming home."

That was a discussion for another time, but I had to say something. "No, it won't always be this way, but for now, it has to be. Can you live with that?"

She sighed. "I can live with the part about you going away to do your job, but I'm not going to deal well with it if you don't come home."

I took her hand. "Sometimes what I do is dangerous. I deal with personalities that aren't particularly socially acceptable, so there's always the possibility of getting hurt."

"Or killed," she said.

"I won't lie. There's always a slight chance that things won't work out the way I planned, but I have Clark to look after me, and remember, I'm not that easy to kill."

"If you don't come home to me, I'll be the one killing you, and not even Clark will be able to stop me." She tried to make it sound playful, but there was no question she was serious.

I kissed her. "I have to get back to St. Augustine today. We'll fly out of NAS Jax tomorrow. You can do whatever you'd like. If you want to hang out here for a while, the suite is available as long as you want it, or you can always go back to St. Augustine. Whatever you want."

"Really?" she said. "Anything I want?"

"Yes, of course."

She lifted the breakfast tray from the bed and placed it on the nightstand. "Okay. In that case, I want to go with you."

I froze. Bewilderment overtook me, and I was certain my face showed the panic I was feeling.

After a full minute of letting me stew in my own juices, she said, "Relax. I'm just messing with you. You couldn't drag me to Russia in November."

I exhaled in marked relief. "It's still October."

"Yeah, well, thirty below is cold regardless of the month. I'm a big girl. I'll be fine. I'll hang out here another couple of days, and then see if I can catch up with Kip and Teri, wherever they are these days."

Teri was Penny's best friend since high school, and Kip was Teri's husband. Their catamaran looked enough like mine to confuse a team of saboteurs, and it wound up on the bottom of the North Atlantic after an explosive device was planted on the hull. I'd pulled everyone from the burning, sinking boat before it'd vanished beneath the waves, but Teri sustained some pretty nasty burns. Fortunately, she'd healed quickly and was already shopping for another boat.

"I'm sure they'd love to see you," I said, thankful she wasn't on the verge of killing me.

She laughed. "The look on your face was hilarious. I thought spies were supposed to be masters of their emotions. You'd make a terrible poker player." She planted her lips on mine, reminding me just how lost I'd be without her. "Yeah, yeah, I know. You're not a spy."

Someone cleared his throat just outside the door of our bedroom, leaving Penny grabbing for a robe and me grabbing for my pistol.

"Don't shoot, Romeo," said Clark. "It's just me."

"How'd *you* get in here?" I growled.

"Unlike you, I *am* a spy, and getting through locked doors just happens to be one of the things we spies know how to do."

Wrapped awkwardly in the bedspread—the closest thing she could find to a robe—Penny said, "The maid let you in, didn't she?"

He ignored her. "Get some clothes on, Uggah. We've got work to do."

Looking down, I realized I wasn't experiencing the same degree of modesty as Penny. "What do you mean, Uggah?"

He laughed. "You went to school at UGA, didn't you?"

"That's it," I said as I started galloping toward him. "You're getting a naked morning hug."

"Oh, no you don't!" he said as he staggered backward.

I discontinued my pursuit and closed the door.

"You guys are too much," Penny said, allowing the bedspread to fall to the floor. "But I'll take one of those naked morning hugs."

Clark would have to wait.

Chapter 11
Peas and Carrots

Clark leveled off at eight thousand feet headed back toward St. Augustine. "So, how'd Penny take the news?"

"Better than I expected."

He set the autopilot and relaxed for the two-hour flight. "She's a keeper, you know?"

"Yeah, I know, but—"

"No buts," he said. "How long are you gonna keep doing this?"

"Doing what?"

He peered at me over the rim of his sunglasses. "Chasing Anya."

"I'm not chasing Anya."

"Look, man. I'd fight a bear for you—not like a grizzly bear, of course—I mean, like a Care Bear. I'd kick a Care Bear's ass for you, but that girl back there with your car and your hotel room—she wants more than cars and hotel rooms. She wants your last name."

Out on the blue waters of the Atlantic, I watched a sailboat enjoying the same southeasterly wind that was adding twenty knots to our ground speed. When I turned back around, Clark had repositioned his sunglasses and was scanning the instrument panel. He was the most hardened warrior I'd ever known, and completely fearless in the face of any threat, but behind that calloused exterior was an unequaled sincerity and understanding of humanity. He may not have had any diplomas hanging on his wall, but I envied how he could read people. Especially me.

"I agree," I said.

He kept his eyes focused on the panel. "That's the surest way to be right…agreeing with me."

I unbuckled his seatbelt and reached across him, pretending to open the door. "That's it. Get out."

He laughed. "Don't tempt me. I know a beautiful girl down there in Vero Beach who'd love to have an old Airborne Ranger land in her backyard. That'd be a lot more fun than keeping you alive in Siberia."

I reattached his seatbelt. "I agree with you that Penny's a keeper. I just worry that what we do for a living makes a real relationship impossible."

Again, over the rim of the glasses. "A living? Are you serious?"

"Yes, I'm serious. Our job is not conducive to family life. Your dad is the perfect example."

"You're right about that, but you don't do this for a living. How much money do you have in the bank?"

He'd never asked about my bank accounts before then, and I'd never volunteered.

"Come on," he said. "I'm serious. How much? Give me the number."

I didn't know where he was going with the conversation, but I had nothing to hide from him. "With the cash Dr. Richter left me, somewhere shy of ten million. Why?"

"Somewhere shy of ten million?" he said. "I also have somewhere shy of ten million in my bank account, but mine is over nine million shy."

"So, what's your point?"

"My point is that you don't do this for a *living*. You do this for some other reason. Your living is already made, Uggah. You can walk away anytime you want, but you're planning to sneak into Russia and cut some crazy deal to get your former girlfriend out of prison."

"It's not that simple," I said.

"Yeah," he said. "It is that simple."

We flew the rest of the trip in silence, and I made a textbook landing back in St. Augustine. We pushed the plane into the hangar, and I began mentally measuring the space not occupied by my 182.

"Have you ever flown a P-51?" I asked.

"No, but I'd like to."

"Dr. Richter left me his Mustang, and I think it'll fit in here."

He froze with a look of utter disbelief.

"I know," I said. "I feel the same."

"Ten million dollars in the bank *and* a Mustang," he said, shaking his head.

"Shy of ten million."

"I know a guy at the Museum of Aviation in Tennessee who has a couple thousand hours in Mustangs. I'm sure I can get him to come down and give us the instruction we'll need in your new toy."

"Great," I said. "Let's give him a call when we get back."

* * *

When we made it back to the boat, I called Skipper. "Hey, there. How's the analyst training going?"

"Oh, my gosh, Chase. It's amazing! You can't imagine all there is to learn. It's so much, but Ginger is an awesome teacher."

"I'm glad you're enjoying it," I said.

"Oh, it's the best. I'm going to rock at this."

"That's fantastic. Listen, I need to talk with Ginger. Is she there?"

"Sure. She's writing some code to task satellites without their operators knowing we're borrowing them. It's so cool. Hang on."

Ginger came on the line. "Hey, Chase. How's it going?"

"I'm great. Skipper tells me she's enjoying what you're teaching her."

"Yeah, she's eating it up, and she's *really* good at it. She's got all the right stuff to be better than me before long."

"That's high praise coming from you," I said.

"She deserves it. You're going to have one hell of an analyst on your hands when I'm done with her."

"I have no doubt, but I need a favor before then."

"Sure. Name it."

"I can't discuss it on the phone. Is there any chance you could come to St. Augustine?"

Her keystrokes sounded like machine-gun fire. "Yep, sure can. We're booked on the six o'clock flight into Jax tonight. Can you pick us up?"

"Thanks, Ginger. I'll send a car for you, and I'll see you in a few hours. Oh, and bring your laptop."

* * *

Skipper and Ginger stepped from the blacked-out Chevy Suburban in Old Town St. Augustine and headed for *Aegis*. Skipper's nearly six-foot frame towered over Ginger, who was barely five feet tall. Had her genetics given her the height, she would have been a supermodel to rival anyone who'd ever worn Victoria's Secret angel wings. Ginger was one of the most incredibly beautiful redheads who'd ever walked the Earth. But neither her tiny stature nor her beauty was the most incredible thing about her—she had the intellect of Einstein and a set of computer skills that was far deadlier than I'd ever be with a rifle.

Skipper came bouncing onto the boat and leapt into my arms. She gave Clark the same treatment and couldn't stop talking about how much she loved learning from Ginger.

When the excitement of the homecoming had waned, it was time to get down to business.

"So, what's this top-secret favor you can't discuss on the phone?" asked Ginger.

I began laying out my plan. "It's pretty simple. We're going to pick up a Russian SVR officer from the Israelis and fly her to Helsinki. Then we're going to smuggle her into Latvia aboard a fishing boat."

Ginger stuck out her bottom lip. "I hope this gets better. So far, a ten-year-old could support that mission."

"Oh, it gets better," I said. "We're going to stuff the SVR officer in a safe house in Riga and take the train to Moscow."

She held up her hand. "Whoa. You're just going to hop on the train and ride it into Moscow? You and Clark? American spies?"

I was tired of denying being a spy, so I let it go. "Well, we don't plan to let anyone know we're on the train."

"Oh, okay. That's reasonable. Go on."

"This is where it gets interesting. We're going to break into Gregor Norikov's house. He's a former Communist Party bigwig who happens to be the father of the SVR officer we're going to stash in Riga." Ginger nodded as I kept talking. "We're going to convince him to release Anya from the Black Dolphin Prison in return for his daughter's safe return to Moscow."

"Sounds reasonable," she said, "but who's Anya?"

I wasn't sure where to start, but I finally made it through a twenty-minute explanation about who Anya was and how she ended up in the prison.

Ginger narrowed her eyes. "Does Penny know what you're doing?"

"She does."

"And is she okay with it?"

I pursed my lips. "I'm not sure if she's okay with the whole thing, but she does understand."

"Hmm."

"So, will you help us?"

Her eyes narrowed even more. "Yeah, I'll help you, but only on one condition."

"Name it," I said.

"When this is done, you put a ring on it."

"Put a ring on what?"

"Penny's left hand."

Clark shrugged. "I told you, Uggah."

"Stop calling me that."

He laughed. "Just be glad you didn't go to South Carolina, 'cause then I'd be calling you Cocky."

I ignored him. "So, here's what we need. A safe house with a dependable team in or near Riga, Norikov's address in Moscow, and a ride home when this is over."

Ginger pulled a spiral notepad from her pocket and scribbled inside. "How about an airplane for the ride from Tel-Aviv to Helsinki?"

"Yeah," I said, "we'll need that, too."

She made another note. "How about a boat from Helsinki to Riga? Do you have that lined up yet?"

"Well, not exactly," I admitted.

She made another note and tossed the pad to Skipper. "Do you have any more questions?"

"No," I said. "That's all."

Ginger shook her head. "No, Chase. I wasn't talking to you. I want to know if Skipper has any questions. This one's hers. I'm just going to look over her shoulder."

Skipper grinned. "I do have one question. Do the Israelis know you're coming to get their prisoner?"

I cocked my head. "I never said she was a prisoner."

"Come on, Chase. I may be new at this, but even I know Mossad doesn't run a bed-and-breakfast. If they have this chick and you're gonna trade her for Anya, she's a prisoner. So, do they know you're coming for her, or not?"

"No, not exactly."

"Okay, then," she said. "That's one more thing you need: a note from mommy to check Little Miss SVR out of school early."

I smiled. "You *are* learning. How much time do you need?"

"I'll need forty-eight hours"—Skipper glanced at Ginger—"but she could do it in, like, eighteen."

"How about we do it together, and you give us twenty-four?" Ginger said.

"Perfect. Twenty-four hours, it is," I said. "We'll book a flight to Tel-Aviv and—"

Skipper cut me off. "No, dummy. Don't book a flight to Tel-Aviv. I'll book you a flight to Cyprus, and then you can catch a local flight into Tel-Aviv."

She was definitely a quick study.

"So, how about some dinner?" I suggested.

Skipper shook her head, "No, we don't have time for that. Just get us a pizza and get out of our way. We've got a lot of work to do."

"Yes, ma'am," I said.

I ordered the pizza and motioned for Clark to join me on the upper deck, where we made ourselves comfortable.

"How do you feel?"

"I'm good," Clark said. "I think your plan is solid, and it'll be a great learning opportunity for Elizabeth."

"I'll never be able to stop calling her Skipper," I said.

"I know, but she asked me to call her Elizabeth, so that's what I'll do."

I motioned toward a bottle of scotch on the counter, but Clark shook his head. I could almost hear Anya saying, "You drink too much, Chase Fulton." I scratched at my chin. "What do you think the chances are of this working?"

He held up his hands. "Maybe twenty percent. There's a lot that can go wrong."

"Yeah, we're going to need a plan B."

"We're going to need a plan Z," he said.

We discussed the operation and finally decided a good night's sleep would be the best option. On our way through the main salon, we found Ginger and Skipper poring over plans and devouring the pizza.

"Good night, guys. We'll see you tomorrow."

Neither woman acknowledged me, and I thought that was a great sign. We would be in good hands.

* * *

Sleep didn't come as I'd hoped it would. I lay in bed, and the thousands of things that could go wrong flooded my mind.

What if we get caught operating inside Russia—in Moscow, no less? Will we end up sharing a cell with Anya?

There were too many bad what-ifs that ended with both Clark and me in a Russian prison. I wondered whether the operation was worth the risk.

* * *

My brain must've endured all the self-torture it could stand, because I obviously drifted off at some point. The sun was coming up. I crawled from my bunk and headed for the galley to start a pot of coffee and found Skipper and Ginger still parked at the table in the main salon. Their laptops hummed, and spiral-bound notebooks were scattered everywhere. Maps of Eastern Europe were taped to the windows, with hastily drawn arcs in yellow highlighter spanning the width of the paper. I wondered where they'd come up with such maps overnight. When I reached the coffee, I was pleased to see a fresh pot had just been brewed, and I morphed into a waiter.

"Good morning, guys. Would you like some coffee?"

Without a word, they shoved empty mugs toward the edge of the table. I took that to mean yes and filled both cups.

"What are those yellow lines on the maps?" I asked.

"Satellite tracks," came their dual response.

"It's going to be yucky. Overcast and snowing for the next two weeks," Skipper said, "so there won't be any live satellite photography. We'll be supporting you blind."

"How about a drone?"

Ginger looked at Skipper as if to say "Why didn't you think of that?" and then typed feverishly on her keyboard.

"That could work," she whispered, "but you'll have to hump it in with you."

"How big is it, and how much does it weigh?" I asked.

She pulled up a data sheet and scanned it. "Less than five pounds, but the batteries weigh almost a pound each. It'll break down no bigger than a shoebox, but that's still a lot of extra cargo."

Clark came stumbling up the stairs and headed straight for the coffee pot.

"You look like you got as much sleep as I did," I said.

"Yeah, it was a tough night. I couldn't stop thinking about what could go wrong."

I laughed. "Great minds think alike."

"Yeah, I guess we're like peas and carrots, but I'm not sure my mind qualifies as great."

"Which one of us is the pea, and which is the carrot?" I asked.

"Does it matter?" he said. "They both turn to crap after they get swallowed up."

"That's one way to look at it," I admitted.

"Can you guys take your act somewhere else? We've still got a lot of work to do here," Ginger said.

We silently obeyed, refilled our mugs, and headed for the upper deck.

It was a glorious October morning on the Matanzas River. The Bridge of Lions drawbridge was on its way up as a tugboat headed north. A pair of sailboats took advantage of the open bridge and followed the tug. I wondered whether the sailors had a destination in mind or if they were simply enjoying the freedom of living on the wind.

My phone chirped, and I pulled it from my pocket to discover a voicemail from Penny. I hadn't heard it ring. I pushed the button and listened. "Hey, it's me. I know you've got a lot on your mind and what you're doing is important, so I want you to know that even though I don't understand what you're doing or why you're doing it, I'm still proud of you for being the man you are. I also want you to know that I'm lucky to be your girlfriend, and I can't wait for you to get home. I really love you, Chase. Okay. Bye."

"That must've been Penny," said Clark.

"How did you know?"

"She's the only person who makes you smile like that."

I thought about what he'd said and wondered how difficult it was for her to stick with me, especially when I was heading to Russia to negotiate the release of my former girlfriend.

"Yeah, it was her," I admitted. "I'm just not sure what I did to deserve her, you know?"

Clark sipped his coffee. "You don't deserve her. She's way too good for you. Are you sure you want to do this?"

"It has to be done," I said, "but I've given what you said a lot of thought."

"I say a lot of stuff," he said. "Which thing are we talking about?"

I looked out over the river as the claxon rang, signaling the drawbridge was on its way back down. "About quitting."

He put on that crooked, knowing smile of his and raised his mug in an unspoken salute.

"I'm thinking about taking a break when we get back," I said.

"A break? You live on a break. Your whole life is a vacation that's occasionally interrupted by work, you playboy. What kind of break are you planning?"

I finished my last drink of coffee. "I thought I might go back to school."

He scoffed. "School, indeed. What are you going to do, become a professor and fill young minds full of wisdom and insight?"

I reached for his mug and stood. "Maybe."

* * *

When I returned from the galley, he asked, "How are they coming along down there?"

"I'm afraid to ask, but they seem to be tidying up the rat's nest they built overnight."

"Good. I'm going to grab a shower, and then we need to get the ball rolling."

He descended the ladder, leaving me alone with my thoughts on the upper deck. It didn't surprise me that my brain went immediately to Penny. I pulled my phone from my pocket and pressed the speed-dial key.

"Good morning," she answered in her sleepy voice. "Have you guys left yet?"

"No, we're still on the boat, but we'll be leaving later today."

"Promise me you'll come back." The helplessness in her voice made her sound like a frightened child.

"Nothing's going to happen to me," I said. "We're just going to have a conversation with a Russian bureaucrat. There's nothing dangerous about this one."

"You promised you wouldn't lie to me."

"I'm not lying. We're simply going to talk with the guy. I'm sure he can be rational."

"I'm not worried about the guy," she said, "and I'm not worried that you'll get hurt."

"Then what are you worried about?"

"I'm worried that you won't come back to *me*," she whispered. "I know what effect *she* has on you."

"Not anymore," I said confidently.

"That's easy to say when you're sitting on your boat and talking with me, but will it still be true when she runs into your arms after you spring her from that prison?"

"I'll never see her," I said. "I'll negotiate the trade—Norikov's daughter for Anya's release. Once that's done, I'll be on a plane and headed back home to you."

"Things always go wrong. Isn't that what you said? No mission ever goes precisely as planned."

"Yes," I admitted, "I did say that, but I can't imagine a scenario that could result in me ever seeing Anya again. And even if I did, I could never trust her. I'm not going to risk what you and I have for anything. I'm in love with *you*, and I'll always come home to *you*."

"Thank you. I needed to hear that. I love you, too, Chase."

We were both silent, unsure of what to say next, until she broke the pause.

"Teri and Kip are coming to Miami this afternoon to meet with a yacht broker. It'll be great to see them."

"That's fantastic news," I said. "I'm sure you'll have a wonderful time. Give them my best, and I'll call you before I leave this afternoon."

As soon as I hung up, a cry came from down below. "Chase, get down here! We've got a plan!"

Chapter 12
Bulldog

Skipper briefed the plan, with Ginger occasionally jumping in with a detail or two. Clark and I sat in silence, listening to Skipper's first real-world mission brief. Her plan was solid, and after an hour of Q&A, we were headed for the airport. *Aegis* would become the tactical operations center for the mission that I hoped would be a quick in and out. The plan was clean, and I had every reason to believe the execution would be just as tidy.

Before we boarded the plane at Naval Air Station Jacksonville, keeping my promise, I pulled my phone from my pocket. "Hey there. I told you I'd call before we left."

Penny's cheerful voice filled my ear. "Hey, Chase. I knew you'd call. Are you leaving now?"

The C-17 cargo plane had her ramp deployed, and the crew was conducting the preflight walk-around.

"Yeah, we'll be getting on the plane any minute now. Ginger and Skipper will run the TOC, and we have some good solid contacts on the ground over there. They've laid the groundwork for a nice clean op. I won't be able to call for the next few days, but I told Skipper to keep you in the loop. I hope that's okay."

I could almost hear her smiling. "Thank you. I'd hoped you'd do that. I know I'm not your wife or anything, but I do worry about you when you're off saving the world."

"Yeah, well, maybe we'll see what we can do about changing that when I get back from Siberia."

She giggled. "Oh, really? And a black lab, too?"

"I love you, Penny. I'll see you soon."

The engines of the C-17 whistled to life as we wheeled our gear up the ramp.

The ten-hour flight stretched the limits of the C-17's range, but we landed at Larnaca International on the coast of Cyprus just before noon the following day. Fortunately, we'd both slept most of the flight, so the jetlag wouldn't take full effect for several hours. The loadmaster told us our gear would be waiting for us in Helsinki, and I thanked him for the ride.

What time I didn't spend sleeping on the plane was spent pondering the questions to which there may never be answers.

Why is Clark so willing to wade through hell with me when he has absolutely nothing to gain from risking everything? Why is a beautiful, brilliant, devoted woman like Penny willing to swallow the pain I dragged her through, and still look into my eyes with such tenderness and unyielding love? How has my life become such a web of danger and confusion, held together by the loyalty and endurance of such incredible people?

A satellite phone call to Skipper and Ginger yielded great news. We'd initially been planning to fly aboard a local commuter into Tel-Aviv, but using commercial transportation tends to leave a paper trail that I didn't particularly want lying around. Skipper, with just a little help from Ginger, was able to score a boat from Psarolimano.

A retired Defense Intelligence Agent living aboard a seventy-foot schooner would be more than happy to have us join him for the two-hundred-mile jaunt across the Mediterranean to Tel-Aviv...for a small fee, of course.

Dennis Crowe met us on the dock in cut-off blue jeans and a Jimmy Buffett T-shirt. He didn't have the look of an intelligence operative, but what he did have was three bottles of KEO, one of the best Cypriot beers on the island.

"Welcome to Cyprus, boys," he said as he handed us the beers and shook our hands. "I'm Dennis. I hear you boys are looking for a ride to the beautiful Hebrew Riviera."

I laughed. "Well, I've never heard the coast of Tel-Aviv called the Hebrew Riviera, but if you're headed that way, we'd love to hitch a ride."

The man raised both hands. "Ah, Tel-Aviv. The city of cathedrals, or whatever. It's beautiful this time of year. Well, that is to say, it's just as beautiful, or not, this time of year as any other."

His boat was enormous. The extra twenty feet of length his boat had over *Aegis* made it feel like an aircraft carrier. Three masts the size of telephone poles jutted skyward, and the array of electronics at the helm station was enough to make an astronaut envious.

"This is quite a boat," I said.

"Oh, this old thing? It's just the spoils of war. If you live long enough and you put away a little cash here and there, this is what retirement looks like. Don't worry, boys. You'll get there someday— if you'll quit this gig and get you a job driving a truck somewhere."

I wasn't sure if our eccentric host was joking, but the beer was good.

"Stow your gear, and make yourselves at home. Whenever you're ready, we'll stick her in the wind. It'll take about twenty-six hours to get you to Marina Herzliya."

"In that case," I said, "let's get some sleep tonight and try to get our bodies aligned with whatever time zone we're in. If we leave at daybreak tomorrow morning, that should give us a nice mid-morning arrival for the meeting with our friends in Tel-Aviv."

Dennis checked his Rolex and nodded. "Sounds good to me. I'll just let Bimini know, and we'll see what we can find to throw in your bellies. I hope you like fish, 'cause there ain't much else around here."

"Fish sounds great," I said, and watched him dance through the companionway like a man forty years his junior.

"Interesting guy," Clark said.

I laughed. "Yeah, you could say that."

We found two unoccupied cabins and stowed our gear. When we made our way back on deck, Dennis was pulling more beer from an ice chest, and a stunning beauty of maybe twenty-five, wearing part of a bikini, was sitting on the coaming with a glass of white wine in her well-manicured left hand.

Dennis passed out the beer. "This is Bimini, my first mate. Well, maybe not my first mate, but my current mate."

We shook Bimini's hand and made our introductions. She pretended to be shy, but no one wearing an eyepatch as a bikini could actually be shy. I doubted her real name was Bimini, but I suspected Dennis didn't care.

I saw the twinkle in Clark's eye, and I knew he was about to push the envelope. He didn't disappoint me.

He raised his bottle toward Bimini. "Also spoils of war?"

Dennis laughed a hearty roar one might expect of Santa Claus, and he raised his bottle. "Here's to spoils of war!"

We touched the rim of our bottles to his and settled into the comfortable cockpit.

Dennis studied Clark and me for a long, uncomfortable moment. "Let's see if an old man has still got it. What do you say?"

Clark looked at me as if I was supposed to know what the old Defense Department spy was talking about. I had no idea what to expect, but I said, "Sure. Why not?"

Dennis cleared his throat and pointed toward Clark. "I first thought Navy SEAL, but you don't walk like a SEAL, so I'm thinking Delta Force. Am I close?"

Clark tried not to smile, but the corner of his mouth started climbing up. "Not bad. You're close, but no cigar."

"Rats!" said Dennis. "I used to be good at this."

"Don't beat yourself up," Clark said. "I was Special Forces, but I got a better offer before I could get accepted into Delta."

"I knew it! I've still got it."

Clark laughed and pointed his bottle toward me. "Let's hear you do him, now."

Dennis closed one eye and sucked the ends of his white mustache into his mouth. "He's a little tougher to figure out, but I think I've got him nailed down."

I finished my beer. "This should be interesting. Let's hear it."

Dennis drained his beer. "Probably lacrosse, or maybe rugby. Definitely rowing. You were an athlete, and probably a good one. A college boy, no doubt. I'm thinking maybe even Ivy League, although your accent hints at the Carolinas or maybe the coast of Georgia. Possibly a Citadel grad, but you don't move like somebody who's ever learned to march, so probably not. Definitely not military. Okay, so here's my FBI profiler's best guess. You're a lawyer by education, but you never took the bar exam. You played lacrosse at either Duke or Penn State. Eagle Scout and National Merit Scholar. The Agency recruited you out of law school at Columbia, and now you're in clandestine services out of Langley."

I winked at Clark. "This guy's good."

The beautiful Bimini leapt to her feet, threw her arms around Dennis, and kissed him as if no one was watching. "I love it when you do that, Papi. It's so sexy."

She tweaked the tip of his nose with her index finger and danced back to her seat.

Clark, Dennis, and I raised our bottles in unison and declared, "Spoils of war!"

Bimini—I was starting to believe that *could* be her name— grilled sea bass, carrots, and olives and served it over brown rice. We ate, laughed, and listened to Dennis's stories as the sun melted into the Mediterranean Sea. I wanted to believe some of his stories actually had a vein of truth to them, but they probably didn't.

* * *

It wasn't the sound of the diesel that awakened me the next morning, but the heeling of the big boat as Dennis and Bimini set the sails. I dressed and climbed the companionway ladder to find Bimini at the helm, this time wearing khaki shorts and a T-shirt with the phrase "How many licks?" below a picture of a Tootsie-Pop.

"Oh, hey! Good morning, Clark," she said a little too cheerfully.

"I'm Chase, but good morning to you, too."

Dennis came from the aft companionway with two cups of coffee in hand and held one out toward me. "Ah, good morning. How'd you sleep?"

I took the mug. "Thanks. I slept great."

I could still see the coast of Cyprus behind us, but it was getting smaller by the minute.

"Is Clark up yet?" he asked.

"I'd be surprised if he wasn't," I said, looking back down the companionway.

Clark came hopping up the ladder and surveyed the horizon. "You guys don't mess around when you say we're leaving at daybreak."

Dennis handed the remaining coffee cup to Bimini and headed back to the galley for more. Back on deck, minutes later, with two more cups and a bottle of Jim Beam, he handed a cup to Clark. "Does anybody want cream?" He poured two shots of the bourbon into his coffee and then held up the bottle. "Well, would you look at that? I got the cream and the bourbon mixed up again."

Clark and I declined, but Bimini held up her mug. She clearly wasn't going to miss out on an opportunity to increase her blood alcohol level, regardless of the hour.

The yacht sailed like an ocean liner—solid, quiet, and fast—and the sea was relatively calm in spite of the twenty-knot wind from the southwest. Clark and I spent the day discussing the details of the mission and standing watch. We agreed that I would stand the ten-to-four watch, he would be on duty from four until ten, and Bimini and Dennis would stand the two overnight watches. While we marked the chart and kept the sails trimmed on our watches, Papi and his arm candy lounged on deck, soaked up the sun, and generally stayed to themselves.

Just after noon, we hooked a fish on a line we'd been trailing behind the boat. Clark had a blast fighting the big fish for nearly half an hour, and when he finally got the monster to the boat, it turned out to be a shortbill spearfish. Dennis gaffed it, and we hauled it aboard. Bimini withdrew a huge filet knife from a sheath near the helm and began butchering the fish. In no time, she had over a dozen steaks cut from its flesh and a bucket of strips she'd cut for bait. We tossed the carcass overboard and saw a shark devour it almost before it broke the surface.

Dennis pointed at the water. "Did you see that, boys? That's a pretty good life lesson for you. Even though you may not see them, the predators are always lurking just beneath the surface and waiting to strike. Don't forget that."

* * *

The coast of Israel came into view a few minutes after nine the next morning. I'd never been to the Middle East, but I thought Penny might enjoy visiting someday.

The sails came down, and we motored into Marina Herzliya. The Cyprus Naval Jack was on the pennant halyard above the Israeli flag boasting the Star of David. I wondered if Dennis had chosen the Naval Jack instead of the official flag of Cyprus—the yellow silhouette of the island above twin olive branches—out of some political belief he held, or perhaps Bimini just thought it was pretty.

I slid an envelope of hundred-dollar bills beneath the Jim Beam bottle—or maybe it was the creamer—and thanked our captain and first mate for the ride.

As we shook hands and stepped from the yacht to the dock, Bimini said, "We'll see you later, Bulldog."

I was unsure what to make of the comment.

She smiled broadly. "University of Georgia baseball star and psych major. MVP College World Series, 1996. I'm better at research than Papi, but I still think he's sexy."

Dennis grinned. "Things are rarely as they appear, boys. Good luck. Let us know if we can do anything else for you."

"Oh, yeah," Bimini said as she tossed our passports down from the deck. "You'll be needing these."

I caught mine and opened it up to find an Israeli stamp already in place.

Chapter 13
Shackles and Chains

"Shalom, gentlemen. I am Nataniel Yochanan. I am here to take you to see Mr. Rabin. Please follow me."

The man was in his thirties with dark, curly hair, and a black yarmulke. The confident stance, scanning eyes, and bulge under his jacket left no question that he was Mossad. In my opinion, Mossad was the world's finest intelligence service, and their agents were, in addition to being some of the deadliest humans alive, a force of supremely well-trained professionals capable of accomplishing things every other intelligence service in the world envied.

We fell in step with him and climbed inside his black SUV. Inside the vehicle was a collection of weaponry, electronics, and communications gear that was like nothing I'd ever seen. Nataniel wasn't just some errand boy.

He pulled to a stop in front of a café off Mordechai Namir Road.

"I thought we were going to—"

Nataniel cut me off. "You will be meeting Mr. Rabin here."

We stepped from the SUV, and Nataniel pulled away almost before we'd closed the doors.

Bureaucrats look the same all over the planet. A slightly overweight, balding man in his late fifties motioned for us to join him at his small table.

Although the temperature was in the sixties, the man wiped sweat from his brow with a yellowed, well-worn handkerchief. He didn't stand or offer his hand. "You are here for the Russian."

I couldn't discern whether that was a statement or a question, so I didn't respond. The man pointed toward a chair, and I took a seat. Clark did not. Instead, he made his way to a corner of the café where he could see both directions up and down the street and keep an eye on Rabin and me.

"What is he doing?" asked Rabin. "We are across the street from the headquarters of Mossad with armed men in every direction."

"He's doing his job," I said, refusing to be intimidated.

Rabin shrugged. "Suit yourself."

A waiter arrived and placed pastries and a carafe of coffee on the table. Rabin poured two cups and raised his in some sort of salute. The coffee was the strongest I'd ever tasted and more bitter than it would be possible to describe. Rabin drank a long swallow and wiped at his mouth with the same handkerchief he'd used for his forehead.

He surveyed the patrons of the café. "Your Russian is at Ben Gurion Airport. She is not cooperative, but she is your problem now. We have arranged for a C-130 Hercules to take you to Helsinki. What you do with her from there is of no concern to the Israeli government, but I am sure you are going to trade her for an equally uncooperative American, no?"

I tried to choke down another minuscule drink of the rancid black muck that was supposed to be coffee. "Mr. Rabin, you are right. What I do with her is of no concern to your government."

I didn't expect him to smile, but he did. "Good luck with that *vild khaye*. Nataniel will take you to the airport."

I stood and pointed toward my cup. "Thank you for whatever that's supposed to be."

Rabin didn't stand, but Clark began moving toward the street. Nataniel pulled up as if he'd known how long the meeting with Rabin would last. We mounted the vehicle and raced through the busy streets like we were running from the devil. Maybe we were, but I had a feeling the devil didn't spend much time in Tel-Aviv.

Ben Gurion Airport was a security stronghold. Armed guards manned every gate, and trucks with mounted machine guns patrolled the perimeter.

Clark surveyed the scene, taking in every detail. "We ain't in Kansas anymore, Toto."

Nataniel never slowed down for a gate or checkpoint. Every guard seemed to know to let us pass. We raced onto the tarmac and screeched to a stop beside a nondescript hangar with a grey C-130 cargo plane parked just outside the doors.

Before we got out, I asked Nataniel, "What does *vild khaye* mean?"

"Ha! Did Mr. Rabin call your prisoner that?"

"He did," I said.

"He is correct, and you will soon find out what *vild khaye* is."

Clark and I walked into the hangar, and my heart stopped beating. Sitting in a straight metal chair with an armed guard on each side of her was the second-most beautiful Russian I'd ever seen. Her hands were cuffed to a chain laced around her waist, and her bare feet were shackled. She wore blue cotton pants and a simple shirt of the same color. Her blonde hair fell across her shoulders and glistened in the light of the hangar. Her high cheekbones, smoky, blue-gray eyes, and sharp features made her Anya Burinkova's doppelganger. Looking at her sent my mind racing through a thousand scenes and emotions.

I pictured Anya standing over me with her knife pressed hard against my tongue. I remembered the feel of her skin against mine and the sound of her Russian-accented English whispers in my ear. I shuddered when I recalled seeing her fall from the staircase in Miami with a bullet in her back.

Instinctually, I shot a glance at the chained woman's feet to make sure she wasn't missing a little toe from a gunshot delivered by my pistol in Charlotte Amalie. To my horror, she had only four toes on her right foot. Had she endured the amputation of a toe solely to pass for Anya? The woman wasn't Anya, but unless they were standing side by side, it would be almost impossible to tell them apart.

The stern, cold expression she wore morphed into what I took to be an almost psychopathic delight when she saw me. Her eyes brightened, and the corners of her mouth turned upward, revealing perfect dimples identical to Anya's.

I took a knee in front of the woman and stared at her. The color and shape of the eyes were the same, but there was enough difference for me to know those weren't eyes fathered by Robert Richter. The tiny gap between her two front teeth was slightly wider than Anya's, and the skin of her neck and upper chest wasn't quite as smooth and delicate as it should have been. The differences were subtle, but they were there…until she spoke.

"Hello, my Chasechka. I knew you would come for me. You are man of honor like knight in armor shining. *YA lyublyu tebya*, my knight."

Hearing her say "I love you" in Anya's voice, with Anya's lips, and in that unmistakable accent left me wishing I'd never seen The Ranch where I became an assassin, an operator, a warrior whose path was destined to cross with that of a beautiful Russian agent bent on seduction, infiltration, and deception. I longed in an instant to undo the past six years of my life and return to the baseball field, crouched behind home plate where I belonged—where I was in control.

"Let's go!" Clark hefted the woman from the chair and began frog-marching her toward the hangar door. The short chain between her ankles made her strides chopped, leaving her incapable of anything beyond shuffling. The rattling reminded me of the sound a chain-link fence made when I threw baseballs against it as a child.

The two guards fell in locked step behind Clark and the chained woman. I watched them go, and I tried to imagine what the coming days of my life would hold.

I heard Penny's frightened voice in my mind. "I'm afraid you won't come back to me." I drove my fist into the cold concrete floor of the hangar and rose to my feet, determined to see it through.

The guards didn't follow Clark and Norikova aboard the C-130. Once the door closed, she truly was no longer Israel's problem.

The turboprop engines came alive, and the plane began to taxi as Clark strapped Captain Norikova into a nylon webbing seat on the side of the airplane. Her eyes never left mine, and she continued to smile and occasionally licked her lips. Even in her chains and behind the apparent pretense of sensuality, she was hypnotically beautiful, but for one of the few times in my adult life, I knew the truth: She was an imposter dedicated to a philosophy that represented the antithesis of everything I held dear, everything I was willing to die to protect, and everything I truly loved.

"Come to me, my Chasechka. Touch my face and brush hair like you did before, and I will do for you all things you like."

I placed one hand on her shoulder and positioned my face inches from hers. Her breath was hot, and her skin smelled foreign to me. She raised her chin and licked her lips, inviting me to kiss her, but I glared at her with undeniable contempt.

"Enough," I said. "No more. I'm taking you home because I have no other choice, but I am not going to play these games with you. I'm not going to listen to your bullshit. And I'm not going to do anything to make this experience enjoyable for you. If you say one more word, you'll spend the rest of this flight gagged and hooded. Nothing about this is acceptable to me, and if I had my way—like your sister was so fond of saying—I would gut you like pig."

The smile she was wearing vanished and was replaced again by the cold stare every Russian girl is apparently required to master by the age of thirteen. Although cold, there was more to her glare than mere insolence. I wanted to know what was happening behind those eyes.

I took a seat, but I couldn't take my eyes off of her.

How can that much hatred exist inside someone so beautiful?

After several minutes, she looked at me with the innocence of a child. "You are taking me to your home?"

"What?" I said, unable to hear her over the roar of the engines.

She spoke louder. "You said you are taking me home. You are taking me to *my* home or to *your* home?"

Finally. A chink in the armor.

I put on my psychologist's hat and decided to have a little fun. "What do you think?" I asked.

She seemed to consider my question. "I think you would not take me to my home in American airplane."

"This isn't an American airplane," I said. "It belongs to the Israelis."

"Why would Israel give to you airplane to take me to Russia?"

I glanced at my watch, strictly as an act of misdirection. "I didn't say we were going to Russia."

"Is that where I have been? Israel?"

Oh, this is getting better by the minute.

"Where did you think you were?"

She frowned. "I think maybe I was in Turkey, but I never hear Muslim call to prayer. Maybe I think now Israel. Why did your CIA not keep me in United States?"

It was a good question, but I wasn't going to give her any useful information.

"What makes you think the CIA cares about you?" I said.

I could see her wheels turning. When she made her decision, it was immediately visible in her eyes.

"I will give to you everything you desire. Tell me what you want, and I will give to you."

I feigned intrigue and moved closer. "What can you give me? What do you think I want?"

"You are young and strong handsome man, and I am beautiful Russian woman. I know how to give to you what every man wants. I can be for only you."

I let my eyes roam across her body, and she arched her back, raising her breasts beneath the simple cotton shirt. I let a boyish grin come across my face. "I can have anything I want?"

"Everything you want, *Amerikanec.*"

"And what do I have to give you in return?"

She raised her hands to the limits of her shackles. "Take from me chains, and take me to your home where I can love you like real man should be loved."

"You'd do that for me?"

"For you I will do everything," she hissed.

"Will you answer one question for me?"

"What is question, Chasechka?"

"Why did you kill Dr. Richter in the hospital?"

Her lips parted, and she tilted her head as if she had no idea what I was talking about. "This is why you are angry with me? This is why I am prisoner?"

"No," I said softly, "you're in chains for an entirely different reason. No one but me cares why you killed Dr. Richter."

"For you, this is important question," she said.

"Yes, for me, it's the only important question."

"He died death of lonely man, but I did not kill him. Only for him deception, not killing. For you this is sad?"

"Yes, for me, it's very sad."

"I am not his killer, but I can take from you sadness and give to you great joy, if only you will remove chains."

I inched nearer until our noses were almost touching and my lips were close to hers. She inhaled, and her eyes gently closed.

I whispered, "There's just one problem. I already have a beautiful woman who'll do everything for me, and she's not a Russian spy who gets off on pretending to be her half sister. Oh, and by the way, your half sister is far more beautiful than you. It's too bad about your toe. The chains stay on, and you will go wherever I take you, Russian."

She glared at me through squinted eyes and spat in my face. I didn't flinch. I licked her spittle from my lips and kissed her forehead. "Close, but definitely not Anya."

She growled like an animal and bucked against her restraints. I watched her with an amused grin on my face and wondered what her life in Moscow would be like. Would her SVR career be over, or would she be heralded as a hero of the Foreign Service? Her lineage as the daughter of a former senior Communist Party official would probably make her life a little more comfortable than most, but spending weeks in shackles at the hands of Israelis, and now *Amerikantsov*, would leave a bitter taste in her mouth.

"What was that all about?" asked Clark as I settled into a seat near his.

"I was just planting a few seeds."

"It looked like you were about to plant more than a few seeds."

"No, it's just entertaining to see how far she's willing to push her game."

"Be careful," he said. "You know what happens when you play with fire."

I laughed. "Yeah, I do. It makes pretty sparks in the air."

"Oh, from where I was sitting, there were sparks, all right."

I turned to check on our prisoner, who was still tugging at her restraints.

"She sure looks a lot like Anya, doesn't she?" I said.

"Yeah, she does. Right down to the missing toe. You gotta hand it to those Russians—they are committed."

"That one needs to be committed to the psych ward."

"I think maybe that's what the Kremlin is—one big psych ward."

"You may be on to something there."

We watched Norikova finally relax after trying to pull free of her restraints.

Clark continued staring at our prisoner. "As difficult as this operation is, she's going to keep making it harder."

"Yeah, you're right," I admitted, "but if we can get to Norikov without getting ourselves captured, shot, or worse, I think he'll do anything to get his daughter back."

"Oh, we'll get to him," he said. "I'm far more concerned about getting back out of there than getting in. It's not like we're just going to waltz right up to a former senior party official, announce that we have his daughter chained to a post in Latvia, and then sashay our way back out. He'll want to keep one of us under his thumb until his daughter is safely back in Red Square."

"No chance," I said. "Neither of us is staying behind, no matter what Norikov demands. We go in together, and we come out together."

Clark closed his eyes, and his nostrils flared. "You have to consider the probability of that choice being taken from us. We'll have the upper hand for a tiny window of time, but if we do anything to let that window close before we're ready, it's going to turn into a Moscow shit show."

Chapter 14

The Norwegian

"Do you have any idea what *vild khaye* means?"

Clark pushed his eyebrows together. "What on earth makes you think I'd know that?"

"Because you're my owl," I said.

"Your owl? What are you talking about?"

"Didn't you read Winnie-the-Pooh when you were a kid? Owl is Pooh's knowing friend. That's you, my knowing friend."

He shook his head. "There's quite a bit wrong with you."

"Maybe I'm wrong. Maybe you're Eeyore. Anyway, I'm going up to talk to the pilots. I'll be right back. Don't let Red Sonja jump out, and don't get within kissing distance. I doubt you have the where-withal to say no."

I headed toward the cockpit, and Norikova said, "*YA dolzhen idti v vannuyu.*"

I eyed the nylon webbing seat she was sitting in and had an idea. "Sure, no problem. I'll be right back."

A plastic trash can was connected to the forward bulkhead. I pulled the bag from the can and removed a yellow bungee cord.

Kneeling in front of Norikova, I slid the can beneath her seat, grabbed the waistline of her pants, and pulled them down to her mid-thigh. "Next time, ask in English with the word *please* somewhere in the request. Got it?"

I made my way to the cockpit and tapped on the door. "Hey, it's Chase. Can I come in?"

"Sure, sure, come on up," the captain said. "I'm Micha, and this is my first officer, Daniel."

"Thanks. What time do you expect to land in Helsinki?"

"We will be making a stop in Frankfurt for fuel, and then it's three hours to Helsinki."

I scanned the instrument panel for the fuel gauges but soon gave up. "Don't we have the range to make Helsinki from Tel-Aviv?"

"We would have the range if we flew direct, but our orders were to not overfly Russian airspace," said Micha.

"I guess there's some wisdom in that because of our passenger. Oh, that reminds me. Can you tell me what *vild khaye* means?"

Both pilots burst into laughter.

Micha asked, "Did someone use that word to describe your prisoner?"

"She's not my prisoner," I said, "but, yes, those are the words they used."

"I would say it is quite appropriate. *Vild khaye* means…ah, in English, maybe…wild animal."

I had to hand it to them. Those Israelis had an interesting sense of humor.

"I'd have to agree. How long before we land in Frankfurt?"

"Just over an hour," Daniel said.

I left the cockpit and made my way back through the cargo hold. Norikova was right where I'd left her with the plastic trash can still in place.

"I am sorry, Chasechka. I will speak only English. Is humiliating like this. Please let me go to bathroom."

"Don't call me that name," I ordered. "You can call me sir or Chase, but nothing else. You went to great lengths to humiliate me and my government, so you'll have to forgive me if I'm all out of sympathy."

An obvious wave of anger came across her face, but she held her tongue. When she'd made use of the plastic can, I repositioned her pants back where they'd been and returned to my seat near Clark.

"We'll be on the ground in Frankfurt in less than an hour for gas, and then on to Helsinki."

Clark motioned toward Norikova with his chin. "What was that all about?"

"She demanded in Russian that I let her go to the can. Instead, I brought the can to her. I think she now understands that we're going to communicate in English, and that she's going to stop making demands."

Clark chuckled. "I doubt that."

I glanced back across the empty space of the cargo plane and into the defiant eyes of SVR Captain Ekaterina Norikova. "I doubt the Israelis showed her a great deal of compassion."

"I'm sure you're right, but the Israelis weren't in love with her half sister, who happens to look nearly identical to her. Are you sure you're not taking some of that hostility out on the wrong sister?"

"Maybe," I admitted, "but I can't think of any reason why she'd deserve any compassion from me or anyone else."

He nodded. "Yeah, but cruelty for cruelty's sake accomplishes little."

"Is that some ancient Buddhist wisdom?"

"No," he said. "It's something my father told me when I was eight. I'd shot a mockingbird with my BB gun."

I tried to imagine Clark Johnson, Green Beret, at eight years old.

* * *

Late October in Frankfurt, Germany, is no time to be standing on an airport tarmac with a sat-phone pressed to one's ear.

When the connection was finally complete, Skipper came on the line. "Oh, hey, Chase. How are things in Germany?"

"It's cold and windy, and I hate it. How are things going there?"

"It's seventy-five and beautiful," she said with a sarcastic giggle.

"We've got Norikova, and we should be in Helsinki in less than four hours. Is the boat still good to go?"

"It is, but there may be a little problem in Riga."

"I don't like the sound of that. We don't have much room for things to go wrong. What's up?"

"The babysitter has turned up missing. I haven't heard from him in like almost a whole day."

Skipper and Ginger had arranged for a Frenchman, who'd been a legionnaire, to sit on Norikova while Clark and I hitched a ride on the overnight train to Moscow.

I pinched the bridge of my nose and squinted to fight off the headache that had suddenly taken root in my skull. Clark was again frog-marching Norikova from the plane with his boots on her formerly bare feet. I watched her close her eyes and inhale the frigid air.

How can anyone enjoy air this cold?

"Okay, so what's the backup plan if we can't find Frenchy?" I asked.

"We're working on that," Skipper said, "but if all else fails, we may have to turn to the Agency."

"The Agency?" The area consumed by my headache expanded. "The CIA isn't going to help us. They don't want their fingerprints anywhere near this."

"Well, that's not completely true. We had to turn to them already. The meeting with Rabin wouldn't have happened without them. They have a vested interest in this going well, so they're gonna play ball with us as long as bodies don't start piling up."

"I can't promise that's not going to happen," I said, more than a little unhappy that she and Ginger had involved the CIA.

"Keep in mind that about two hours after you get on that train, you'll be inside Russia without a visa or an invitation. You can't afford to start turning breathing bodies into corpses. It'll be hard enough to get you out if you stay clean, and practically impossible if you don't."

"I know, I know. It's just that Norikova isn't remotely cooperative, and that's making everything harder than it should be. I know we could've trusted Pierre, or whatever his name is, to keep her quiet and still. I don't have the same faith in the Agency boys."

"I know, but like the crazy Norwegian at the marina says, you gotta work with whatcha got."

There was a guy named Bob who'd been insane enough to buy a fifty-foot sailboat in Nova Scotia and sail it back to the Gulf of Mexico by himself. I think he was from Boston or somewhere up there, and he had a lot of fun spouting wisdom in his Beantown accent from beneath his nine-pound mustache. He spent a few nights in the marina in St. Augustine telling us grand stories of his glory days, and he and Clark struck up a quick friendship because of their similar military experience. Bob was a Green Beret in Vietnam and had the battle scars to prove it. Skipper started calling him "the Norwegian" for some reason, and the moniker just stuck.

"Yeah, well, how about you work with what you've got and find the Frenchman? I'll call you from Helsinki."

I joined Clark and Norikova beside a hangar sheltered from the driving wind. She was standing on one foot, smoking a cigarette, while he stood just beyond her with his Glock in one hand and a boot in the other.

I liked the way he played good cop. He let her have a cigarette and some fresh air, and had even been kind enough to provide her with boots, but he wasn't taking any chances of her turning into a rabbit and jetting off into the German countryside. If the Glock didn't stop her, wearing one boot in subfreezing conditions would.

"Smoking will kill you," I said.

"I think probably you will kill me first."

"It's possible. Now let's get back on the bus. It's time to go."

She locked eyes with me, dropped her cigarette to the tarmac, and then ground it out with the ball of her bare foot.

"You don't have to convince me you're tough. I'd much rather you convince me you're smart and start cooperating with me. I'm taking you home. To *your* home. The least you could do is pretend to be happy about that."

"Why would I be happy to go home? A disgraced agent who failed her only mission? I will be punished. Going home for me is torture."

Her response intrigued me and left me with more than a few questions, but I'd have to save them for a more strategic point in time.

Back on the airplane, Norikova asked, in English, if she could sit in one of the airline-type seats on the passenger pallet. I agreed, but laced a nylon cord through her waist chains and fastened it around the seat back so she couldn't stand and do her best to kill everyone on the airplane.

I stuck a piece of gum toward her mouth. "Here, chew this. You smell like an ashtray."

She opened her mouth and took the gum, allowing my fingers to slide between her lips. She could have easily bitten to the bone, but she slowly let my fingers slip from her mouth, and she let out a sound that would send most men to their knees. She was an unmistakable study in extreme contrasts. Her physical beauty and sensuality were breathtaking, but her utter disdain and hatred for the freedoms and indulgences I'd dedicated my life to preserving left a dangerous, contemptuous core inside the body of one of the most beautiful women alive. I was fascinated by her, but not remotely tempted.

"Please don't do that again," I said, determined to avoid the cruelty Clark had warned me was unnecessary.

"*YA ponimayu, pochemu Anastasiya tak naslazhdalas' svoim zadaniyem.*"

I was unsure if she was speaking Russian in defiance of my order, or if it was an innocent oversight.

"Forgive me," she said, appearing embarrassed. "English is not sometimes so good for me. I mean to say, it is easy to know why Anastasia enjoyed pretending to love you. I think maybe she did not have to pretend. I think maybe for you it is first instinct to be kind, and to be cruel is not so easy for you."

I was being played by an actress of the highest skill. She'd been trained and conditioned to morph into whatever her intended victim wanted and desired. She was a master of her craft. It seemed to run in the family.

"You're wrong about me," I said. "It isn't my nature to be kind. I want to throw you out the back of this airplane. It takes every ounce of self-control I can muster to let you continue to live. Don't fool yourself into thinking I'm anything less than the man who represents everything you hate. I'll deliver you back to the Kremlin, not because I think you deserve the privilege of going home, but because it's my duty. I will not make sacrifices to make you more comfortable, nor will I play along with your silly games."

"I am not playing games. I know position I am in, and also you. You think my father will trade to you the life of Anastasia if you will give to him me, yes?"

I knew better than to get suckered into a conversation with her, but I had to know where she was going with that question.

"I think your father will do anything in his power to get his daughter back, including releasing a political prisoner."

She locked eyes with me. "You are on fool's errand if that is what you believe. My father's men will kill you, and his—I do not know English word—*soldaty* will come for me."

"Soldier," I said. "The English word is soldier, but I don't think we need to worry about that. Daddy dearest may kill me, but if he does, you'll be dead long before his *soldaty* can get to you. You see, we're pretty good at this cloak-and-dagger stuff. If I don't check in at the allotted time every few hours, your body will find its way to the bottom of the Baltic Sea, and life will go on without both of us."

"What is cloak and dagger?" she asked, feigning both innocence and ignorance.

I wondered if it was possible for her to answer any of my questions honestly. Clark was watching us intently.

"Does Anya know you've been running around pretending to be her?"

She furrowed her brow. "Anastasia does not know of me. She has never seen me, but I have seen her. It is like looking to mirror. She is beautiful, yes?"

My mind raced, trying to piece together the scene. I couldn't imagine an intelligence service creating a nearly identical agent solely for the purpose of making them interchangeable, but not training them side by side. How could Norikova move, sound, and behave like Anya if they'd never trained together? Perhaps the genetics were enough. From across the room, I doubt I could tell them apart, and I knew Anya's mannerisms and body as well as anyone on Earth. Although they were practically twins, I couldn't understand why I wasn't smitten with Norikova the way I was with Anya the first time I saw her atop the water tower in New York.

Seeming to sense my uncertainty, she said, "Why did you kill Colonel Tornovich?"

"He planned an operation specifically designed to destroy my life and the lives of people I care about very deeply. He used Anya like a worthless pawn and lied to her about her own father for twenty years. He attacked my country, and me personally. No one gets to do that and survive."

"I did not attack you, but you say you want to throw me from airplane. I did for you things to help you."

I shook my head. "What have you ever done to help me?"

"I killed Michael Parchinkov on island to save life of your friend, Elizabeth. I went to bedside of Robert Richter to comfort him before he died."

"Michael Parchinkov?"

"Yes, is his Russian name. In United States, he is Michael Anderson."

I kept shaking my head. "You didn't go to comfort Dr. Richter. You went to kill him."

"No. He is father of my sister. She is traitor to Russia, but to me, she is still sister. She feels love for him, and when there is love, there is comfort in being together. For my sister, I give comfort to her father at end of life."

Nothing was making sense. Either she was luring me into believing she was honorable so I'd lower my guard, or she was the most screwed-up person who'd ever lived. I couldn't trust anything about her.

"It's not going to work," I said.

"What is not going to work?"

"You're very smart, and even more manipulative. I'm not getting sucked into your trap. You're an SVR intelligence officer. Deception, disinformation, and assassination are what you do. Every word and every action are designed to achieve your goal, and I'm not green enough to fall prey to your game."

"Is no game, Chasechka." She slowly blinked and lowered her head. "I am sorry. I will not call you that name again. Is no game, sir. I am going home to be no more your prisoner. I do not have to manipulate you to get what I want. You are giving to me."

It was time for me to gain the upper hand. "Okay, then. If you're not playing a game, then answer some of my questions."

She glared straight into my eyes. "I will not break trust of my country, but I will answer if possible."

"Was that you or Anya at the safe house in Virginia?"

"It was both," she said quickly.

"Both? What do you mean, both?"

"Your CIA was holding my sister at safe house, but we came for her. I was to be changed with her, but she escaped into forest. We captured her in forest and take her clothes for me. Your CIA found me and took back to safe house. Anastasia was taken away to prison in Russia."

"Wait," I said, holding up a hand. "Just wait a minute."

I waved Clark over. "You've got to hear this. She says Anya escaped from the safe house and into the woods in Virginia before we got there, and the SVR had a team capture Anya and exchange her for Norikova."

Clark cocked his head. "So, you're telling me the guards didn't know you weren't Anya?"

Norikova set her gaze between the two of us. "That was plan, but I did not know names and routine. That is why I had to kill them in upstairs."

I locked eyes with Clark, and it was clear we were having the same stroll down memory lane of discovering the murdered CIA safe house babysitters piled in the attic.

"Did you steal the airplane?"

"It was not airplane. It was helicopter. And yes, I take."

My clever attempt at tripping her up on the details didn't work. Maybe she was telling the truth.

"Okay," I said, "why did you kill Michael Anderson...or Parchinkov?"

He was going to kill your friend and then kill you. I could not let him kill you. It was my duty to get to you to continue what my sister started."

I decided to change gears. "So, you know your sister is in prison, then."

"Yes, I know this. This is for me sad, but is necessary. She is traitor."

"What made her a traitor?" I asked.

"Is same for United States, same for you. She tells to CIA what she is doing. If you tell to SVR or FSB what you are doing, is traitor to United States. Is same, yes?"

"So, the Kremlin thinks Anya surrendered to the U.S. Is that what you're telling us?"

"Yes, she turn from Russia for you and defect."

"Wait a minute," I said. "You think she defected to the U.S.?"

"I do not *think* this. This is truth. This is what she did. That is why I say she maybe was not pretending to love you. Maybe, I think, she does love you, and for me, is easy to see why. You are not like him." She flicked her chin toward Clark. "He is killer who pretends to be kind. You are kind and pretend to be killer."

I sprang to my feet. "I've heard enough."

Clark and I settled back into our seats at the other end of the plane.

"Don't let her get inside your head, man. That's what she does. Every word she says, true or not, is designed to manipulate you. And I can see it's working." He tapped his finger to my temple. "Do not let her in there."

Chapter 15
Upgrade

We landed in Helsinki and stepped off the plane into a frozen world of darkness. The wind carried a thousand tiny razors that tore at every inch of exposed flesh, and I never wanted to be back in the Florida sun so badly. The airport was almost completely dark, and that didn't make sense.

"Is this the international airport?" I asked Clark as we peered through the darkness.

"Definitely not. This must be Helsinki-Malmi."

"I should've paid more attention in Nordic Geography class."

"Maybe you should look at a map every now and then," he said.

I ignored him and powered up my sat-phone. Three minutes later, Ginger answered with no pleasantries. "I've got good news. Our babysitter is in place, but he's not in the place we thought. It's much better."

"Hello to you, too," I said.

"There's no time for that. I see you're at Malmi. That's great. Your ride will be there shortly. I've arranged with the Finnish Border Guards to have someone pick you up and take you to the port where you'll meet Jurek Josephson. He'll take you to the babysitter."

"The Finnish Border Guards? Are you serious? I can't imagine they'd jump at the chance to get involved in this."

"Are you kidding?" she said. "They love any opportunity to stick it to the Russians."

"Okay, so where are we meeting the babysitter?"

"That's the best part. The reason he disappeared was so he could find a spot to hold your girlfriend with no chance of her escaping."

"She's anything but my girlfriend."

"Yeah, well, whatever she is, she's a flight risk, and we've found the perfect spot to diminish that risk. In the Gulf of Riga is Ruhnu Island, and there's only a handful of people there. Satellite imagery suggests there's less than fifty who actually go outside."

"Okay, go on."

"Pierre will be waiting for you at the ferry dock at the south end of the island. He's got just the spot for Goldilocks. His sat-phone number is programmed into yours. Oh, and the Finnish Border Guards are probably going to speak a lot better Russian than English, so keep that in mind."

"Thanks, Ginger. Where's Skipper?"

"Taking a nap. She's been awake for almost two days."

"How's she handling all of this?"

"Like an old pro. She's a natural. You've got a good one on your hands. Oh, and speaking of good ones, how much can we tell Penny?"

I smiled. "Tell her I said to start picking out names for her black lab puppy." I disconnected and powered down the phone just as an SUV came to a stop near the door of the C-130. I quickly briefed Clark on the conversation with Ginger and headed for the plane.

Two extremely Scandinavian-looking young men stepped from the truck and introduced themselves in broken English.

I shook each of their hands, and in Russian I said, "Thank you for your help tonight."

Their eyes lit up at discovering a common language, and relief poured across their faces. Their night just got a lot easier.

I explained that I needed to get my prisoner to the ferry terminal. "We've got a long, cold boat ride ahead of us to Ruhnu Island."

The guard raised his eyebrows in utter disbelief. "Ruhnu? On a boat? With a prisoner?"

"Unfortunately," I said, "that's the best we could arrange on short notice."

He looked at his partner, and they shrugged.

The first guard turned back to me. "What if I can get you a helicopter to Ruhnu?"

"If you can get us a helicopter, we'll be in your debt for the rest of our lives."

"Your prisoner is Russian?" he asked.

I nodded.

"In that case," he said, "I can get you a helicopter, but in return, I would like to speak with your prisoner…alone."

I was instantly skeptical. "I'm not sure you'd get anything meaningful out of her. She's not what you would call cooperative."

"*Her?* Your prisoner is a Russian woman?"

"Yes," I admitted.

"Are you going to give her back to the Russians by chance?"

"Maybe," I said. "If they give me what I want."

He grinned. "In that case, I must speak with her. If you will give me just five minutes alone with her, I will have your helicopter here in twenty minutes."

I turned to Clark, who bobbed his head in agreement.

"Done," I said.

The man snapped his fingers at his partner, and the younger man climbed back into the truck and stuck the radio microphone to his lips.

The Israeli pilots came down the ladder as the border guard and I approached the plane. The look of uncertainty on their faces told me they weren't interested in having the Finnish Border Guard on their airplane.

"He needs to speak with our guest," I said, hoping they'd change their minds.

The pilots didn't appear to understand a word I'd said. It occurred to me that I was still speaking Russian, and I told them what was going on, this time in English.

Both pilots shook their heads.

Daniel said, "I'm sorry, but we cannot do that on the aircraft. You can unload your gear and your guest, but I can't allow this man aboard my aircraft."

I didn't fully understand the reason for his adamance, but I had no standing to argue. He'd just given me a ride that would have been almost impossible without him and his airplane, so I didn't put up a fight. We unloaded our gear and walked Norikova from the plane.

She asked Clark for another cigarette, but instead of complying, he tucked her into the back seat of the Border Guard vehicle. The guard motioned for us to load our gear in the back, and he slid onto the seat beside Norikova.

Five minutes later, he returned, red-faced and obviously furious.

"I warned you," I said.

He scowled. "If the Russians don't give you what you want, bring her back to me, and I'll make sure she never sees Mother Russia again."

Clark rounded the vehicle and slid into the back right side while I climbed in from the left. Norikova's lips were pressed into a thin, horizontal line, and her body was trembling with a negative emotion I took to be either anger or disgust.

"Be nice," said Clark. "If you misbehave, this is going to get a lot uglier than any of us wants."

She gave no indication of either hearing or caring what Clark had said.

A few seconds later, the ground lit up as a helicopter approached and landed. Clark helped Norikova out of the vehicle. Her expression hadn't changed, but whatever transpired between her and the border guard obviously left a bitter taste in her mouth. We walked toward the helicopter, flanking Norikova closely between us. Even cuffed and shackled, I didn't want her getting away from us in the dark. She had made no attempts to escape, but that didn't mean the thought wasn't dancing around in her head. I wondered if she believed we were actually taking her home.

The Bell 412 was a variant of the Huey that had served us so well in the wilds of Panama only weeks before. I doubted the Finnish pilot had the personality or the aeronautical skill of our old Central-American pilot, Leo, but it was nice to see a familiar aircraft so far from home.

With the engines still running as we climbed aboard, the border guard from the SUV leaned into the cockpit and yelled to one of the pilots. Seconds later, we were climbing into the Scandinavian night.

The dim red lights inside the cabin of the helicopter cast an eerie glow onto everything, especially our faces. Norikova was still scowling from the interaction with the border guard, and Clark wore an inquisitive look. I watched him peer into the cockpit and then back at his watch.

His eyes met mine, and we leaned toward each other with Norikova between us. Just loud enough for Norikova and me to hear, he said, "*Ich denke, wir sollten sie jetzt töten.*"

Clark had said "I think we should kill her now" in German. If she had understood, there would've been some involuntary reaction in her expression. We'd discovered a new method of private communication.

"Something's not right," Clark said in German. "I don't like how this feels."

I peered into the cockpit, but I couldn't see the instruments well enough to piece anything together. In English, I asked Norikova, "What did that guard say to you?"

In perfect German, she said, "He said he will do things to me worse than death before I see sun again."

So much for our private method of communication.

Clark groaned. "I knew it. We walked right into a trap, and we're headed northeast."

Ruhnu was southwest. There was nothing to the northeast except millions of square miles of frozen Finnish countryside.

I leaned toward Norikova. "Have you ever heard the phrase, 'lesser of two evils'?"

She slowly nodded.

"It's time for you to make a choice. I might make you pee in a bucket, but I'm not going to do whatever that Finn has in mind. Help us get out of this, or we all end up frozen to death."

"I will do what is better for me," she said. "Until something changes, I am better with you than with them."

Anya's chances of ever getting out of the prison were fading quickly, and I had no idea what the Finn had against Norikova, but whatever it was made her nervous enough to temporarily change sides. Perhaps Sun Tzu was right when he said, "The enemy of my enemy is my friend." Or some craziness like that.

One of the pilots climbed out of his seat, stuck his head and shoulders into the cabin, and yelled in Finnish. Recognizing that none of us spoke that language, he tried again in Russian. "Get some rest, and we will be on Ruhnu in about ninety minutes."

"*Spasibo*," I said, hoping he couldn't detect my suspicion. "Okay, Geography Boy, what's ninety minutes northeast of Helsinki in a Huey?"

Before Clark could get a word in, Norikova said, "*Tuohisaari*."

"What's *Tuohisaari*?" we asked.

"Is island and secret training area of the Special Jaeger Battalion."

Clark closed his eyes and sighed.

I was lost. "What's the Jaeger Battalion?"

"Finnish Special Forces," he said, "and they're no joke."

Things were going from bad to worse with every passing minute, but the beginning of a plan was coming together in my head.

"Okay, listen up," I said. "It's too much risk to try to take the chopper while we're in the air, so we have to take the fight to the ground."

Clark and Norikova leaned in.

"They think we believe we're still going to Ruhnu, so they won't be expecting a fight from us when we hit the ground. Do you think they'll hit us as soon as we land?"

"That's what I'd do—take full advantage of the element of surprise."

"They will not," said Norikova. "They own only two helicopters in all of Border Guard service. They will not take chance of hurting this one."

"How do you know?" Clark asked.

"It is, for me, job to know these things."

"Okay," I said, "so that will give us a small window of opportunity to disable any ground forces we encounter and take the chopper. Are the pilots armed?"

"The right seater has a pistol," Clark said, "but the left seater didn't appear to be strapped. Though I can't say if they have anything stashed in the cockpit."

"They have to assume we're armed."

"Probably not," he said. "They would've asked for our weapons if they thought we had any."

Norikova moved uncomfortably in her restraints. "I agree with him."

"Ekaterina, listen very closely to me. I'm going to uncuff you, but if you run, I swear to you I will kill you, and you'll never see Mother Russia again. Is that clear?"

Chapter 16
Kat Nap

The red glow of the bulb above Norikova's head cast strange shadows across her perfect features.

"Kat," she said.

"What?"

"I would like for you to call me Kat. I will not run. I will fight, but I will fight for *my* life and not for yours."

I squinted against the red glow. "I think it's safe to say our lives are inextricably linked right now. We probably can't overcome whatever is waiting for us without your help, and you'll never survive the night without ours. So, Kat, don't make me shoot you."

I pulled the two keys from my pocket and handed one to Clark. After unlocking Kat's shackles and handcuffs, she rubbed at her wrists and stretched her legs. To create the illusion that she was still bound, we laced the restraints loosely back around her ankles and wrists, taking every advantage we could get.

We'd been in the air for almost ninety minutes. I wasn't afraid of a fight, but I didn't like walking into an ambush outmanned, outgunned, and with no support. That's when it occurred to me that we weren't completely without backup—Skipper and Ginger were just a sat-phone call away.

Ensuring the pilots couldn't see what I was doing, I powered up my phone, and just like E.T., I phoned home. It would take several seconds for the call to go through, but Ginger would immediately know we weren't on a boat when she tracked the call. No boat on the Baltic Sea would be traveling at two miles per minute like our helicopter, and it certainly wouldn't be headed through the Finnish wilderness.

After pressing the call button, I felt the chopper begin to descend, and I shoved the phone deep into the interior pocket of my coat. Ginger and Skipper wouldn't be able to hear what was happening, but they could track my position as long as the battery lasted.

The skids of the chopper touched the ground, and the rotors spun to a stop. One of the pilots removed his helmet. "*Dobro pozhalovat' v Ruhnu.*"

Welcoming us to Ruhnu was a nice addition to the charade, but I doubted the pilot expected us to believe he'd taken us where we wanted to be.

"*Spasibo,*" I said as I unbuckled my shoulder harness and reached for the door.

"No!" he yelled, and I retracted my hand.

Our arrival was about to turn into a fireworks show, and I hoped us going up in flames wasn't the grand finale.

I saw Clark reach inside his coat, obviously gearing up for the coming gunfight, so I did the same. The left and right doors of the chopper opened simultaneously, and four men lunged into the cabin, two on each side. Before we could react, Clark and I were in their grasps. One of the men yelled in Finnish, and the second pilot leapt from the cockpit with his pistol trained on Kat's face, though I didn't have time to worry about her; I was about to be in the fight of my life.

I heard Clark's boot make contact with an attacker's chest, and an instant later, I heard the man hit the ground. I wanted to see what was happening, but my hands were full on my side of the chopper.

The first of my abductors quickly wrapped me in a bear hug, and the second grabbed my ankles. I was outside the chopper in an instant and breathing in the frigid Nordic air. I twisted with all my strength, hoping to break his grasp, but the first man wasn't only strong, he was enormous. He outweighed me, and judging by the length of his arms, he was at least six foot six. Overpowering him wasn't possible; I would have to outwit him. I tried to force a glance back into the chopper to see if Kat had revealed her freedom, but I couldn't turn my head far enough to see.

The man holding my feet stumbled slightly as he backed through the darkness, and I took full advantage of my enemy's mistake by yanking my right foot as hard as possible, attempting to free it from his vice-like grip. It almost worked, but the giant recognized what I was doing and lunged forward, giving his partner the chance to reclaim his grasp on my ankles. These two had obviously practiced their teamwork for years. I was in far bigger trouble than I wanted to admit.

I took inventory of my situation and resources and realized the two men weren't trying to kill me—they were trying to get me away from the helicopter. I hoped the same was true on Clark's side of the chopper. I decided to stop resisting long enough to gather my wits and come up with a plan. My eyes were well-adjusted to the darkness because of the dim red light under which I'd spent the last hour and a half of my life. My captors stopped, threw me down, and rolled me facedown. The ground was covered with a couple inches of frozen snow, but it felt like I'd been shoved onto concrete.

I expected to feel the giant kneel on my back and pin me to the ground, but what happened next was much worse. Each of the men placed a booted foot on the inside of my elbows, effectively pinning me to the ground and eliminating any chance of me using my hands or arms. I tried to remain calm and listen for signs of a struggle. If Clark were able to overpower his abductors and get free, he'd be coming for me within seconds. I could faintly hear him cursing and struggling against the men, but it was obvious he wasn't winning the fight.

The sounds of the struggle continued and grew closer, and I heard the men trying to catch their breath while wrestling with Clark. He was clearly giving them more fight than they'd expected. If I could get just one of my captors to believe I'd surrendered, he might rush to the aid of his buddies to help subdue Clark. That would give me the window I needed to get my pistol out of its holster. I didn't care if I could aim. I just wanted to point the muzzle toward anybody who wasn't Clark or Kat and squeeze off a few rounds.

Since I couldn't speak their language, I let out an audible sigh and let every muscle of my body relax, hoping they'd recognize the physical signs of surrender. They were either too well trained to fall for my trick, or they had faith that their comrades didn't need their help.

Clark's struggle continued to draw nearer and louder until I heard the unmistakable sound of a baton being extended. The combination of the *swoosh* and *click* of the weapon is one of the most ominous sounds imaginable during a fight in the dark. I dreaded the next sound I knew I'd hear.

The sickening thud of the weapon finding its mark against Clark's skull silenced the struggle. Did the blow kill him or just render him unconscious? Either way, he was no longer capable of being involved in the rest of the fight.

Clark's body came to rest on the ground near me, and I listened closely, hoping to hear him breathe. The men chatted incessantly with their teammates, and I made a mental note to learn Finnish if I survived the night.

After their breathing returned to normal, the men lifted Clark from the ground and hefted his body onto a metallic surface. I tried to focus in the dark to determine what was happening as I waited for my window to fight.

Four hands grabbed me—one at each elbow and ankle—and I was amazed they hadn't searched me for a weapon or taken my satphone yet. They were brutes to be sure, but they weren't particularly thorough in their tactics. They hurled me into the darkness, and I landed against Clark's body in what must have been the bed of a truck.

I heard the shaft of the baton tap the edge of the truck bed several times before I felt it connect with the back of my skull.

* * *

When I returned from the spirit world, I heard six or seven shots. I assumed it was pistol fire, but I couldn't be certain. My head was pounding, and what little vision I had in the dark was too blurry to make out any distinct objects. I felt for Clark and found him still prone and motionless. I grabbed at his neck and held my breath, hoping to feel his pulse. The regular, slow rhythm of the blood still pumping through the veins in his neck was one of the most welcome feelings I'd ever experienced. He wouldn't be much help, but he wasn't dead.

I tried to shake off the spiderwebs from my brain and take in my environment. It appeared that no one was guarding us. When I sat up, I saw the outlines of two bodies running away from us and toward the helicopter. Clark stirred beside me, but I had more important concerns. With my pistol drawn, I tried to focus enough to put a bullet in at least one of the running men, but Clark's hand fell limply against my wrist.

In a groggy, pain-filled voice, he said, "No. That's our only way out of here."

He was right. If I put a bullet through the turbine engine of the chopper, we'd never make it out of Finland. As I lowered my pistol, the engines of the helicopter whistled to life, and I saw the blur of the spinning blades.

"Dammit, they're going to get away with Kat." I brought my pistol back to bear on the helicopter.

The skids left the ground, and the nose of the chopper turned abruptly toward us. The searchlight hanging beneath the helicopter burst to life, filling the air with blinding white light. The two men who'd been running raised their arms to shield their eyes from the assaulting light, but little did they know the light would be the least of their concerns.

Seconds later, the silhouettes of their headless bodies tumbled across the frozen ground, and the nose of the chopper rose until the light was trained directly on Clark and me. I immediately threw my body back to the bed of the truck, hoping the tips of the blades didn't hold the same treatment for me as they had for the two Finns.

To my relief and surprise, the chopper came to rest fifty feet behind the truck, and the searchlight went dark. The outline of a form was coming toward us through the darkness, and I raised my pistol in defense until, over the whine of the turbine engines, I heard Kat's voice cut through the cold night air. "Come now! Get in helicopter!"

I helped Clark to his feet, and we stumbled toward the idling chopper. Kat helped me put Clark in the cabin and then buckled herself into the right seat. She brought the throttle to one hundred percent, and in seconds, we were climbing out of Tuohisaari and heading south.

"Kat, I can't read Finnish, so I won't be much help on the instruments."

"Is okay. I do not need your help. Go to Clark. He is hurt."

"Are you sure you're okay up here alone?"

"Yes, I am very good pilot."

I pulled off my headset and crawled from the cockpit into the cabin. "How you doing back here, old man?"

Clark rubbed at his neck. "I took a pretty nasty shot to the noggin, but I think I'll be okay. Where's she taking us?"

I turned around, and Kat was standing in the cabin pointing my pistol at us. "Sit beside him and put shackles on ankles. One on you, one on him, and chain through seat frame. Do it now!"

She must have lifted my pistol when she helped me put Clark in the cabin. I could only assume she'd set the autopilot for Saint Petersburg.

I followed her instructions, knowing she'd shoot us both if we didn't comply.

"Now also handcuffs. Same."

We did as she ordered and cuffed our wrists together.

"Good, now give to me satellite telephone."

I reached into my coat to retrieve the sat-phone as she extended her hand toward me. Clark lunged forward, and with every ounce of strength that remained in his battered body, clamped her wrist with his free hand and pulled her thin frame. She stumbled forward, and I thrust my free hand behind her neck, pulling her face into the bulkhead between Clark and me. Blood exploded from her nose, and she let out a painful groan as her body collapsed between us and my pistol fell from her grip.

I swiped the gun from the floor and held it tightly as Clark retrieved the shackle key. After releasing the bindings from our ankles, he replaced the shackles on Norikova's feet and positioned her limp body on the seat.

There was no sign of the handcuff key in my pockets, and I questioned the decision to have shackles and cuffs without matching keys. I considered shooting the cuffs off, but the risk was too high, so I set about searching for anything to use as a pick.

Clark pulled a sheaf of papers from a packet hanging behind the cockpit and removed a paperclip. "Give this a try."

I straightened the clip and fed it into the keyhole, struggling with the simple mechanism for far longer than I should have, but it finally surrendered, and the cuff fell from Clark's wrist. I went to work on mine and soon had myself free. Clark cuffed Norikova's wrists to the seat and tried to stop the blood flowing from her nose. The beautiful woman she'd been only minutes before would soon be well hidden behind a badly broken nose and two black eyes.

Clark rubbed at his neck while occasionally digging his knuckles into his temples. We climbed into the cockpit, Clark on the left, and me on the right.

"Everything is in Finnish," I said, "but I think we can figure it out enough to get back to Helsinki."

"To hell with Helsinki," he said. "I never want to see that place again. Do we have the gas to make Ruhnu?"

I fumbled with the GPS, wishing I'd learned Finnish in my spare time. "It looks like it's just over five hundred kilometers, and we've got about twelve hundred liters of fuel. How's your grasp of the metric system?"

Clark was still wincing from the pain in his head. "There are two kinds of countries on Earth: those who've never lost a war, and those who use the metric system. You're the college boy. You figure it out. In the meantime, I'm going to point us toward that little island."

After five minutes of struggling with the conversion, I said, "Okay, I think we can make it, but it's going to be close."

"In that case, it sounds like we'll either make it, run out of gas over the Gulf of Riga, or get shot down over Estonia. One out of three ain't bad."

Clark set the autopilot, and I began taking notes, calculating our fuel burn against our distance remaining to Ruhnu. With every liter we burned, I lost a little more faith in our ability to make it.

I glanced over my shoulder and saw Norikova still unconscious on the seat. "Wouldn't it be nice if just once everything went the way we planned?"

In spite of the pain, Clark laughed. "Oh, grasshopper, you have so much to learn. I've been on three dozen real-world missions in my life, and never—not once—has it gone as planned. Something always gets screwed up. Somebody always gets hurt or killed. There's no way to plan for everything that might go wrong. The key to staying alive is what I've seen you do every time things start to fall apart. You stay calm, think, plan, and execute. That's all we can do. It's never going to go as planned. Never."

"I thought it was just me," I said. "I thought I was a bad luck charm."

"Bad luck charm? Ha! That's funny. We haven't had any *real* bad luck yet. We were only captured once, and only two people tried to kill us. Those border guards, or whoever they were, screwed up when they just knocked us out instead of shooting us, and Kitty-Kat back there messed up when she got too close. All in all, this has gone pretty smoothly."

I shook my head and sighed. "If this is smooth, I'm not looking forward to rocky."

"Speaking of getting rocky," he said, "you might want to see if you can get the girls on the phone."

I immediately dialed Ginger.

Skipper answered. "Are you there?"

It was nice to hear her voice. "Yeah, I'm here, and we're okay."

She hit me with a barrage of questions about why we weren't on the boat and how we ended up so far off track and going so fast.

I tried to explain it to her, but the noise in the chopper made it challenging. "What can you do about paving our way through Estonian airspace? We don't have the gas to go around if we're going to make Ruhnu."

"I have no idea how to do that, but I'll tell Ginger. How about if we get you some fuel in Estonia? Would that help?"

"I'd rather not stop," I yelled into the phone. "I think we have fuel to make it, and I don't want to risk anything else going wrong on the ground."

"Okay, I'll see what we can do, and we'll call you back in twenty minutes."

I clicked off and went back to work on my fuel burn calculations. "It's looking pretty good. Did we pick up a tailwind?"

Clark scanned the instrument panel. "Yeah, a little one. Eight or nine knots."

"That's enough to make a big difference," I said.

We crossed the Baltic Sea and watched the lights of the Estonian coast fall beneath our nose.

"I really hope they don't start shooting."

Clark peered over the panel at the few ground lights scattered across the landscape. "Estonia is an ally."

"Yeah, so is Finland," I said. "And we saw how well that worked out."

Chapter 17
No Ground Fire

"Okay, the ambassador said nobody's going to be shooting at you, but we owe him a big favor."

I was thankful for even a little bit of good news. "Thanks, Skipper. I knew you'd come through for us. I'll let you know when we're feet dry on Ruhnu."

We flew across the entire peninsula of Estonia without so much as a flashlight shining up at us. I checked on Norikova to find her wincing and licking blood from her lips.

"It looks like sleeping beauty has finally awakened," I said. "I think I'll go say hello."

Clark glanced over his shoulder and chuckled. "Don't get too close. You know how she gets."

I crawled from the cockpit and knelt safely away from her. "Welcome back. How does your face feel?"

"You know I had to try, yes?"

"Yes, I know, but it didn't work out for you, and I'm going to recommend you not try again."

"You are still taking me home, yes?"

"We'll see about that."

"I saved your life. I could have left you there to die, but I did not."

"No, that's not what you did. You saved your life, and then you got greedy."

"What does that mean?"

"It means you shot four or five guys and chopped the heads off of a couple more. You could've flown away and made Saint Petersburg in an hour, but you decided to pick up some trophies for your wall. Did you think bringing home American operatives would get you off the hook for screwing up?"

"My nose is, I think, broken."

"I think so, too," I said, "and from where I sit, you're pretty lucky that a broken nose is all you got for the stunt you pulled. I told you we're pretty good at this cloak-and-dagger stuff."

She refused to look at me.

I leaned a little closer, but still well outside her reach. "Regardless of your reasons, thank you for not leaving us back there."

Her eyes met mine, and although her expression wasn't a smile, it wasn't a frown, either.

"How's she doing?" asked Clark when I'd settled back into my seat.

"She's in a lot of pain."

"Yeah, I bet. A broken nose will do that. We've got some morphine in the kit if you're in the mood to show some mercy."

"I'm running low on mercy for people who point guns at me," I said.

"I know, but it might make her a little easier to deal with when we get back on the ground…if we make Ruhnu."

I climbed back into the cabin. "I have some morphine. It'll help with the pain of your broken nose if you want it."

She seemed unsure of how to respond. "This drug will make me sleep, yes?"

"Sometimes it makes people sleepy, but I can give you as much or as little as you want. You don't have to sleep."

"Why are you kind to me?"

"It's not me," I said. "It's Clark. He's the one who thinks I should give you the morphine. I told him I didn't like the idea of helping people who point guns at me…especially when the gun is mine."

She dropped her gaze to the floor. "I am sorry for pointing gun at you, and I would like to have drug to stop pain. Please."

I pulled the med kit from my gear and stuck a syringe into the vial of morphine. "How much do you want?"

"I would like same dose you would want in same circumstance."

That was a pretty good answer. I drew up enough morphine to make an elephant dream of unicorns, capped the needle, and tossed the syringe to her.

She let it land on her lap and then pulled the top from the needle. With one swift motion, she pierced the cloth of her pants and the muscle of her thigh, emptying the syringe with a long, slow press of the plunger. She capped the needle and awkwardly tried to toss it back to me in spite of her cuffed hands.

"*Spasibo, Amerikanec.*"

"You're welcome, Russian."

Those words echoed in my head. An almost identical exchange took place between me and Anya the night we first kissed aboard *Aegis*—the same night I shot off her toe.

Back in the cockpit, I was pleased to discover my fuel calculations had been a little too conservative. It appeared we would make Ruhnu with fuel to spare.

"Did you save any morphine for me?" asked Clark.

"You know you can't have morphine after a head wound."

"You spoil all the fun."

A few small lights came into view on the horizon ahead, and I checked the GPS. "Look at that. That's just how I expect Ruhnu to look in the middle of the night. I think things are finally going our way."

"Don't get excited just yet. We still have to find a place to land in the dark, and my head feels like somebody's beating a bass drum inside it."

"Believe it or not, there's an airport on the southern end of the island. I can't think of a better place to land a helicopter. Can you?"

"You're just full of good answers tonight," he said, "but with my head thumping and my blurred vision, I'm not sure I can make much of a landing. You'll either have to put us back on the ground or get your dream girl look-alike back there to do it."

I glanced into the cabin. "The first runner-up for Miss Russia 2001 is dancing with Sugar Plum Fairies back there on her morphine trip, so I guess it's up to me."

He rubbed his temples. "Just try to keep all the big parts on the helicopter, okay?"

I was comfortable landing almost anything with real wings, but helicopters weren't my strong suit. "I'll do my best, but I can't make any promises."

The GPS, even in Finnish, would get us to the unlit airport on the frigid island in the Gulf of Riga, so finding the airport would be the easy part. Getting us back on Earth, in one piece, in the dark, would be the challenge.

We flew south along the eastern shore of the island until the coastline fell away to the west. The GPS showed the airport at the extreme southern tip of the island.

I slid my boots onto the pedals and gripped the cyclic and collective with my gloved hands. "I have the controls," I said, a little less confidently than a competent pilot should.

Clark muffled what sounded like a nervous laugh. "You have the controls."

"Let's get the searchlight on and the instrument lights dimmed," I ordered as I settled on the controls.

Clark adjusted the lights. The clearing where the airport was supposed to be looked like a postage stamp—probably a mile long and a quarter mile wide—but I would've preferred a South Georgia peanut field. There were no buildings under the searchlight, so that left trees as my only obstacles. As we approached the airport, I saw the vague outline of a runway, but I had no illusions about actually being able to hit it. I'd be happy just keeping us out of the tree line and icy water.

I pulled the nose up to bleed off some airspeed as we approached from the south. The ink-black sea gave way to uncertain terrain, and finally, the barren airport.

The nose kept coming up, and the speed kept bleeding off. Everything was going far too well. I had to be on the verge of hitting

Bigfoot or a flying unicorn—which were just as likely as me pulling off the landing.

I brought the chopper to a condition resembling a hover at tree-top level, and I was pleased to see the beam of the searchlight holding relatively still on the ground. I slowly lowered the collective to descend toward terra firma, but as we settled, the world beneath me started spinning. I stomped the pedal, and the spinning turned into spinning *and* swaying in the opposite direction. After four or five, or maybe fifty attempts to get the chopper under control with wild combinations of hands and feet moving in every direction, I realized I was chasing the helicopter, overcorrecting, and generally doing everything wrong. I had to calm down and get ahead.

I felt Clark on the controls, and the aircraft finally stopped trying to tear itself apart.

"There you go. Just hold on to her," he said. "I'm going to bring the light up a few degrees. That'll give you something to focus on. Don't chase her. If she gets out of control again, we've got plenty of clearing ahead to climb out and give it another shot."

I took a long, slow breath and relaxed the tension in my arms. The beam of light gradually settled and then came to a stop in front of us. As I relaxed and decreased my death grip on the controls, the aircraft settled until we were, what I believed to be, only inches above the ground. In fear of having to do it all again, I dumped the collective, and the skids hit the ground in a bone-jarring collision. Everything stopped moving. I rolled off the throttle and watched the gauges spin down. It wasn't pretty, and we were far more than a few inches above the ground when I committed to the landing, but we were safely on deck, and I believed the chopper was still intact and relatively undamaged. I wasn't sure I could say the same for my pants.

Clark clubbed my left shoulder. "Well, I'll be damned! I can't believe you did it. I was sure we were all going to die."

"Sorry to disappoint you, but we can't die today. We've got too much work to do."

An old flight instructor once told me, "There's no such thing as a crash landing, kid. You either crash or you land, but sometimes it's hard to tell the difference." I wasn't sure which category the last two minutes of my life fell into, but for reasons I can't explain, I was glad Ekaterina Norikova wasn't awake to witness my so-called landing.

"It looks like Kat's still sleeping like a baby back there," Clark said. "How much morphine did you give her?"

"Enough to ensure her cooperation."

We finished shutting down the chopper, and all the moving parts became stationary. As we stepped from the cockpit, a single bobbing light approaching from the south caught my eye.

I grabbed Clark's arm and pointed toward the light. "What's that?"

"I can't tell, but let's get some cover until we find out. I don't want to be out in the open when whatever it is gets here."

"What about her?" I asked, pointing to an unconscious Norikova.

"She's not going anywhere. Follow me."

We moved to place the chopper between us and the approaching light, and then, with pistols drawn, sprinted for the tree line, where we took cover behind some fallen trees. We were able to conceal ourselves almost entirely while still seeing the opening well enough to watch our quarry. The dim light continued its approach but stopped bouncing five hundred feet beyond the chopper.

"Did it stop?"

I squinted and tried to focus on the light. "No, it's still coming, but it's on the runway now."

As the light grew closer and finally stopped beside the helicopter, I heard a man's voice with a decided French accent call out, "Monsieur Fulton! Monsieur Johnson! Where are you?"

"It's the Frenchman," I said as we climbed over the tree trunks and headed back for the chopper. Neither of us holstered our weapon, but we were happy to hear a friendly voice.

As we approached the helicopter, we kept the fuselage between the Frenchman and us. Clark maneuvered to come up from behind while I rounded the nose of the chopper.

I raised my weapon to bear on the man's feet and hit his eyes with the beam of my flashlight. "Show me your hands!"

He calmly held out his empty hands, palms up. "I am Pierre Arnoult, monsieur. I am armed, but I mean you no harm. If I were trying to assault you, do you think I would have ridden that old bicycle?"

I cast my light toward his bike and lowered my pistol. "I'm sorry for the scare," I said, "but we've had a rough night."

"That is what I heard from your analyst, Elizabeth. She says you had a little trouble with some Finns. Ah, their bark is worse than their bite. I thought you were coming by *bateau*, not *avion*."

His French accent was amusing, but I was starting to believe it wasn't completely authentic. "Yeah, well, we opted for the chopper instead. It was a little more exciting, and a lot warmer and dryer."

"Ha ha! Exciting, it was. I saw the landing—if that's what it was…a landing."

Clark stepped from the shadows.

I said, "Our pilot took a nasty blow to the head, so his skills aren't at their peak tonight."

Clark scowled. "Yeah, you might even say someone else was trying to fly the thing."

Pierre pulled a penlight from his pocket and shined it into the cabin of the 412. "So, this must be the guest of honor I am to entertain, no?"

"Yeah, that's Ekaterina Norikova, and she's a handful. She's currently sleeping off a big-boy dose of morphine, but she'll be feisty when she wakes up and gets her wits about her."

"Ah, I know how to deal with feisty. She will be no problem for me."

"Don't be so sure. She's a well-trained assassin and as crafty as they come."

"Oh, my boy. I have been dealing with Russians for thirty years. They are all well trained and crafty, but not so much so as to outwit Pierre."

It finally hit me. Pierre sounded like the crazy cat man from Mallory Square in Key West. His bizarre act with the two dozen cats every night at sunset was only slightly more insane than Pierre. I don't think his accent was authentic either, but he nailed the crazy part.

"So, where do you want her?" I asked.

"I will take her in the motor car. It is just down by the water."

Pierre disappeared on his ancient bicycle without another word. By the time he'd returned, Clark and I had Norikova unlocked from the seat frame and resting comfortably on the floor of the chopper.

What Pierre had called a motor car turned out to be a black Land Rover with a bicycle rack affixed to the rear. We hefted Norikova into the vehicle, ensuring her cuffs and shackles were still securely in place, and climbed into the truck. Clark took the front, and I sat in the back seat with Norikova's head in my lap. I fully expected her to wake up at any moment and chew through my thigh.

"If you don't mind," said Pierre, "I would like to hover your helicopter out of the way—just in case someone else happens to need the runway before you leave."

"Knock yourself out," I said. "You can't do any worse than I did."

"I don't believe I will have any troubles."

We sat in the warmth of the Land Rover while Pierre expertly hovered the chopper clear of the runway.

When he returned, I said, "You're just full of surprises, Pierre."

"Don't be surprised, my boy. When you are my age, you will have more skills than you can count."

"So, where are we taking our guest?"

"There is a very old church, beneath which is a very old cellar. We are taking her there."

We wound through the narrow dirt path that apparently passed for a road on Ruhnu, and pulled up in front of what was, indeed, a very old church. I wished the sun would come up so I could see the building in the daylight.

"This is the Ruhnu wooden church," Pierre said. "It was built in the sixteen-forties and is most likely the oldest wooden building in all of Estonia."

"I'm not sure what day it is, and I'm even less sure how long we'll need you to hold her," I said. "Won't the parishioners get a little nervous about a Frenchman holding a Russian spy in the basement of their church?"

"Oh, no no no. This is a Lutheran church, and the congregation meets in that stone building just there." He pointed toward a more modern structure that still must've been a hundred years old. "But this not a thing to worry about. They will not be meeting for church until April of next year. There are only about two dozen people here on the island through the winter."

I hefted Norikova over my shoulder, and then followed Pierre and Clark around the back of the ancient church, to equally ancient wooden doors opening onto a set of stone steps. The steps looked like they could lead into the pits of Hell…if Hell were a lake of ice instead of fire.

We made our way into the dungeon-esque cellar and discovered that someone—possibly Pierre—had gone to great lengths turning the space into a prison ward worthy of belonging to the gulag.

Pierre pointed into a makeshift metal cage with iron rings welded inside. "Put her in there."

A small metal bucket rested beside an old iron bedframe. I was relieved to see I wasn't the only person making Norikova pee in a bucket. Minutes after we'd secured her into her new home, she began to stir, pulling at her restraints and swearing in Russian.

Pierre watched her with practiced attention, taking in her every movement and listening intently to her language. A smile lit up his weathered face. "Welcome, Mademoiselle Spy, to my humble home that is now your home. Eh, for maybe a little while."

She winced as the pain from her broken nose reclaimed its place in her brain, and then she twisted and turned in either a wasted effort to escape or an equally wasted attempt to gain some measure of comfort.

"*Gde my?*" she growled.

I waggled my finger in the air. "No, no. English. Remember?"

"It is okay," said Pierre. "My Russian is good, and we are going to spend a lot of time together. I think she should speak any language she wishes. I will keep up."

"Who are you?" she hissed.

"That is up to you, mademoiselle. I may be your roommate or your jailer. It is most entirely your decision."

She turned to me with a look that I supposed was meant to appear appealing. "How long?"

As beautiful as she'd been before her nose encountered the bulkhead in the chopper, it was difficult to find her seductive in her current state.

"That depends on how your father reacts to my offer."

Chapter 18
All Aboard

Clark and I took advantage of nearly frozen church pews and used them as cots. Wrapped in several woolen blankets, we were able to get a few hours of shut-eye. Our bodies appreciated the gift of sleep, and our minds demanded it.

I examined the knot on Clark's skull and was relieved it wasn't as serious as I'd feared. "Your head must be harder than I thought."

He pressed his palm against his forehead and groaned. "That doesn't stop it from hurting."

"How's your vision?" I asked, hopeful he'd be more mission-ready than he'd been the previous night.

"It's better, but still not perfect. That was a nasty shot I took."

"Yes, it was, but I need you at full strength. The next couple of days are going to suck."

He chuckled. "Well, that's nice to hear since the last two days have been so delightful. We've still got thirty-six hours before we get to Moscow. I'll be fine by then."

We couldn't show up in Riga in a stolen Finnish Border Guard helicopter, so we opted for Pierre's boat. It was a forty-eight-foot, steel-hulled commercial fishing boat with enormous diesels. It wasn't anything close to luxurious, but it would certainly get the job done.

What sufficed as a marina on Ruhnu was little more than two dozen wooden pilings, and an extremely weathered, somewhat-floating dock. The ferry landing was adequate, but the ferry wouldn't be running again until spring—except for the few times during winter when an icebreaker would cut a swath through the frozen Gulf of Riga to deliver meager supplies to the inhabitants of the island. The Gulf wasn't frozen yet, but there were sheets of ice forming near the rocky shoreline. The thought of a frozen ocean made me cringe. I was really starting to miss the tropics.

The old workhorse of a boat made the sixty-mile trip to Riga look like a Sunday afternoon joyride. Ginger and Skipper provided us with Canadian passports with Latvian immigration stamps already inside. I had no intention of showing our actual passports when we crossed the Russian border, but getting through the Port of Riga would be challenging without some pretense of authenticity. How we'd get back out of Russia would depend on a thousand unpredictable variables, so I hadn't bothered to think that far ahead yet.

I piloted the boat, which is immensely easier than landing a helicopter in the dark, while Clark packed our go-bags from our larger kits. We couldn't hump all of our gear into Moscow, so the smaller go-bags had to hold everything we needed.

Although neither of us spoke Latvian, my Russian, along with a wad of cash, was enough to make arrangements to keep our boat in the marina in Riga for a few days. A boy by the docks insisted that two weeks was too long because the Gulf could turn into a million-acre sheet of ice before then. I assured him that we'd be back before it froze, and if we weren't, he could keep the boat. He heartily agreed to my terms.

We found a café and ordered enough coffee to thaw the parts of us that had frozen on the boat ride from Ruhnu. Latvian coffee, I learned, was much better than Israeli coffee, but I preferred the climate of Tel-Aviv.

Skipper answered my sat-phone call. "Hey, Chase. It's good to see you made it to Latvia."

"We made it, but it hasn't been easy. Norikova is in the loving arms of your Frenchman, and we plan on catching the four-fifty overnight train to Moscow this afternoon."

I heard keystrokes through the sat-phone.

"Okay, that should do it," she said. "You'll have two first-class tickets waiting at will-call."

"Don't you think first class is a little too obvious?"

"Nope. Ginger says first class is important. It'll give you the privacy you need, and a window large enough to climb through if you need to get out in a hurry."

"Okay, you're the boss. I'm just along for the ride."

She ignored my comment. "Do you need Norikov's address again?"

"No, I have it memorized."

As if she didn't hear me or just wasn't listening, Skipper read the address one more time. My memory was correct. The house would be on the Moscow River, and the young Swedish beauty who believed Gregor Norikov was her ticket to supermodel stardom would be occupying the old communist's full attention on a cold Moscow Saturday night.

Skipper was right. The prepaid tickets were waiting at the will-call window for the two Canadians. The bored redheaded ticket agent barely glanced up at me, but locked eyes with Clark and tried to suppress a shy smile.

"You've got to stop doing that," I said.

"What can I say? It's a curse that I'm saddled with. Beautiful women can't resist me."

I shook my head. "You'll know just how bad that curse is when a ticket clerk, the one person in all of Eastern Europe, remembers us when the FSB starts asking questions about the handsome young Canadians."

The equally bored security agent not smitten with Clark searched our backpacks and found nothing more than extra mittens, a change of clothes, and a rolled-up comic book. What he hadn't discovered was the concealed compartments containing two Glock 26 subcompact 9mm pistols, extra magazines, Ka-Bar fighting knives, lock picks, sat-phones, and a handheld GPS. The X-ray machine also missed them, thanks to the lead-thread woven baffles designed to look like insulated socks. Things were starting to go our way, and that scared the hell out of me.

We settled into our cabin and double-checked our inventory. Chalk up another good call to Skipper. She was right about the first-class compartment. Not only was it comfortable and would give us the privacy to catch up on much-needed sleep, but the sliding window was of adequate size to allow even me to get off the train should the Russian *der'mo* hit the proverbial fan.

As trains tend to do, ours pulled out of the Riga-Passajieru station precisely on time and began her nightly sixteen-hour trek toward Moscow.

I had never been closer to the Russian border. I sensed the motion of the train, but the movement I felt in my embattled heart was from the memory of the man who taught me how to perceive the world, who sacrificed so much for his country, and who loved a beautiful woman who was born, served, and died behind the Iron Curtain that once figuratively hung less than two hundred miles ahead of me, where I would cross the border between Latvia and Russia for the first time in my life. Dr. Robert Richter spent his life fighting for the freedoms my country was founded upon, and in the midst of the Cold War, he had fallen in love with Katerina Burinkova, a Soviet KGB officer. He fathered a beautiful daughter who would grow to become one of the world's most elite assassins and most accomplished agents of the SVR—the Russian Foreign Intelligence Service. Fate, or perhaps depravity beyond measure, would deliver that beautiful young assassin into my arms, and ultimately into Dr. Richter's life, as if from the darkest depths of his anguished memory of loving her murdered mother. The web of deception woven so skillfully by the Russian masters had collapsed, sending Anya Burinkova—my mentor's daughter—into the pits of a prison so unimaginably horrible that no one, not even Anya herself, could imagine she would ever again see freedom. I held in my hands the power to set her free, and the weighted responsibility of facing the consequences of doing so. I bore that weight with the unquestioned faith that Dr. Richter would have given his last breath to save his beloved daughter from the hell in which she suffered, and I owed it to him to make that impossibility a reality, no matter what the cost. I would see Anya Burinkova walk again in freedom, but I would do so at the cost of delivering Ekaterina Norikova, an enemy of my country and freedom, back to her father, and back to the Rodina to continue her fight against everything I held dear.

"Chase! Do you want two or three?"

Clark's words yanked me from my stupor. "Huh?" I mumbled.

"Do you want two or three spare mags? I'm only taking two. If we get in a gunfight so bad that two extra mags won't solve it, the third one sure won't make any difference."

"Oh, yeah. Just two is fine."

He took on that confused puppy look he wears so well. "Are you all right?"

"Yeah, I'm fine. I was just thinking about Dr. Richter."

"You're going to need to focus. We're not in Kansas anymore, and it ain't the Wizard we're off to see."

"You're right," I said. "I'm sorry."

We heard a rough knock, and Clark grabbed every piece of hardware he could and shoved it beneath the mattress of the bunk.

I slid open the door, and the conductor asked a question in what I assumed was Latvian, so I answered in Russian. "Everything is perfect. Thank you."

"*Spasibo*," he said, and continued through the train car checking on passengers.

Announcements were made over the intercom of the train in Latvian, Ukrainian, Russian, and butchered English. I ignored most of them, but the mention of dinner in the dining car caught my attention. I pushed the call button for the conductor, and he arrived a few minutes later. I asked if we could have dinner in our cabin, and he was obliged to happily say, "*Da.*"

Our dinner arrived half an hour later, and it wasn't what I'd expected. I'd never spent any time aboard passenger trains, especially not in Europe, so I imagined the food was similar to airline fare. I was wrong.

The salad and soup courses arrived simultaneously, delivered by a uniformed steward wearing white gloves. Precisely eleven minutes later, the main course of roasted lamb, steamed baby carrots, and a rice dish I couldn't identify arrived in the arms of the same steward. He cleared our salad plates and soup bowls, poured an Italian Zinfandel, and disappeared. We ate as if we'd just come off of a hunger strike. Dessert of chocolate pie with caramel and vanilla ice cream arrived twenty-five minutes later with two cordials of vintage port and two cups of steaming black coffee.

"I need to spend more time on trains," I said through a mouthful of chocolate pie.

"Oh, yeah. The food is always amazing. I wonder why the airlines can't get it right."

The steward returned to clear our dessert and asked if we wanted anything else. We tried to avoid eye contact and waved him off. Not only did I not want the redhead at the ticket counter to remember us, I also didn't want to plant any roots in the memories of anyone aboard the train. If Clark's theory of something always going wrong were to hold true, there would be a plethora of questions after the two Canadians had come and gone.

Chapter 19
Friends in Cold Places

Some decisions are always made during the planning stage of any operation, and likewise, some must be made based on conditions in the field. We discussed whether we should ride the train to Moscow Rizhsky station, or if we should make our exit on the outskirts of Moscow when the train slowed to enter the city. We had no way of knowing the level of security we'd encounter at the station or if the place would be littered with surveillance cameras. I wasn't particularly fond of having our faces plastered on every fencepost and telephone pole in Eastern Europe, so I decided getting off the train would be the better option.

Snow had fallen overnight and continued into the morning. The countryside looked like a postcard winter wonderland, but the beauty of the landscape belied the truth of the country. Russia had one hundred forty million people, most of whom lived in poverty. Most Americans could never have understood the conditions the people of Russia endured, nor how they withstood some of the harshest winters on the planet. Although Bernard Baruch coined the term "Cold War" in 1946 to describe the ever-diminishing relations between the U.S. and the Soviet Union, he could just as well have been describing the yearly battle the Soviet people fought against Mother Nature from October through April every year of their lives.

There would be nothing easy about getting off the train on the outskirts of Moscow. I didn't know how much it would slow when we approached the city, but I was confident the train wouldn't continue the pace we'd made through the night. Aside from the possibility of getting hurt when we jumped, we had to consider plenty of other factors, as well. The most obvious was the need to acquire transportation. We couldn't just walk into Boris and Natasha's Rent-A-Car, throw down a credit card, and sign for a Chevy Cavalier. We had to survive the jump with no injuries, determine our position, and requisition a car, none of which would be easy in the best of conditions, but doing it in the snow added an element that neither of us was looking forward to.

We agreed it would be better to step from the back of the caboose to avoid being run over should we roll the wrong direction when we hit the ground. I set out to explore the train in an effort to find the easiest way to get through the caboose and onto the aft platform without drawing too much attention. Most of the passengers were either staring out the window at the snow-covered landscape or busy with their newspapers from around the world. I made the most of the opportunity to move about relatively unnoticed. The escape looked straight forward, and the sliding doors at the rear opened easily on their tracks.

I returned to our cabin and briefed Clark on what I'd found. We agreed if the train slowed sufficiently, we'd turn the caboose into our exit ramp.

The schedule put us at Moscow Rizhsky station at 9:42 a.m., so we estimated we'd make the outskirts of Moscow a few minutes after 9:00. We made our way separately through the dining car and coach class cars to the end of the train. Clark went first, with me following about four minutes behind. No one offered so much as a glance at the six-foot-four, backpack-wielding Canadian. I hoped Clark had garnered no more attention, although I imagined if there were any fair maidens along the way, he wouldn't have passed up the opportunity to wink and smile.

Reaching the last door of the train, I estimated we were doing over sixty miles per hour—far too fast to survive a fall unscathed.

"At what speed are you willing to risk a jump?"

"I was just about to ask you the same thing," I said.

"It's risky, but I still think it's a better plan than dealing with security at the station."

"I think we need to consider the possibility of one of us getting hurt. If I go first and don't fare well, maybe you should consider continuing and taking your chances at the station."

He shook his head. "No way. I'm not leaving you alone and wounded on the side of the tracks in Moscow. Are you kidding me? I've seen how Russian girls swoon over you. You'd have half the women under eighty tending to your wounds, and the other half pregnant. I'd never see you again. We're going together."

I chuckled. "I have to admit, I am big with the over-seventy Muscovite girls. It's a burden, but we all have our crosses to bear."

The train began to decelerate.

Clark said, "Okay, Playboy. It's time to shit or cut bait. Or maybe fish or get off the pot. Whatever it is, it's time to do it."

I slid the door to its stops and stepped onto the platform with Clark half a step behind me. The ground was whirring by as we continued eastward, still at forty miles per hour.

I glanced over my shoulder. "What do you think?"

The look on his face told me what he was thinking before he said it. "It's too fast. A few bruises are okay, but a broken bone any bigger than a finger is going to send this operation down the crapper."

I nodded in agreement and watched the frozen, snow-covered earth continue past the toes of my boots. That's when the gods who hear the prayers of an assassin came to our rescue.

The speaker above our heads crackled, and the conductor spoke again in every language he knew. "I'm sorry, ladies and gentleman, but we are forced to make a temporary sidetrack delay to allow another train to pass. We will be back on our way in just a few minutes, and we will still make our scheduled arrival time at Moscow Rizhsky station."

Clark slapped me on the shoulder. "See, good things do happen to bad people sometimes."

As the train left the main track onto the sidetrack and began slowing, the door behind us slid open with enough force to make me fear Stalin himself was coming through. Clark took a knee and drew his pistol while I drew my fighting knife and pinned myself to the wall, ready to plunge my blade into the chest of whoever came through the door. Clark was looking up to make sure I was in position. We'd been in plenty of fights together, but never one on the back of a train approaching Moscow.

A black, glossy brim of a uniform hat broke the plane of the door, and my heart stopped. I was about to be forced to kill an innocent train conductor to keep him from blowing the whistle on us.

I grabbed his gloved hand coming through the door, and forcefully pulled the rest of him through, propelling his body toward the iron railing of the platform. He hit it with such force that he bent at the waist, and the upper half of his body hung off the back of the train while his legs and feet remained aboard.

"Wait!" he yelled in English.

English? Why did he yell in English?

When humans yell out in fear or surprise, they do so in the first language they learned as a child. I wasn't the only one to notice the discrepancy. Clark reacted by grabbing the man's belt and stopping him from continuing over the railing, though I didn't believe Clark was entirely sold on the man's act. The instant he grabbed the conductor's belt, he also aggressively sent the barrel of his pistol between the man's legs, leaving no room for doubt that he would send a 9mm round straight through his goozle if he misbehaved.

Winded and still bent over the railing, the conductor said, "Ginger said you might like to leave the train before we make the station. Will this little sidetrack fiasco do?"

With that, Clark holstered his pistol and pulled the man upright. I lowered my knife but didn't sheath it yet.

The conductor straightened his coat. "It's nice to have friends all over the world, isn't it?"

The train had almost come to a stop when I decided the small talk was over. I nudged Clark and then followed him down the pair of slick metal steps and onto the snow-covered gravel of the railbed.

I picked up the conductor's hat from the snow, dusted it off, and tossed it toward the train.

He caught it, inspected it, placed it back on his head, and then pointed to the south. "Less than two kilometers that way, follow the stream. You'll find what you need."

We never looked back as we scampered down the embankment toward the stream. When we reached the bottom, I was pleased to see the train and tracks were invisible through the trees and falling snow.

"Why didn't Ginger tell us she had a contact on the train?" I said.

"Maybe she didn't know he'd be on the train until the last minute. I don't know, but never look at a horse's teeth if you've got a gift cat and some rocking chairs."

"What's wrong with you?" I asked, trying to suppress my laughter. "Do you know any sayings?"

"I know all the sayings," he said. "I just can't always keep them straight."

I pulled the handheld GPS from my pack, hoping it wouldn't take long to initialize. "What do you think the conductor meant by, 'You'll find what you need'?"

"I don't know, but I hope it's got four-wheel drive."

We followed the stream and found it frozen where the water slowed and the banks widened. I didn't like being in a place where ice was part of the natural landscape. I belonged in the Caribbean where ice came in the form of cubes under scotch or froth in a daiquiri. I'd never been more distant from everything I considered my home in either geography or my heart.

Clark had, no doubt, been trained to operate in arctic conditions, but I had not. I'd never let him hear me complain, but the unbearable cold painfully penetrated my body and soul. It all but destroyed my will to continue and left me longing to feel the sun on my skin. I ached and trembled more violently by the minute. The only things driving me onward were my limitless loyalty to Dr. Richter and the obligation I felt to repay the debt Anya had so willingly paid on my behalf.

The GPS came to life and delivered a dose of terrible news. We were heading directly toward a heavily populated suburb, and worse, the Moscow River was less than half a mile away. Crossing a river of any size in those temperatures would lead to hypothermia in minutes. Our friend, the conductor, had sent us in the worst possible direction.

"We need to come up with a better plan," I said. "This way is going nowhere fast."

"It's starting to look that way, but maybe we should push on until we know for sure he screwed us."

I agreed, and we continued southward, careful to stop every few steps, listening for any movement in the trees. The snow was dry and crunchy, so we would easily hear anyone walking nearby. Fortunately, it was snowing hard enough to cover our tracks within minutes after making them, so we would be difficult to track. I just hoped we weren't walking into an ambush. The closer we got to the river, the fewer avenues of escape there would be. Getting arrested or killed within our first twelve hours in Russia was not in the plan.

There were sounds of traffic in the distance. We needed to find transportation and orient ourselves enough to find Norikov's house, but I wasn't looking forward to trying to blend in with the locals. The traffic sounds soon gave way to the sound of falling water. I didn't know if that was good or bad, but it was definitely new.

The trees began to thin as we approached the river, and we could see a hundred yards or more in every direction. That made us more vulnerable than I liked, but the walking was getting easier.

When the Moskva came into view, my heart sank. There were no roads between us and the river. That meant we would either have to find a way to cross the thirty-three-degree water or follow it either east or west.

Clark pointed to the southwest. "That's it!"

"What's it?"

"That's exactly what we need, and it's definitely not four-wheel drive."

I moved beside him so I could see what he was pointing at. "I guess the conductor was right after all."

Lying at anchor, just off the riverbank, were four pilothouse workboats bobbing in the slow current of the Moscow River. Driving a stolen car, in the snow, eight thousand miles from home, in a city I'd never seen, was not on the list of things I understood, but boats and water…they were a different story. If we could get to one of the boats and stay dry while we did it, our day would look a whole lot brighter.

"Whoever put those there had to get ashore somehow," Clark said.

"I was thinking the same thing. Let's find ourselves a launch."

We scanned the riverbank for anyone who might catch us. I doubted the snow and temperatures were keeping Muscovites inside, but luckily, there wasn't a living soul in sight.

"That'll work," I said, pointing toward a dinghy lying upside down near the bank of the river.

I grabbed the bow to flip it over, but it was frozen to the ground. Clark found a wooden plank and began prying at the gunwale to free it from its icy bonds. After several attempts, the tundra-like earth gave up and surrendered the boat to us. The drain plug was missing, so I drove a broken limb into the hole and snapped it off, hoping it would keep the boat dry for the fifty-foot trek.

With no paddle in sight, Clark said, "It looks like my pry bar is going to have to do for a paddle."

"Let's do it," I said.

We slid the boat into the edge of the river and managed to stay mostly dry as we climbed aboard. The current was stronger than it had appeared, and we started downstream faster than Clark could paddle with his makeshift oar. It soon became apparent the current would be impossible to overcome, and we would likely float past all four boats before we could reach any of them.

Clark dug at the water, paddling as hard as his arms would allow. "This ain't lookin' good, cowboy. Do you have any ideas?"

I yanked the board from his hand and beat it violently across my knee. Clark looked bewildered, but soon realized what I was doing. Seeing that my plan was flawed, he grabbed the board and propped it against the gunwale, immediately giving it a swift, well-aimed kick. The board cracked in half. Two short paddles were better than one long paddle, so we each grabbed a piece and began digging furiously into the frigid water.

It was working, and we made slow progress toward the anchored boats, but we'd never reach the first boat in time. We focused our efforts on boat number two and kept digging. As we came alongside, I reached out to grab the railing of the anchored boat and dropped my board. I instinctually grabbed for and recovered it, but soaked my gloves in the process. I quickly threw the board into the bottom of the dinghy and reached back for the metal rail of boat number two. I squeezed with all my strength, but it wasn't enough. The combination of the water on my gloves and the temperature of the rail made gripping it impossible. My hand slid down the railing as if it were greased, and we soon drifted past.

I shed my dripping wet gloves into the bottom of the dinghy and started paddling again. The near-freezing water stung my hands and left me shivering in spite of the sweat forming on my brow. Boat number three was only feet away.

"Let's aim for the stern," I said. "If we can get behind the boat and out of the current, we can paddle right up to it with no problem."

Clark shrugged. "Okay, let's give it a try. Nothing else is working."

We aimed for the port stern quarter of the anchored vessel and paddled for our lives. The line was looking good, and our speed was perfect. Our plan was strong, and our odds of pulling it off were improving with every stroke. Motivated by our progress and impending success, Clark and I paddled harder, driving our dinghy faster through the water. We hit the sweet spot perfectly and slipped behind the boat. The current immediately died in the shadow of the much larger boat, and I dug my paddle in to turn our bow toward the boarding ladder hanging over the stern. At that instant, I realized we'd been a little too zealous with our strokes. We'd built up enough speed to shoot past the stern and back into the current on the other side.

Discouraged, and with hands on the verge of frostbite, I started paddling toward boat number four—our last hope.

"I'm going to steer for the bow," Clark said. "Grab whatever you can, and get aboard no matter what it takes. If I can't make it, I'll head for the bank, and you can come get me."

There was no time to come up with a better plan, so I nodded my agreement. We headed directly for the bow, and I planned to grab the anchor chain, even if I had to wrap both arms around it since my hands were becoming more useless by the second.

"Get ready!" Clark yelled. "We're going to hit pretty hard. You just make sure you get on that boat, no matter what."

I leaned over the bow of our dinghy, stretching for the anchor chain. I missed it by inches, and we collided with the hull of the boat in a colossal crash, sending us listing and shuddering. As we came to an instant stop, the dinghy began filling with water that would, in minutes, suck the life from our freezing bodies if we didn't get aboard the larger boat.

I threw my pack aboard the boat and turned to reach for Clark's, but I was too late. He launched his over my head and sent it sliding across the deck of the workboat. The water rose in our dinghy, and I lunged for the railing above my head, landing with both arms across the bar and my feet dangling above the surface of the river. The dinghy broke free and drifted again, half full of the deadly water.

Clark grabbed my thigh and shoved me up and over the rail. I landed on the frozen metal deck and spun, quickly thrusting my right arm toward Clark, who was standing in the dinghy's knee-deep water as our hands met. He shoved his arm up my wrist and clamped onto my forearm. I squeezed at his arm with what I hoped was all the grip I had.

"Jump," I yelled as I forced myself backward, pulling as hard as I could. I fell onto the deck just as Clark came soaring across the rail.

He landed with a thud beside me and moaned, "Go to Moscow, they said. It'll be fun, they said."

Chapter 20

Anchors Aweigh

We sat up as our abandoned dinghy drifted downstream in the coldest water I'd ever touched.

"You know we're screwed if this thing doesn't start."

Clark watched the dinghy. "We were screwed when we got on the plane to Greece. If it doesn't start, we'll find another way. That's kinda what we do."

My hands had gone from cold, to tingling, to burning, and finally to numb. "Why don't you see if you can get this tub started? I need to find a way to get some feeling back in my hands."

He climbed to his feet and headed for the pilothouse. Of course it was locked. Clark turned to me as if I was supposed to have the key.

"I've got a pick set in my bag," I said, "but you'll have to do it. My hands are glaciers. I couldn't pick my nose, let alone that lock."

He glanced at my bag and back at the door before delivering a powerful kick to the handle. The lock gave way, and the door flew inward on its hinges until it crashed into the bulkhead.

"It would've been nice of them to leave us a set of keys," Clark said as he scanned the instrument panel and empty ignition switches. He pulled off his gloves and lay on the deck beneath the helm station. After two minutes of touching wires together and cursing, he slid from beneath the console. "It's dead. There's no power at all."

I maniacally rubbed my hands together. "Maybe the battery switches are off."

We searched for the switches and finally found them inside the engine room, mounted high on the forward bulkhead. Hanging from small, brass hooks beside the battery switches, were two sets of keys on chunks of brown cork.

"Nice." Clark pulled the keys from the hooks and flipped the battery switches. Lights illuminated, and several small fan motors whirred. Those were encouraging signs.

We looked for the through-hull ball valves that would allow river water to be drawn into the engines for cooling. Opening the valves proved more challenging than expected since the mechanisms were nearly frozen shut. I just prayed the water in the lines wasn't solid ice.

Back in the pilothouse, Clark reconnected the wiring to the ignition switch and slid in the keys. One counterclockwise turn of the port side key illuminated an orange light above the switch, indicating the glow plugs in the diesel engine were warming up.

"Here goes nothing." Clark turned the key to the right. The port side diesel slowly turned over, battling against the cold. The RPM gauge rose, and the engine coughed its way to life. "One down, and one to go." He turned the key to warm up the glow plugs for the starboard engine, and just as number one had done, the second engine initially resisted but finally opened its eyes.

The pressures and temperatures were settling into the green arcs, and a quick scan of the riverbank revealed no unwanted attention being cast our way.

Still rubbing my hands furiously together, I made my way to the head and opened the valve for hot water. The boat's plumbing system was designed to allow flow through a heat exchanger on the port side engine, delivering hot water to the sink and shower. The head was filthy and smelled as if something had recently died in there, but the water pouring from the spigot was clean, and it was definitely warm. I adjusted the cold water flow to avoid scalding my nearly frostbitten hands and let it cascade over my knuckles. I slowly decreased the stream until the feeling came back to my fingertips.

When I returned topside, I found Clark cranking the manual

windlass on the bow to raise the anchor. I was surprised it wasn't electric, but Clark was making short work of the job.

Just as the anchor came to rest on its roller, he turned to me. "Anchors aweigh. Now let's go house hunting."

One more scan of the engine instruments reassured us that everything was running as it should. If the rest of our day would follow suit, we'd be on our way back to the Western world in less than twenty-four hours.

I found a cigarette lighter plug that actually worked, and used it to maintain the charge in our GPS. The handheld unit wasn't designed for navigation on the water, but as long as it would show our position and Norikov's house, we could manage the nautical work.

"Uh, Chase. You might want to take a look at this."

I joined him at the helm where he was pecking on the fuel gauges. There were three of them, presumably for three different tanks somewhere aboard the boat. One indicated nothing in the tank, and the other two were oscillating between an inch past full and an inch below empty in random, swinging arcs.

"No way can that can be good," I said as I joined him in tapping on the gauges.

He dropped to the deck and shimmied beneath the console again. "Maybe I screwed them up while I was trying to hotwire it."

I watched the devices closely as he tinkered with the wiring. The gauge indicating empty went dark, and the others kept dancing.

"The wiring for the one on the left is falling apart, but the others look fine," he said, crawling from beneath the console.

"I guess it's time to find and dip the tanks."

He agreed, and we scoured the bowels of the boat for the aluminum fuel tanks. As it turned out, they weren't challenging to find. They were arranged neatly and conveniently beneath a deck plate near the stern. As is almost always true of rigidly installed fuel tanks, there was no easy access to open up the tanks and look inside. Each had circular inspection plates on the top of the tank with twelve screws in each.

"I don't think we should do this here," I said. "Let's get some-place a little less conspicuous. One of us can work on the screws, and the other can drive. Which job would you prefer?"

"Well, since your soft little hands can't stand the cold, you'd bet-ter do the driving. I'll do the screwing...or unscrewing."

I wasn't going to argue. We found a nicely stocked toolbox in the pilothouse, and while Clark worked on the plates, I checked the GPS. Heading west would take us away from the congestion of the city, but it would also take us away from our target. Forward progress is always preferred, so I eased the transmissions into gear and slowly added throttle. I didn't want to jostle Clark around in the back, and I didn't want to do anything to draw attention to the solitary workboat making its way down the Moscow River.

"Good news!" Clark yelled from the stern. "The starboard tank is full, and the sending unit for the gauge is rotten."

"How big are the tanks?"

He glanced down. "Maybe six by three by three."

I gave the okay signal as if we were underwater, and Clark's head disappeared beneath the deck as he went back to work.

I ran the rough calculations. Six by three by three is fifty-four cu-bic feet, and there are seven and a half gallons per cubic foot. That meant there would be about four hundred gallons in each tank if they were full. Even if the engines burned a hundred gallons per hour, we'd have twenty hours of running time. I liked those numbers.

Clark came through the pilothouse door, shivering.

"How do the other tanks look?" I asked.

"I don't know yet. I stripped the head of one of the screws in the center tank. I came in to warm up. It's frigid out there."

"Come on, Green Beret," I said. "It's time to embrace the suck."

"You embrace the suck, wussy-hands. It's nice and warm in here."

"Fine. Just keep us heading that way, and I'll pick up your slack, slacker."

He put up no argument and took the wheel.

I found dirty but warm gloves in a locker and headed for the stern where I went to work on the remaining screws in the plate.

Except for the one Clark had stripped, I was able to get all of them out. With the blade of the screwdriver beside the plate, I tapped until the metal disc rotated far enough so I could see the fuel level while the stripped screw remained in place. I was relieved to find, that just like the first tank, this one was also full. Knowing it was unlikely the owner of the boat would've filled only two of the three tanks, I tapped at the aluminum chamber with the handle of my screwdriver and compared the sound of the third tank to the first two. Satisfied with my results, I secured the plate back in place and headed for the helm.

"It looks like we've got more diesel than we'll ever use," I said.

He glared at me. "How'd you get the plates off so fast?"

I grinned. "Those are the things they teach us college boys in school. You should've gone."

"Ha! Let's see how that college learning feels when bullets start flying."

I patted him on the shoulder. "I'm thankful I've got you when bullets start flying."

It was just past 2:00 p.m. We wouldn't have much light left, so finding Norikov's house was of utmost importance. I pulled the GPS from the console and scrolled until I saw a map presentation showing our position relative to Norikov's address. We were less than ten miles as the crow flies, but the winding river would more than double that distance. I spent the next several minutes thinking of everything that could go wrong in the next two hours on the water.

Clark snapped his fingers in front of my face. "Stop it."

"Stop what?"

"You're doing that thing where you worry about stuff that'll probably never happen. Stop doing that, and start thinking about your speech for dear old Gregor tonight."

"How do you do that?"

"It's just one of those things they teach us Green Berets in Special Forces College."

I couldn't have asked for a better partner, but his mind-reading skills always freaked me out.

We continued until I saw the spires of Saint Basil's Cathedral in the distance. I'd seen thousands of pictures, but no camera could capture the feel of Red Square. I'd never agree with the politics of the Kremlin, but I had no choice but to respect the history of the majestic city.

The snow had almost stopped, but as we approached the coordinates I'd entered into the GPS, the sky was still gray with low-hanging clouds.

"It has to be that dark building on the right," I said, pointing over Clark's shoulder.

He checked the map. "Yep, that has to be it. So, now we wait."

He pulled the throttles back to just above idle, and I focused down the river toward the heart of Moscow.

"I know this is probably stupid," I said, "but I'd like to take a look at the Kremlin since I may never have another opportunity. Something tells me that my connection with this country has almost reached its end."

He tried not to grin. "The right thing to do is hide and wait."

"Yeah, I know."

He set that crooked, mischievous smile of his. "But doing the right thing rarely results in great drinking stories, so let's go have a look at Putin's office."

We motored on as if we had every right and reason to be driving down the middle of the Moscow River. Nothing about my idea was good, but it was an opportunity too rare to pass up.

The cathedral spires grew larger and more dramatic as we neared. The wall made it impossible to get a good look at the Kremlin from the deck of the boat, but what I could see made goosebumps rise on my arms and neck.

Somewhere beyond that wall had been the beating heart of Communism, where gods of war plotted and schemed against the West. Colonel Victor Tornovich, the mastermind of the elaborate operation to infiltrate American covert ops with Anya Burinkova as the tip of his spear, had lived and worked behind those walls for decades. I'd quite literally sent him to Hell in an elaborate operation of my own that cost the lives of not only Tornovich, but a dozen or so other Russians and enough American CIA agents to bring a lump to my throat.

"Have you seen enough?" asked Clark.

I was speechless, and all I could do was nod.

By the time we set the anchor a quarter mile from Norikov's home, the sky was dark, and the snow had begun falling once again. Night fell not only on Clark and me, but also on the city that embodied the philosophy that had taken everyone I'd once loved. Moscow had great potential to send its mighty foot atop my head and crush the life from my body, just as it had crushed my soul by murdering my family and destroying the final days of my dear mentor and beloved professor's life.

Chapter 21
Kiss Me, Fool

Any covert operator will confirm that he'd rather be in a gunfight than a holding pattern. We weren't interested in waiting, especially in twenty degrees on the Moscow River.

"We can't tie up to Norikov's dock," Clark said. "Do you have any ideas how we're going to get ashore and stay dry?"

I'd been thinking about that problem for an hour or so. "We should've kept the dinghy, but there's nothing we can do about it now. I think our best bet is a modified Mediterranean mooring."

Clark got the confused puppy look again.

"In a Mediterranean mooring, we drop an anchor a hundred feet offshore and then back up to the dock, where we tie crisscrossed lines from the stern. Then, we haul in on the windlass, hauling the anchor rode tight."

"What's the difference in that and just tying up alongside the dock?"

"The difference is that we aren't tying off the stern to anything. We're going to drop anchor, go back to the dock, secure a line to a stern cleat, and step off the boat. We'll then let the line out until our boat—or whoever's boat this is—drifts downstream against the anchor, and then we'll tie off the stern line to whatever we can find. That'll make the boat appear to be resting at anchor offshore. When it's time to beat a hasty retreat, we'll haul the boat back to the dock using the stern line, and then we'll hop aboard and run like smoke and oakum."

"Smoke and oakum? What the hell is that?"

"I don't know. It's something Captain Jack Aubrey says."

"Who's Captain Jack Aubrey?"

"Oh, never mind," I said. "I don't have time to teach an English lit class. Let's just see if we can make this work."

I maneuvered the boat into position off the bank of the river in front of Norikov's house, and Clark dropped the anchor. The boat drifted downstream until we put out a hundred feet of chain rode, and then I pulled the starboard transmission into reverse and added enough throttle to start us moving slowly toward Norikov's dock. Clark pulled a hefty coil of line from a locker and secured one end to a stern cleat while I kept inching us toward the shore.

I killed the engines, grabbed our packs, and we were ashore, standing on an old-school communist's riverfront dock less than two miles from the Kremlin. I was supposed to be wearing an Atlanta Braves uniform and catching at Turner Field. Who could have ever guessed my life would come to this?

The plan worked just as designed. We watched the boat trail off downstream and settle against the anchor and chain rode. Our stern line sank, leaving it almost invisible except at the cleat on the boat and where it ran out of the water and across the frozen ground. If the next few hours of our lives went as we planned, we'd be on the boat and headed back toward the equator, where the temperatures were on the other side of freezing.

Norikov had apparently done well for himself since the fall of the Soviet Union. While most of his neighbors lived in cramped, multi-family homes, his was almost palatial in comparison. In addition to the size of the house, the waterfront side was private, thanks to a stand of poplar trees on one side and a high fence on the other. That privacy was a welcome surprise. Not only was I going to have to spend a little time picking the lock on the back door, but we'd also make the most of the privacy when it was time to exit the scene.

I knelt in front of the door and inserted my tensioner and pick into the single lock. "I hope there's no security system."

"I would think he's probably got personal security with him most of the time, but who's brave enough—or stupid enough—to break into Gregor Norikov's house?"

I raised my eyebrows. "That would be us."

I spent longer than expected picking the lock, but the knob finally turned, and the door swung inward a few inches. I listened for the beeping of a security system or the barking of a dog. Thankfully, neither came.

With my pick set back in my pocket, I drew my pistol and stepped through the door with Clark close on my heels. Room by room, we silently cleared the house until we were confident we were the only living souls on the property.

I pulled out my sat-phone and dialed Skipper. "We're inside and alone."

"It's about time you called. Our man on the train said you got off eight hours ago."

"Thanks for letting us know the conductor was an inside man, by the way. We almost threw him off the train."

"We weren't sure if we could actually get him on the train. It was a last-minute thing."

"It worked out," I said, "but we scared the hat right off his head."

"Okay, back to new business."

I was impressed by how quickly she was learning the trade. Ginger must have been a phenomenal teacher.

"Since you left the drone—and most of the other stuff I needed you to take with you—in Estonia, we're flying blind a little bit. We've got a guy, though, and he says Norikov is having dinner with his favorite Swedish bikini-team girl at seven o'clock."

"Did you say a *guy*?"

"Yeah, a guy—you know, a reliable source or whatever. Anyway, before you rudely interrupted me, I was trying to tell you that our *guy* says Norikov likes to have his arm candy tuck him in around nine thirty. He says the dude is usually snoring like a lumberjack by eleven, and then Little Miss Thing makes the Saturday night club circuit."

I cataloged the information in my mind and tried to decide if it would be safer to wait until the girl left before having our chat with Gregor. I didn't like the idea of being in Moscow any longer than absolutely necessary, but involving a young, frightened woman wasn't my idea of a good plan.

"Can your *guy* let us know when Norikov leaves the restaurant?"

"Hang on."

She was talking with Ginger, but I couldn't make out what they were saying. "Keep your sat-phone on," she said. "I'll call you back in twenty minutes if we can put that together. Is there anything else you need right now?"

"I could use a sandwich."

"You're in a rich man's house in Moscow. Surely he has a refrigerator."

I turned to Clark. "She just hung up on me. I think this analyst gig is going to her head."

"I think she's doing just fine," he said.

I filled him in on the details Skipper had passed along, but he didn't seem to listen to anything after the word *refrigerator.*

The kitchen was well stocked, so we grazed on anything we could eat with our fingers without producing scraps or garbage.

Further investigation of the house revealed plenty of places to hide, but Clark's earlier comment about Gregor having personal security kept running through my head.

What if they sweep the house before he comes inside? What if they discover Clark or me? Will we have to kill the guards?

The idea of killing anyone while we were in the country illegally didn't sit well with my logical brain. I wanted to get in, negotiate with Norikov, and get out with no bread crumbs, and especially no dead bodies in our wake.

Skipper called with an update. "Okay, here's the deal. We've got another guy—not the same guy as before – but anyway, he says he'll let us know when Norikov leaves the restaurant. You should have fifteen or twenty minutes from the time we hear from him until Norikov shows up at home—if he goes straight home. Based on what our guy said, Norikov will be in a hurry to get his beauty queen in the sack."

"You're the best, Skipper. Thank you."

"Nope, Ginger is the best, but I'm learning. I'll call you and let you know when the lovebirds are on their way back to the nest."

I slid the phone back into my pocket and checked my watch. "If Skipper's timeline is on the money, we've got a little less than an hour before our friend Gregor arrives. Just as we thought, he'll be bringing home a playdate who, most likely, won't be sleeping over after our boy conks out."

Clark was still pillaging finger foods from the refrigerator. "So, are you thinking we should wait until his little mattress monkey scampers away, or do you want to hit them as soon as they get comfortable?"

"I think we should wait until she leaves, but we should also have a plan in case she stays the night."

"I agree," he said, finally closing the refrigerator.

"Okay, so here's the plan. Regardless of the scenario, we're always in complete control. We never, under any circumstance, let anyone get the upper hand. If we have to hit him while the girl's here, she's either going to scream her head off and fight like a wild animal, or she'll freeze. Nothing in between."

Clark was staring intently. "Agreed."

"Good, so let's play it like this. If the girl isn't in the picture, we'll wake him up with a gun in his mouth and stay in his face as much as possible. We can never let him believe he has a way out. Total domination is the play. Nothing less."

Clark nodded. "Absolutely."

"If the girl is in the equation, she's the wildcard. We'll have only three options with her. One, we put her down. Two, one of us escorts her out or subdues her. Three, we make her watch. The problem with option one is that I don't feel good about killing an innocent girl. I don't like option three because that brings the element of ego into play. Our boy, Gregor, may want to show off and play tough if she's in the room. He's more likely to roll over and beg if we're on him two-on-one."

"I think you're spot-on. So, plan A is to wait for the girl to leave."

"Exactly," I said, "but if she stays, I've got a newly acquired tool in my box that just might come in handy." I pulled a syringe and vial of ketamine from my pack.

"Whatcha got there, Doctor Fulton?"

"Oh, nothing much. Just a little something to help people get some much-needed rest."

Clark grinned and nodded his approval.

We walked through the house twice more to make sure we knew every nook and cranny. If things got wild, we would need to know precisely how to get out or where to hide. There would be no time for exploring if things started going downhill.

Skipper called to let me know Norikov had left the restaurant.

"All right, we've got about fifteen minutes."

Clark checked his watch. "Let's get in position."

As much as I dreaded the cold, we had no choice but to wait outside in case Norikov's personal security swept the house. We re-donned our coats, hats, and gloves and headed back out the door. On the way out, I parted the drapes just slightly so we could get a picture of what was happening inside.

I quickly glanced out onto the river, relieved to see our boat was still resting like a good little getaway car. Our modified Mediterranean mooring was working perfectly.

Minutes passed like hours as we hunkered in the shrubbery near the dock. Every breath felt like daggers in my lungs, and I was forced to consciously control my shivering. I didn't belong that far from the equator.

"Look," Clark whispered.

The first floor of the house lit up like a concert hall, and I squinted to see through the break I'd made in the drapes. Two men in dark suits carrying flashlights and sidearms were sweeping the house. One of the men opened the back door, placed one foot outside, and gave a cursory glance across the yard and dock area. I held my breath. If the man caught a glimpse of the cloud that formed every time either of us exhaled, we'd be sitting ducks. Fortunately for us, he wasn't the thorough type and quickly retreated inside.

We low-crawled toward the door and peered inside. I saw the heels of two men ascending the stairs and one man still standing in the opening formed by the front door. I'd been wrong about my count. The man by the door made three. In less than a minute, the two men I'd watched climb the stairs came back down and headed for the front. Although I couldn't hear what they were saying, it was clear Gregor Norikov was dismissing the men for the night.

He looked younger than his seventy years and fitter than I expected. The woman on his arm was, indeed, a world-class beauty. In her heels, she was an inch taller than the old communist, and her blonde hair fell perfectly down her shapely back. Gregor removed her floor-length fur coat and placed it on an antique hall tree by the door. The woman's dress probably cost more than the average Russian family's annual income.

She slid off her heels, reducing her height by three inches, and left them by the door. The woman placed two glasses side by side on the countertop and dropped ice cubes into each. Never taking her eyes from Gregor, she covered the ice with vodka and then offered him the glass. He greedily accepted, and she poured half the contents of her own drink into her mouth. Her diamond-adorned hand then slid around Gregor's neck as she pressed her painted red lips to his. The vodka found its way from her mouth, into his, and then down his throat.

Clark whispered, "We should try that later."

I shook my head. "Sure, but that shade of lipstick would look terrible on you."

When the vodka-laced kiss ended, the pair headed for the stairs. I was thankful our opportunity to get back inside the house and out of the cold was approaching. I slid my pick set from my pocket and inserted the tensioning arm into the lock, but before I could begin putting pressure against the tool, Clark reached for the knob and gave it a twist. The door swung inward on its hinges, revealing the fact that the so-called security team would never qualify as tier-one operators.

We removed our coats and gloves but left our watch caps in place to hide our faces. As we approached the stairs, we could already hear the woman having either the greatest night of her life, or demonstrating her Oscar-worthy acting skills. Either way, we were confident Gregor was focused entirely on the woman's performance. We crept up the stairs in silence and made our way to a pair of alcoves outside the master suite, well out of sight of the bed.

The woman's vocal extravaganza went on for twenty minutes, punctuated at random intervals with ecstatic cries of soul-shaking pleasure.

If that's real, I need to get some tips from old Gregor.

Finally, I heard the woman collapse in apparent exhaustion following dinosaur noises from Gregor. I didn't want to imagine what that looked like. Clark was trying not to laugh but doing a poor job of it.

Although her Russian was terrible, the woman shoveled compliments on the communist Casanova, who was still breathing like he was on the verge of a heart attack. In a mix of Swedish and painful Russian, the woman said something about how much she liked going out to the club after a night with Gregor so all the other men would know, just by looking at her, what he'd done for her.

Norikov either bought the lie or didn't care. I suspect his Swedish was just as bad as mine, but there was no mistaking his Russian. "Take all of my money and go dance until you drop dead for all I care. Just don't you dare let any other man do to you what I just did. Do you understand?"

"*Da, moy dorogoy,*" she said.

"Do not call me darling, you whore. I am nothing more than your banker. Now, get out!"

We tucked ourselves further into our holes and waited for the woman to come through the door. We didn't have to wait long. Even after what she'd been through for the past half hour, she was still a knock-out. Being a seventy-year-old Russian oligarch has its benefits, but I think being a twenty-seven-year-old American spy in love with Penny Thomas trumped anything Miss Sweden could dish out.

The woman made a brief phone call, poured four fingers of vodka into an iceless glass, and then downed it in one shot. She stepped into her high heels, pulled on her coat, and danced through the front door. I locked eyes with Clark as he pointed to his watch and then held up five fingers. I was thankful those five minutes would be spent in the warmth of the house and not huddling in the bushes by the river.

Three minutes later, the sound of a snoring buffalo came rolling from the bedroom. Gregor was out, and it was time to party.

Chapter 22
Rules of Negotiation

I slid the muzzle of my pistol into Gregor Norikov's mouth, and in the most feminine Russian tone I could force out of my throat, I said, "Wake up, darling."

He didn't move a muscle.

I tried again in a slightly more aggressive and less feminine tone. "Wake up, asshole!"

Clark, who had already lost his patience, launched a lamp against the headboard, sending shards of porcelain against Norikov's face. Even our favorite snoring buffalo couldn't sleep through that.

He sprang upward, forcing the barrel of my pistol deeper into his mouth until he gagged and reflexively grabbed for the gun. I caught his left hand, and Clark seized his right as I withdrew the pistol from his mouth. Each of us twisted a wrist half an inch further than wrists can be comfortably twisted. With panic-filled eyes, the man groaned in pain. It was safe to say we had Norikov's attention.

"Hello, Gregor," I said as cheerfully as possible. "I'm sorry to wake you like this, but we have some things we need to discuss."

"*Kto ty, chert voz'mi?*" he roared.

"Who we are isn't important, Gregor. What *is* important is who we have," I said. "When was the last time you saw your beautiful daughter, Ekaterina?"

In that tone old communists are so good at using, he roared, "If you hurt my daughter—"

I stuck the gun back in his mouth. "We'll be making the threats tonight, Gregor. You'll be listening and giving us what we want. Now, I'm going to take my gun back out of your mouth, and you're going to be a good little boy, aren't you?"

His eyes narrowed in rage, and Clark added enough additional pressure to his wrist to garner submission from almost anyone, especially a naked, seventy-year-old communist.

His face morphed from defiant to compliant in an instant.

"That's the look I want to see," I said. "I think you're starting to get the picture, Gregor. You're not in charge anymore."

Clark eased the pressure, and I did the same.

Norikov's face relaxed, and his shoulders sagged. "What do you want?"

"It's not what we want. It's what our superiors want. We're just low-level implements—sharp tools you might even say. We're just the people who do the dirty work our bosses don't want to soil their hands with."

"What is it?"

"It's a girl who looks a lot like your daughter. You see, she's in the Black Dolphin Prison. That's a men's prison, Greg. And that's no place for a beautiful young woman."

He shook his head. "I do not know what you are talking about."

"In that case," I said, "you're of absolutely no use to us, and we'll have to kill you *and* Captain Ekaterina Norikova. Thanks for your time." I released his wrist, holstered my pistol, and backed away from the bed. I pretended to press a few buttons on my sat-phone. "Go ahead and shoot him in the head. I'm ordering our friends to do the same to his daughter."

Clark raised his pistol to the man's temple.

I said into the phone, "Kill the girl. Norikov can't help us."

"Stop! I'll do it!" Gregor cried out. "Whatever you want, I'll do it."

I put the phone back to my ear. "Belay my last order…temporarily."

Clark shoved two fingers up Norikov's nose and pulled him from the bed. "Get up, you piece of shit. If you tell us *no* one more time or refuse anything we demand one more time, there will be no more second chances. You'll die, your daughter will die, and we'll simply move up the chain until we find someone powerful enough to give us what we want."

Clark's negotiating tactics weren't necessarily diplomatic, but he had a way of getting his point across while leaving no room for misunderstanding. The fact that there was no chain and we had no leverage against anyone but Norikov didn't matter. All that mattered was getting Anya out of the Black Dolphin Prison at any cost.

Norikov had no choice but to follow Clark or have his nose ripped from his face. He chose wisely and let Clark stand him up beside the bed.

Negotiating 101 for spies is a simple course. The rules are these: 1. Dominate the environment. 2. Physically control the subject. 3. Humiliate if possible. 4. Make demands and accept nothing short of full compliance. Oh, and 5. Have fun while doing it.

We'd dominated the environment by invading Norikov's home and specifically his bedroom. Our environmental dominance in that case was expanded by the make-believe phone call to have his daughter killed. The physical control was covered by the nearly broken wrists, mouth wounds from my gun barrel, and leading him around by his nose. We'd accomplished the humiliation by standing the man beside his own bed, completely naked, and in fear for his life. It was time for the demands.

I looked the man up and down, intentionally laughing as I did. Okay, maybe I was still applying the humiliation step, but I was also starting to have a little fun. "I'll confess that I don't know much about you, Gregor, but I know I have your full attention. You know even less about me, but you do know I won't hesitate to kill both you and your daughter if you hiccup one more time. That's all you need to know about me."

I picked at my front teeth and then pretended to look at an imaginary speck on my fingertip. "Well, there is one more thing you probably need to know about me."

I took three steps toward him until we were inches apart. I towered over him by eight inches and wasn't going to let that fact be lost on him.

His hatred for me returned to his eyes.

I whispered, "Remember Colonel Victor Tornovich? I set him on fire and watched him burn while screaming like a terrified child. Then I shot him in the head, Gregor. That was me."

More environmental dominance…and a little fun.

I licked my lips and took a step back. "So, here's what you're going to do." I paused and glanced around the room. "Do you need a pen and paper, or can you remember this?"

Clark chuckled as if we'd rehearsed the act. "I think he'll remember."

I cleared my throat. "You're going to have Anastasia Burinkova released from the Black Dolphin. You have ten hours to make that happen."

Clark chimed in right on cue. "Why does he have just ten hours?"

"I'm glad you asked," I said, and stepped back into Norikov's face. "You have ten hours because that's the number of fingers your daughter has, and I'm going to have one finger cut off every extra hour Anya spends in that prison. And when I run out of fingers… Well, Gregor, do I really have to tell you what I'm going to do when I run out of fingers? I would include her nine toes in the party, but keeping her alive for nineteen hours in that much pain would be cruel. Don't you think, Gregor?"

"Okay, okay. I will make it happen, but it will take several hours," he said.

"That's fine. Take all the time you want. I'm sure Ekaterina will understand. I think I'll start with the thumbs. Those are particularly handy digits. Aren't they, Gregor?"

"Please don't hurt my daughter."

As Marlon Brando did in *The Godfather*, I patted his face several times. "I'm not the one who's hurting your daughter, Greg. You're the one who's taking his time. You might even say you're giving your own daughter the finger."

Clark laughed again.

Norikov sighed, apparently realizing he was out of options. "Okay, just let me use the telephone."

"Now you're starting to grasp the sense of urgency of the situation. I knew you were smarter than they said you were. Sure, go ahead. Make the call. Just keep in mind, my Russian is strong, so be very careful what you say."

"May I?" he asked, pointing to the phone on the nightstand.

I motioned to the phone with my palm up. The next two seconds were the longest seconds of my life.

Instead of reaching for the phone, Norikov turned his back to me, reached behind the nightstand, and drew a Makarov pistol. He stuck the gun under his left arm and blindly sent two rounds toward Clark. I threw a front kick to Norikov's kidney, sending him careening forward. His right shoulder hit the massive headboard and spun him toward me. Although I was ultra-focused on Norikov, I heard Clark bellow in pain. I wanted to see how badly my partner was wounded, but taking my eyes off my target would've been a fatal mistake. Another shot rang out from Norikov's pistol, and the bullet grazed the top of my left ear. It took what felt like an eternity to draw my gun, but I pulled my trigger twice, sidestepped to the right, and then squeezed off two more rounds.

The naked man melted to the floor, wedged between the bed and nightstand, and a pool of blood formed around him. I turned my attention immediately to Clark, who was grasping his left side with his right hand and hopping on one foot, cursing every other breath.

"How badly are you hit?"

He raised his hand to reveal a few ounces of blood. "It's not going to kill me, but it hurts like hell."

Though my ears were ringing like church bells, the next sound I heard was unmistakable. From downstairs came the Swedish-accented, terrible Russian, "Is everything okay, sweetheart?"

Clark and I cast our eyes toward the door, and he ordered, "Get her!"

I sprinted from the bedroom and down the staircase just as she started up. The look on the woman's beautiful face when she saw me, dressed in black with a watch cap pulled down over my face, was one of sheer terror. She screamed, spun on one foot, and bolted for the front door.

I launched my body forward, covering eight steps per stride, and caught her just as her trembling hand grasped the doorknob. My momentum carried the two of us face-first into the heavy oak door, and she collapsed in my arms, unconscious.

I checked her pulse, and she was alive but out cold. I lifted her from the floor and placed her on one of the sofas near the fireplace. In seconds, I was back in Norikov's bedroom, where Clark was still grabbing his wounded side and lighting candles.

"What are you doing?"

He glanced up. "Covering our tracks. Are you hurt?"

"No, I'm fine. What do you mean, covering our tracks?"

"Did you kill the girl?"

"No, she's unconscious on the couch," I said. "How badly are you hurt?"

"It's a through-and-through above my left hip. There's nothing much to hit there. We're lucky he wasn't shooting hollow-points."

I checked his wound and discovered small trickles of blood coming from the entry and exit wounds. I found a roll of tape and stuck a field-expedient bandage in place until we could get some time and distance between us and that house.

When we reached the bottom of the stairs, Clark pointed to the girl. "Find something to wrap her with. I'm turning on the gas."

"You're doing what?"

"Just find a big, heavy blanket and wrap her up."

I did as he said, and watched him yank the stove from the wall and disconnect the gas line, leaving the metallic hose to spray natural gas into the house. The candles he lit upstairs were beginning to make sense.

We put on our coats and gloves, and I carried the well-wrapped Swedish beauty over my shoulder, oblivious to the near-zero temperature as we headed for the dock. We soon had the boat hauled in with minimal effort.

"What are we going to do with her?" I said.

Clark looked over her cocoon-like form. "We can't leave her here. This place will be a fireball in no time. Hit her with your tranquilizer. We don't need her waking up in the middle of this."

I followed him aboard the boat and carried the Swede into the pilothouse. I had no idea what the drug would do to an unconscious, already drunk woman, but he was right—her waking up was not an option.

I drew out a few CCs of ketamine and sank the syringe into her thigh. Thirty seconds later, I was hauling the anchor chain in with the manual windlass. The hundred feet of anchor rode still in the water would take far too long to get aboard, so I opened the brake on the windlass and let the chain play out until the bitter end ran overboard and sank to the bottom of the river.

Clark eased the throttles forward as soon as the chain hit the water, and I carefully made my way back to the pilothouse on the cold metal deck.

Without a word, we motored downstream past the Kremlin, through the heart of Moscow, in the bitter night air, with Norikov's girlfriend breathing deeply and never offering to stir. The lights of the massive city kept us from seeing Norikov's house go up in flames, but the fire was inevitable.

The house wasn't the only thing going up in smoke that night. I'd watched any chance of getting Anya out of prison melt into a bloody heap. The thought of her dying in the unthinkable conditions of the Black Dolphin was more than I could bear. With my jaw clenched and fury rising in my chest, I drove my fist into the wooden hatch leading to the forward cabin. Splintered wood flew in every direction, and the remains of the hatch swung loosely on the single hinge.

Clark watched my tantrum but didn't say a word. There was no question in my mind that he understood everything I was feeling, and that he had undoubtedly had his share of outbursts over the years.

He finally put his hand on my shoulder. "Let's find a place to leave the girl."

The lights of an industrial dock came into view on the south side of the river. "How about there?" I said. "Surely somebody will find her there before she freezes to death."

He pointed the boat toward the dock, and we were soon pulling away with one less soul on board, but still without a plan.

"Obviously, the train back to Riga isn't an option," Clark said, "and the Moscow River to the west turns into a creek before we could get anywhere meaningful."

I couldn't decide if he was asking me to come up with a plan, or if he was justifying running deeper into the largest country on Earth.

"If your math is any good," he said, "we've got enough diesel to keep running for days, but we've got to get someplace a little friendlier than Mother Russia."

I kicked myself for not knowing everything there was to know about European geography. The GPS wasn't much help, but it did paint a rough picture of what lay ahead.

I studied the screen. "We'll hit the Oka River if we keep going. It looks about seventy miles, straight-line distance."

"It has to be twice that far on the river, so that's six or seven hours, best case."

"Which direction does the Oka flow?"

He glared at me. "Downhill." Recognition flashed in his eyes. "Wait a minute! See if you can find the city of Ryazan."

I scanned the tiny screen.

Clark tapped his foot and bit at his bottom lip. Those two ticks, when combined, meant he was trying to recall something important.

"Got it!" I found Ryazan fifty miles southeast of the convergence of the Moscow and the Oka Rivers. I handed him the GPS and pointed toward the town.

"That's it," he said. "There's a military aviation museum just southwest of there, but I can't remember the name of the airport."

I leaned in, hoping he was about to announce a brilliant plan to get us anywhere other than Russia, but he kept tapping his foot and biting his lip.

"It doesn't matter what the name of the airport is. Just tell me what you've got in mind."

"I've got Ginger in mind," he said.

I had the sat-phone burning up prepaid minutes in no time, and Skipper's anxiety poured through the earpiece. "Is everything okay? Are you both okay? Did he get Anya out? Where are you?"

"We're fine," I said, "but the mission has gone all to hell. Listen to me. Find an airport southwest of a town called Ryazan. There's an aviation museum there. We can be there inside of twelve hours if everything goes well. See what you can do to get us out of there, and call me back."

I hung up, not wanting to answer any more questions or explain what had gone wrong. None of that mattered unless we could get out of Dodge.

Forty minutes later, Ginger's voice came through the sat-phone. "I've got an operator who's willing to trade places with you. He'll bring you a flying machine. I don't know what kind yet, but it doesn't matter. All you have to do is trade passports with him. You've still got the Canadian passports, right?"

"Ginger, I love you! You're brilliant. That's how we'll get Anya out of the Black Dolphin."

"Chase, what are you talking about? I'm talking about getting you—not Anya—out of Russia."

"I know, but now I know how to do both. Get your guy headed to Ryazan, and we'll be there as soon as we can. I'll call with updates every three hours."

Clark glared at me. "What was all that about?"

"I just figured out how we're going to get Anya out of that prison, but we'll need some more firepower and a little white lie."

Chapter 23
The Ukrainian Express

The convergence of the Moscow and Oka River came into sight just as the morning sun broke through the overcast. The sun was a godsend, but the silhouettes of the two gunboats bearing on us from the east were quite unnerving.

"That can't be good," I said.

Clark shifted his eyes between the boats. "Ditch the pistols over the stern. They're going to stop us, and it'll be impossible for two Canadian tourists to explain having pistols that smell like they were used to kill an old communist."

He shoved his holstered pistol into my palm, and I pulled mine from my waistband. I watched them hit the white, foamy wake behind our boat and disappear instantly.

A glance at the depth-sounder showed eleven feet under the keel.

"Someone might find those someday, and I'd love to be a fly on the wall when they do."

Clark was clearly more focused on the problem at hand. "What do we tell those guys when they ask us what the hell we're doing?"

"Maybe they'll want to debate who has the better hockey team."

Clark shook his head. "Yeah, I'm sure that's what they'll want to discuss."

In the States, Coast Guard regulations say boats should pass port to port just as if they were cars passing on the street, but those were the rules several thousand miles west of where we were that day. The gunboats kept coming in their staggered formation about fifty feet apart, clearly oblivious to the U.S. Coast Guard regulations.

Clark turned the wheel slightly to the right, demonstrating our willingness to surrender the center of the river to them, and I hoped they'd make some similar move and drift slightly toward the opposite bank. But I knew it wouldn't be that simple. Instead of veering to the right, the two boats turned directly toward us, narrowing their opening. They were only a few feet apart and coming our way.

"I'm starting to regret throwing the guns overboard," I said.

"With only two pistols, we'll never win a gunfight with those guys. Do you think we should stop?"

"I'm thinking we should maintain course and speed until a collision is imminent, and then give way."

Clark raised his eyebrows. "That imminent collision part is coming sooner than you think."

The massive gunboats plowed through the water with their bows high and their deck guns trained on us. They showed no indication of slowing down.

"I'm not risking it." Clark pulled the throttles to idle. Our heavy boat settled in the water and continued drifting forward in a slow deceleration.

"Try not to look guilty," I said as the boats drew closer.

"I'm not guilty. You're the one who shot Norikov. I was busy dancing around like a jackass and trying not to bleed to death."

"Yeah, but you're the one who ate half the food in the man's refrigerator."

He smirked. "Okay, so I'm a little guilty."

The gunboats plowed through the water until they were just off our bow, and then they split and roared down each side of our boat. The machine gunners kept their weapons trained on our hull. As they passed, the enormous wakes rocked us around like a cork. Clark eased the throttles forward to keep enough speed to maintain steerage, but he was careful to show no signs of trying to run away.

I watched the gunboats as they each turned aggressively toward the other, crossing each other's wake behind us. Rolling out of the turn, they roared past us again, missing us by only a few feet. The crew of each boat laughed hysterically at the pair of frightened idiots in the workboat. It obviously hadn't been reported stolen yet, and Clark gave them the universal single-finger salute as the Russian boat crews accelerated back toward the Oka.

"That was way too close," I said.

"You're telling me. That could have been an international cluster—"

"Yeah, it could've been," I said, "but it wasn't…this time."

We turned northeast into the Oka River and erupted in nervous laughter.

Clark wiped imaginary sweat from his brow. "Let's not do that again. What do you say?"

"I couldn't agree more. Let's check in with the girls."

Skipper's cheerful voice had a way of making everything better. "Good morning. I see you've made good progress."

The state-of-the-art tracking software on Ginger's laptop allowed them to see our current position and track our motion in real time. It was powerful and reassuring.

"Yeah, we're in the Oka now and headed for Ryazan. Do you have any more information on the swap?"

"I do," she said. "You won't be going to the Muzey Dal'ney Aviatsii. That would be stupid. There's way too much that can go wrong there. We have a much better plan."

I could hear her shuffling paper. "Write down fifty-four degrees, fifty-three point seven-five minutes north, by thirty-nine degrees, thirty-one point three minutes east."

"Okay, I got it," I said. "Where is that, and what are we likely to find when we get there?"

"The Ukrainian Express."

"The Ukrainian border is over three hundred miles from here," I protested.

"Oh, I know where Ukraine is. I've been studying. Those coordinates won't put you in the country, but they will put you at the spot where a seaplane is going to splash down just before dark, and I happen to know the pilot of that plane would love to trade it for a nice Russian riverboat."

"You're amazing."

"You keep telling me that. Can't you come up with something better than amazing?"

I laughed. "I'll see what I can do. Thanks for the good news."

"Don't forget to check in every three hours. All of this is fluid."

"You got it," I said.

Clark glanced up from the helm. "Well, that sounded positive."

"It was. We're trading up. Skipper gave me coordinates where we were supposed to meet a seaplane just before dark. She says that Muzey Dal'ney Aviatsii is too dangerous."

"She and Ginger haven't led us astray yet, so I trust them. Where are the coordinates?"

I typed the lat and long into the GPS and waited for it to plot the position on the screen.

"I like it," I said. "It's just twenty-five miles."

"More like fifty on the river, but I like it, too."

We pushed the boat a little harder than we normally would have, but the encounter with the patrol boats reminded us not to spend more time than necessary on the open water. If we could find a place to hide near the coordinates, we could take turns getting some sleep while we waited for the seaplane.

* * *

There had never been a finer stretch of water on which to land a seaplane. The river was dead straight for almost five miles, and nearly two thousand feet wide. A small peninsula jutted into the river from the south bank and gave us the perfect place to take cover. We were able to maneuver the boat out of sight and tie her to a tree. It was still bone-chilling cold, but we were tucked away nicely and waiting for what Skipper had called the "Ukrainian Express."

I phoned home, and Skipper wasted no time on pleasantries. "Are you there yet?"

"Yes, we just arrived and got ourselves dug in."

"Great," she said. "The weather window is closing, so we're moving up the timetable. There's another snowstorm coming late tonight, and we need you in Kyiv before that happens. Our guy is in the air now and should be arriving in less than ninety minutes. Will that work for you?"

"You bet it will. The sooner I can get where nobody wants me dead, the better. As far as I know, I've never pissed anybody off in Ukraine."

"Great," she said. "I'll pass the word along, and I'll call you just before he should be landing. What else do you need?"

"Put me on speaker with you and Ginger. We've got a change of plans, and I'm going to need a lot of help."

The phone clicked.

"Hey, Chase. What's up?"

"Hey, Ginger. We need some serious support here. I have a plan, but you're not going to like it."

"Okay, let's hear it."

"Everything fell apart last night. Norikov took some shots at us, and we had to put him down. He's no longer a factor in this."

"Are you both okay?"

"Yes, we're fine," I said, "but now we have to come up with another way to get Anya out of the Black Dolphin. That's where you come in. I need detailed maps of the interior and exterior of the prison, as well as your best guess as to where she's being held. I need to know yard schedules—if she ever gets to see the sky—and I need topo maps of the surrounding terrain."

"You don't want much, do you?" she said.

"I'm not finished. I also need two tickets to Riga from Kyiv, and then some way to get into Kazakhstan, but I don't know where yet. We'll figure that out from Riga. I'll also need you to get a message to the Frenchman. Tell him to stop feeding Norikova."

"What?" she protested. "He can't starve her."

"Oh, yes, he can," I argued, "and he's going to. I need her hungry, dirty, and generally miserable. Oh yeah, and I need some cold-weather gear for her—boots, gloves, thermals, hat, everything. Can you do that?"

"Sure I can, but what are you planning?"

"Don't worry about that right now. It'll all make sense in time. Just get me what I need, and make that call to Pierre, okay?"

"Okay. Anything else?"

"Yeah, there's a lot more, but that's it for now. Call me when the plane is fifteen minutes out."

Clark was sitting on an overturned bucket, shaking his head. "You're insane. You know that, right?"

"Yeah, I know, but do you have a better idea?"

"Ha! Hell yeah, I've got a better idea. We catch a red-eye to Bangkok from Kyiv, party like rock stars for a week, and then fly home."

"That sounds like a good idea, too" I admitted, "but I have to get Anya out first."

"What are you going to do with her when you get her out? *If* you get her out."

"I'm going to hand her a pistol and a check for two million bucks, pat her on the butt, and wish her luck."

"The most dangerous part is what Penny will do to you when she finds out you patted that girl on her little Russian butt."

I smiled. "Okay, maybe I'll forego the Russian butt patting, but I have to get her out. I owe that to Dr. Richter...and to Anya."

He nodded slowly. "You don't owe either of them anything, but what you're doing is a noble thing, and nobility has to come before Bangkok...this time."

We rummaged through the lockers and found nothing to eat. I was starving, and we were still several hours away from any possibility of a meal.

"So, just hypothetically, if you were to freeze to death, would you mind if I ate part of you?"

He pointed his finger at me. "Oh, I can think of a part of me you can *bite*, but you're not eating me, College Boy."

The sat-phone put an end to our banter.

"Chase here."

"Your trade-a-plane should be arriving any minute, and you're booked on the eight a.m. Lufthansa flight from Kyiv to Riga with a layover in Frankfurt. I've even booked you a hotel in Kyiv tonight. I figured you could use a hot shower and a soft bed."

"Did you call Pierre?"

"Yes, we called him, and there will be no feeding time at the zoo. I'm still working on the cold-weather gear, but we'll have it arranged for you by the time you get to Riga."

"Thank you, Skipper. You're...phenomenal."

She giggled. "Okay, I'll take that. Call me from Kyiv."

"You got it."

"Things are looking up," I said. "Our ride out of here should splash down any minute, and Skipper booked us a hotel in Kyiv. We're on the plane to Riga tomorrow morning."

* * *

The PBY Catalina came in low over the treetops and skimmed the glassy surface of the river, settling into the water in just a few hundred feet. The plane wore a French registration and looked like it just came from a warzone.

The engines went silent, and a thirty-something guy about my size stuck his head and shoulders through the hatch.

We motored alongside and tossed a line to the man. He hastily tied it off to a pad eye and threw down a pair of worn, green seabags. I sidestepped the falling bags and let them land with a thud on the deck of the workboat.

The man stepped from the seaplane onto the rail of our boat. "Permission to come aboard?"

"Of course," I said, as if any other response would've made a difference. He hopped to the deck, and I stuck out my hand. "Chase Fulton."

He looked at my hand, then at Clark. "Don't care. Plane's full of gas. Here's your new passport. Where's mine?"

I stuck my Canadian passport in his hand. He quickly thumbed through the pages and then pointed toward the southwest. "Ukraine is that way." He pointed southeast. "Kazakhstan is over there." He pointed north. "Well, you already know what's up there."

I shouldered my backpack and climbed aboard the Catalina with Clark right behind me. Before we had the hatch closed, the man had already tossed the line from the boat into the water and motored away.

"Who *was* that guy?" I asked, watching him head back toward Moscow.

"Don't care." Clark pointed to the southwest. "Ukraine is over there."

I laughed and secured the hatch. We settled into the cockpit and started familiarizing ourselves with the instrumentation and controls. It was nice to see English on an instrument panel. Clark dug out a checklist, and we soon had both engines purring like kittens —very big, very noisy kittens. In no time, the Ukrainian Express was pointed toward Kyiv.

Chapter 24
To Be Somebody

I don't know what felt better—the shower, the bed, or the food. Any one of the three would've qualified as a temporary heaven, but the combination was all we could've wanted. The human body still functions when dirty, but the lack of sleep and calories tend to leave us less than optimum.

We were finally able to properly clean and bandage Clark's gunshot wound, which looked remarkably healthy already. He'd fallen asleep within minutes of hitting the sack, but I still had a lot on my mind and decided I'd make a call home.

"Nice job on the hotel," I said when Skipper answered.

"Thank you. I'm glad you approve. Are you doing okay?"

Sometimes she still sounded like the teenage girl I'd known a decade before, but she was quickly becoming an astonishing young woman, a brilliant analyst, and an integral part of the team.

"We're tired, battle-weary, and still shaking off the cold, but it's nice to be back in civilization. How about the cold-weather gear for Norikova?"

"You're all business, aren't you?"

"It's what we do," I said.

"You'll be pleased to know there will be a package waiting for you at the airport in Riga tomorrow afternoon. It should contain everything you need, but if anything's missing, just call the number inside the package."

"I knew I could count on you."

"I'll be tracking the airline passenger manifest, so I'll know when you get on and off the plane tomorrow, but call me when you get to Riga for an update."

I hung up and felt my eyelids turn to lead weights. Minutes later, the sat-phone rang, and I stuck it to my ear. "Yeah, what did you forget?"

"Chase?"

I couldn't believe what I was hearing. "Penny? Is that you?"

"Yes, I'm sorry. I know I'm not supposed to be doing this, but I need to hear your voice and know you're okay. And I need to tell you I love you."

I couldn't hold back the smile. "I'm fine."

"You promised you'd never lie to me," she said softly.

"Okay," I confessed, "I'm tired, cold, sore, and a little homesick, but other than that, I'm fine and not hurt or in any danger right now. I was just falling asleep in the amazing hotel Skipper scored for us."

"I wish I was there with you."

"No, you don't," I said. "You wish we were together, but you don't want to be here. It's cold and nasty."

"I want to be everywhere you are, Chase."

"I love you, Penny."

"Good night, Chase. Come home to me soon, okay?"

"I promise."

The line went dead, and I cradled the phone against my chest.

What am I doing halfway around the world, freezing my butt off, getting shot at, and sneaking in and out of a different country every other day? I should be anchored off Key West with Penny in one hand and a margarita in the other.

* * *

Morning came far too quickly, and we devoured the offered breakfast. I hadn't expected first class, but the Lufthansa gate agent insisted that our seats were up front.

The flight attendant couldn't keep her eyes off Clark. "Can I get you gentlemen anything?"

His patent-pending crooked grin was doing its thing. "I'd love a black coffee."

"Coffee for me, as well, please," I said, interrupting their moment.

I gave him the eye.

"What? It's not like it matters if a Lufthansa stewardess remembers me."

"Flight attendant," I corrected him. "Have you always been such a slut?"

"Hey now, that's hurtful. I'm just über-friendly. That's all. I can't be held responsible for the animal magnetism I put off."

"Oh, you put off all right, but I'm not sure there's anything magnetic about it."

The two-and-a-half-hour flight to Frankfurt was pleasant and left us in the airport for a two-hour layover before the connecting flight to Riga. I was enjoying the peek at a normal life, even though there's little that's enjoyable about airline travel. At least we weren't cold, and as far as I knew, no one in the airport was going to try to kill us. I'd been wrong about that sort of thing before, but I felt relatively safe in the middle of Germany.

We landed in Riga and picked up the package of cold-weather gear just in time to make it to the marina and catch the boy I'd left in charge of Pierre's boat. Fortunately for me, the Gulf of Riga hadn't yet frozen, and the boat was still moored offshore. The look of disappointment on the boy's face when he realized he couldn't keep the boat was unmistakable.

"I'm sorry to disappoint you by coming back before the big freeze, but I think I can make it up to you."

The boy frowned at me with uncertain curiosity. "Make it up to me?"

The language barrier was a hurdle, but I believed we could overcome it. "How many more days do you think until the Gulf freezes completely?"

He looked out over the water with ice already forming in the shallows. "I know it will be frozen enough to walk to Finland in two weeks."

I surveyed the Gulf. "Two weeks, huh? I'll tell you what. I'm going to give you one hundred American dollars right now, and I'm going to take my boat back to Estonia. If the Gulf freezes over in two weeks, you can keep the money, but if it doesn't, I'm coming back in my boat, and you'll owe me my one hundred dollars, plus one cup of coffee."

The boy thought about my offer. "But what if you can't find me when you come back?"

"Oh, I'm much better at finding people than you are at guessing when the sea will freeze."

The boy stuck out his hand. "It's a bet."

I stuck the money in his gloved hand and thanked him for watching my boat. There was no question that unless a meteor hit, the Gulf would be a solid sheet of ice in two weeks. I'd never see the boy again, and he'd spend the rest of his life thinking he outsmarted a dumb Canadian…American…whatever he thought I was.

I checked in with Skipper, and she immediately apologized for letting Penny get the sat-phone number.

"Don't apologize," I said. "It's perfectly fine. There are times that would've been a terrible idea, but last night I needed to hear her voice. This time, it was a good thing. So, we're headed across the Gulf now. Call Pierre and let him know we're coming. Give him position updates as we get closer, and tell him we need Norikova and the chopper. Oh, and how are you coming along with the maps and plans of the prison?"

She sighed. "I'm thinking about finding myself a new operator. You're too demanding."

"Yes, but I pay a lot better than the other guys."

"We haven't discussed that yet, but you can bet your buns we'll be discussing it when you get home."

"Okay, discussion planned. Now, about those maps."

"You haven't opened the package of cold-weather gear yet, have you?"

"Not yet. Why?"

She huffed. "If you had, you would've found a laptop with a satellite modem. You can download the maps, floorplans of the prison, guard schedules, yard schedule, and all sorts of other goodies we thought you might need."

"You're amazing."

"I thought we agreed on phenomenal."

"You're better than phenomenal."

"I know," she said. "Call me from the island. I'm working on a little surprise I think you'll like. We may have a way to get the three of you into Kazakhstan without using a stolen helicopter. Besides, that chopper would make a nice bonus for Pierre."

"Sounds good to me. I'll call in a couple of hours."

After paying a fisherman to ferry us out to our boat, we were relieved to hear the engines start on the first attempt. Making our way across the Gulf was a miserable experience in the frozen night air, and it ended with us breaking through a thin crust of ice as we entered the marina back on Ruhnu Island.

Headlights flashed from the wall of darkness behind the marina. It was our favorite Frenchman in his Land Rover.

"Welcome back, and *merci* for the helicopter," he said as we thawed out.

I furrowed my brow in confusion. "What do you mean?"

His eyes widened. "Mademoiselle Ginger said when this is all over, the helicopter is for me to keep if I can get it safely back to France. I assured her I could do that, and I would never forget her kindness."

"Oh, sure. We get knocked out, kidnapped, shot at, beaten up, and nearly freeze to death, and Ginger gives away our only trophy."

Pierre laughed. "*C'est la vie.*"

"How's our special guest?" I asked.

"She is hungry, dirty, angry, and generally miserable, but otherwise, she is fine."

"That's just what we'd hoped for, Pierre. I'm sure you'll be sending us a bill."

The man scratched his chin. "Oh, I think the helicopter makes us about even, don't you?"

"Do I want to know what you plan to do with the chopper?"

"Oh, I am going to sell it back to the Finns, of course. They will pay a handsome price to have back their helicopter and not admit to the world that it was stolen. It is a win-win as you say in America. I get paid, and the Finns get to save face and get back their helicopter."

Clark said, "I like your style, Frenchy."

"And I like yours, Monsieur Clark."

Back in the dungeon-esque environs of the church cellar, we were greeted with a barrage of angry threats from Captain Norikova. I tore a bit from a baguette Pierre had sticking from a bag and tossed it to her.

"Your father told us he wasn't interested in any deal, and he didn't care if you lived or died."

"Bullshit!" she hissed. "My father would never say that."

I turned to Clark. "That's what I took away from the conversation. How about you?"

Clark nodded. "Yeah, there's no question about it. He had no interest in negotiating with us for your safe return. In fact, he did everything in his power to see that we left the country quickly and in the most uncomfortable manner possible. He's not a nice guy."

"You did not see my father. You are lying. My father would have killed you before you could make your threats," she roared.

Clark lifted his coat and shirt, revealing the gunshot wound to his side. "Oh, he tried to do that, but let's just say things got a little heated for him after that."

"Yeah, it's safe to say he got screwed more than once the night we saw him."

She began another barrage of insults and threats, but I stepped toward the cage, grabbed her wrist, and yanked her against the bars. "You listen to me. I am the only reason you're still alive. I still have a job to do, and I'm going to damned well do it. I'm taking you back to Russia, and I'm getting your sister out of that prison. You can play nice and come willingly, or I can exercise one of two options. Option one, I can sink you in that soon-to-be-frozen sea out there. Option two, I can knock you out and drag you back to Russia by your hair. The choice is yours."

She narrowed her eyes and glared at me through the bars. "You will never live long enough to regret what you have done to me. I swear to you I will—"

I cut her off. "It sounds like you choose the frozen sea, so let's go."

I reached for Pierre's keys, and she immediately opted for a far more civil tone. "I know you will not kill me. You are American, and you must play by rules."

I pulled out the passport the pilot of the PBY gave me. "I'm not an American. Let's see what I am." I flipped open the ID. "Oh, look at that. I'm an Egyptian. That's convenient. Now, let's go for a little stroll by the sea. What do you say?"

She swallowed hard. "I will go with you to Russia, but—"

"No buts! You will do what I say every time I speak. Anything more or less than that gets you a bullet to the brain. That is, if there's no sea handy. Got it?"

She sat silently, neither agreeing nor arguing. I took that as a concession, but we'd have to wait and see how she behaved.

I spent the next several hours upstairs in the ancient church, poring over schedules, plans, and sketches of the infamous Black Dolphin Prison, and maps of Sol-Iletsk, the city where the prison had existed since the eighteenth century. The town was basic enough with relatively good infrastructure, including maintained roads, parks, and public utilities. The area to the south, toward the Kazakh border fifteen miles away, was barren and would be simple enough to cross with an ATV or light truck. Kazakhstan was definitely the best way into the city. What I couldn't come up with was a way into the prison; there simply were no weaknesses. The inmates were never outside concrete block walls, and when they were allowed to see the sky, it was within high, block-walled courtyards with horizontal fencing well above their heads, and razor wire above that. When the prisoners were moved, they were handcuffed, blindfolded, and marched bent over at the waist so they couldn't resist or learn their way around the interior of the prison. No one could leave unless someone unlocked the four or more doors behind which everyone lived at the Black Dolphin.

* * *

Clark came up to the church where I'd been for hours, and he sat beside me. "What have you come up with?"

I shook my head. "Nothing. I don't know how to get her. There's simply no way to get in or out."

"Mind if I take a look?"

"Of course not. Maybe you'll see something I'm missing."

He studied the plans and maps. "I think you're right. The only way out is in a coffin or a prison transfer."

I slapped him on the back. "That's it! We clearly can't break her out, so we'll get the Russians to drive her out. Where's the satphone?"

He looked confused. "It was in your pocket earlier."

I slapped at my pockets and yelled when Skipper answered. "Put Ginger on!"

"She's sleeping, Chase. What do you need?"

"I need you to wake her up and put her on the phone right now."

Thirty seconds later, Ginger was on the line. "What is it?"

"Get something to write on, and listen closely."

"Okay, go ahead. I'm listening."

"I need you to get me connected to the embassy in Moscow with somebody way down the chain—nobody with the words *deputy* or *chief* in their title. I need an unencrypted line with a mid-level nobody who wants to be a somebody. Can you do that?"

"Yeah, I can do it, but it's going to take a while. There's nobody like that awake in Moscow right now."

"Okay. Set up the call, but don't warn them what's coming."

"Okay, Chase. You got it. But what *is* coming?"

"A little misdirection is all."

"I'll call you back within three hours. Oh, and Chase, whatever you're doing…be careful. There's a beautiful woman here who can't stop talking about a black lab puppy."

Clark and I went to work planning every detail. I'd had enough of running into the fray and hoping everything would work out. It was time to play chess instead of red rover, red rover.

The call came soon after.

"Okay," Skipper said. "It's all set up. The next voice you hear will be Oliver Conner, second assistant to the military attaché. Is that mid-level enough for you?"

"That's perfect. I'll call you back as soon as I bait the trap."

The phone clicked over, and Oliver Conner spoke. "Attaché office, Mr. Conner."

In an intentionally menacing voice, I said, "Conner, listen to me. It's on. We're hitting the Dolphin on Friday at fifteen hundred hours. We're getting your girl out of there, and casualties cannot be avoided. Make sure Burinkova is in her cell no later than fourteen forty-five, and make damned sure your two inside-men are not on shift. Do you understand?"

He stammered and started to ask, "Who is this?" But I'd already disconnected, and the trap had been fully baited.

Chapter 25
Geronimo!

"You're getting good at this spy gig," Clark said.

"I'm not a spy," I replied, trying not to laugh.

"I'm starting to understand why no one believes us when we say that."

"I have to call Skipper back."

I dialed the number and waited. I'll never understand why sat-phone calls take so long to connect.

"How'd it go?"

"Perfect," I said. "Now here's what I need you to do. Monitor the chatter from the embassy about the Black Dolphin, especially the back-channel stuff."

Realizing Skipper may not have fully understood what I was talking about, I asked, "Is Ginger listening?"

"Yeah, Chase. I'm here. We copied everything you said to Conner, and I've already got feelers out. I expect the buzz to kick off in a matter of minutes."

"Great, Ginger. Conner will immediately report the call to his superior, and it'll rocket up the chain until it finds its way outside the embassy. If the Russians buy it, they'll have Anya out of that prison long before fifteen hundred hours on Friday."

"It's brilliant, Chase. There's no way they'll ignore it," she said. "What else do you need?"

"Now we need a ride to Kazakhstan. That's our only way into Sol-Iletsk. As soon as we know when they're moving Anya, we'll know our timetable, but the sooner, the better. I'm going to need a heavy truck, some bigger guns than the guards on the prison transport will have, and a couple of ATVs that aren't afraid of getting wet. I'd like to round up some cavalry so it won't be just Clark and me hitting the transport."

Ginger chuckled. "None of that is a challenge, and there's never been a bugle that could call up the cavalry better than I can. How many do you want?"

"How many can you get?" I asked.

"Just answer my question, and tell me how many you want."

"Yes, ma'am," I said. "I want four knuckle-dragging trigger-pullers who know how to follow orders. Oh, and preferably ones who can at least understand Russian."

"We're on it. We'll be in touch in an hour. In the meantime, get ready to move out."

I hung up, hoping to get some indication of approval or trepidation from Clark. Instead, I got, "This is going to be more fun than Bangkok."

We headed back into the cellar where Norikova was on a cot in the fetal position and Pierre was staring intently at her.

"Is everything all right?" I asked.

"I'm concerned," the Frenchman said. "I don't think she is well."

"I can assure you she's quite unwell in the head."

"No, no. That is not what I mean. She did not eat the baguette you gave her, and she is quickly losing weight."

"That's not our problem," I said. "We just need her to stay alive for three more days, or maybe less. After that, she's Mother Russia's problem."

We inventoried our remaining gear and repacked everything for a hasty departure. Ginger and Skipper would have us in Kazakhstan soon, and then time would really start to fly. I secretly hoped Norikova wasn't well. The worse she felt, the easier she would be to control.

Skipper called at exactly one hour. "There's an abandoned airfield just north of the town of Jelgava. Do you know where that is?"

"I don't even know what country that's in," I said.

I asked Clark, "Have you ever heard of Jelgava?"

He shook his head, but Pierre spoke up. "Certainly. I know Jelgava. It is just southwest of Riga."

"Okay, Pierre knows where it is," I said into the handset.

"Be there at sunrise, and make sure there's nothing on the runway that would ruin the day for the crew of a cargo plane."

"Outstanding," I said. "How about the trigger-pullers and equipment?"

Ginger came on the line. "You can handpick your squad. Clark probably knows some of them. They're all Brinkwater Security guys, and they're just itching to help."

"I'm pretty sure I love you, Ginger."

"Don't say that. There's a tall blonde here who'd kill me in my sleep if she heard you professing your undying love to me."

"Come on, Ginger. I'm not sure I can put much stock in you calling someone tall. Everybody's tall compared to you."

"Oh, is that how it is? Now we're doing little people jokes?"

"No, not at all. I'm just celebrating the fact that you're not short. You're fun-sized."

"I'll show you fun-sized. You just wait."

"Okay, Ginger. I'm sorry. Tell that tall, beautiful woman I love her and I'll be home in a few days."

"I wouldn't be so sure about that coming-home-in-a-few-days business. Your travel agent may not be tall enough to see over the keyboard to book your flight."

I hung up and turned to Pierre. "So, where's this Jelgava?"

"It's about seventy-five miles south of here. We used that airfield for training when I was a legionnaire."

"Can you get us there before daybreak in the chopper?"

"*Oui, monsieur.*"

I didn't speak French, but I knew what a *yes* sounded like.

* * *

That night, we slept as well as possible with one's blood congealing from the cold. An hour before daylight, we lifted off from the Ruhnu airport, in Pierre's new helicopter, and headed out over the Gulf of Riga.

The abandoned airfield came into sight just as the sun was starting to brighten the eastern horizon. There was no question the site had once been a serious airport. Norikova was back in her chains for safekeeping, but we allowed her to change from her Israeli blues into the cold-weather gear Ginger and Skipper provided. When I cuffed her, her skin felt hot to the touch. Pierre may have been right about her condition.

A slow hover taxi down the runway revealed nothing more than snow and dead foliage. We believed a cargo plane could've easily made use of the formerly grand runway.

We landed at the upwind end of the airfield, well clear of the runway, and watched for Brinkwater's finest to descend from the heavens. The long shadows on the pearly white snow shortened as the sun rose higher into the morning sky, and I questioned whether anyone was actually coming.

Clark put his hand on my shoulder. "Don't worry. They may be late, but they'll be here."

Norikova's chains rattled ever-so-slightly, and despite her cold-weather gear, she was shivering on the seat of the helicopter.

Before I realized the words had come out of my mouth, I said, "Are you all right?"

She shook her head. "No. I am badly sick. I have terrible fever."

She's playing a game with you, Chase. Don't get sucked in. She'll make you regret it.

That's what I told myself, but as usual, I didn't listen. I pulled off my glove. "If you move, I'll end your suffering right here, even if I have to clean up the blood. Do you understand?"

She nodded, and I placed the back of my hand against her forehead. She wasn't pretending.

"If I feed you, will you eat?"

She nodded.

"If I give you antibiotics, will you take them?"

Again, a nod.

I rearranged the chains so she could reach her mouth and handed her a canteen of water and a horse-pill antibiotic. She swallowed the pill with a drink of water and motioned the canteen back toward me.

"Keep it," I said. "You'll need it." I handed her crackers with peanut butter smeared on top that I'd scavenged from an MRE.

"*Spasibo*. I am sorry. I mean to say thank you."

"Just don't die," I said, trying to sound harsher than I felt.

"Tallyho!" Clark yelled, and I turned to see a C-130 Hercules rolling out on final approach for the snow-covered runway. The silhouette of the airplane against the morning sun was a welcome sight.

A billowing cloud of snow churned up around the plane as it roared down the runway and came to a stop abeam our position. The rear opened, and a pair of mercenaries in full battle rattle with M-4s strapped across their chests strolled down the ramp.

"Well, I'll be damned if it ain't Baby Face Johnson," said an enormous man as he approached.

Clark grinned and embraced the giant. "Look at you, all dressed up like a real soldier. It's good to see you, Mongo."

Clark turned to me. "Chase, meet Marvin Mongo Malloy. This dude and I jumped into Panama together the first time I went down there."

I stuck out my hand. "Nice to meet you, Mongo."

"Nice to meet you, too, Chase. They told us you had a prisoner. Where is he?"

I pointed toward the chopper. "*She* is chained to the back seat of the four-twelve over there."

"*She*?"

"Yeah, *she*. And she's a lot more dangerous than most *he's* I know. She's an SVR captain."

"Holy shit, man. They didn't tell us that." He glanced toward the helicopter. "Well, I guess it don't matter much. Let's get her on-board."

I unchained Norikova from the helicopter and watched the two commandos march her up the ramp and chain her to a seat near the front of the plane.

I shook Pierre's hand and thanked him for his work.

"I saw what you did back there," he said. "Be careful, young Chase. That soft heart of yours makes a big target."

With that, he climbed aboard his helicopter and disappeared over the treetops.

Clark and I humped our gear up the ramp and sat where we could stretch out for the long ride to Kazakhstan.

In the center of the cargo bay were pallets of tactical gear rigged with parachutes. At the rear of the plane, on pallets all their own, sat a pair of Chenowth Desert Patrol Vehicles, virtually indestructible tactical dune buggies that are commonly referred to as DPVs. There were nine warriors aboard the plane, and each of them looked eerily similar to the others, with full beards, the highest quality gear, and the look of men who understood what it was like to stand in front of an enemy and say, "Not on my watch, you won't."

These guys were the Clark Johnsons of the world. They weren't afraid of wading through hell and would stand in line to take turns trying to kick the devil's ass. My plan to play chess was coming together quite nicely.

Over the noise of the engines, I yelled to Clark. "How many of these guys do you know?"

"Just Mongo, but I'm sure they're all tier-one operators like him."

A tier-one operator is a soldier who is trained to the highest standards, pushed beyond the limits any sane human could survive both mentally and physically, and has proven himself under fire. For Clark to express that measure of faith in these men gave me an excellent feeling about what was to come.

The ramp closed, and the plane began its takeoff roll. I soon felt us leave the ground and heard the landing gear clang into their wells.

"I've never been to Kazakhstan," I said. "Where do you think we'll land?"

Clark pointed to a pallet of parachutes. "Wherever those put us."

With the ramp closed, the interior of the C-130 was much quieter and even had heat. That was a welcome change.

"I'd better go check on Kat," I said, standing from my seat.

Clark grabbed my arm and spun me around. "Look at me. She's not Kat. She's Captain Ekaterina Norikova of the Russian SVR, and she's not remotely our friend. You got me?"

"I got you." I appreciated his willingness to get my mind right when I started to stray.

Norikova was barely conscious and still had a fever. I pulled a med kit from the bulkhead, found Tylenol, and got four pills down her throat. "This should help your fever. Do you want me to take you out of that coat?"

"Thank you, but no. I am very cold."

I turned to head back to my seat, but she stopped me. "Mr. Fulton. Even when you want to be cruel, you are a good man. A weak man can be cruel, but compassion comes from strength. I am not sorry for doing what my country demands of me, but I am sorry for you being hurt in this thing."

I wanted to talk with her. I wanted to know what her life had been like, but I kept hearing Pierre's words ringing in my head: *That soft heart of yours makes a big target.* Without another word, I returned to my seat.

"Is she okay?" Clark asked.

"No, she's burning up with fever. I gave her some Tylenol and antibiotics. Maybe that'll help."

"She's not Anya, Chase. Don't forget that."

For the remainder of the flight, we talked with the operators to get a feel for their individual skillsets. They were all battle-hardened and anxious to do it again. We selected four of them: Snake, Smoke, Singer, and Mongo, the big, retired, Green Beret who looked like he could snap a wing off an airplane. Snake could get into and out of holes and crevasses like no one else. Smoke had turned down a division-one football scholarship as the fastest running back in America, choosing instead to join the Marines, and ended up in Force Recon. He didn't want to talk about why he wasn't a marine anymore, but I didn't care. His speed on foot was more than enough incentive for me to want him on the team. Singer, a scout sniper and devout Southern Baptist, had the voice of an angel and the skill of a surgeon behind a long gun. As for Mongo, well, I wanted him in case I need to tear a tree out of the ground.

My ears popped as we started our descent, and the plane became a beehive of activity. The soldiers who weren't going with us began double-checking the rigging on the parachutes for the gear, while the rest of us strapped on chutes of our own. Clark wore a tandem rig with clips in the front so he could carry Norikova to the ground.

"What is happening?" she said in a weak voice that could have been Anya's if I'd closed my eyes.

Clark held up the nylon harness in front of Norikova. "We're taking you home. You've got two choices. You can ride with me or step out and take your chances without a parachute."

She weakly held her arms away from her body so he could fit the tandem harness on her, and then he walked her toward the back of the plane. "Have you ever done this?"

She tugged at her harness. "Never like this"—she motioned toward the rest of us in our conventional parachute rigs—"but many times like that."

"Well, then," he said. "This should be fun, 'cause it's my first time, too." Clark clipped Norikova's harness to his, and they shuffled toward the edge of the ramp.

The jumpmaster peered out the back of the plane and into the Kazakh wilderness. He turned back and yelled, "Stand clear!"

Three seconds later, the pallet carrying the first DPV slid toward the ramp and disappeared out the back. Immediately, the second DPV was sliding rearward. A pallet containing our gear followed, and then Clark and Norikova stepped off the ramp. The remaining four operators leaning out the back disappeared.

I stepped from the ramp and allowed gravity to draw me from the relative comfort of the cargo plane and into the frigid air. I felt my chute deploy, and I looked up to see a beautifully formed canopy above my head, slowing my descent rate to a survivable speed. Between my feet were three huge canopies above the DPVs and the equipment pallet, and five other parachutes carrying my team toward the Kazakh mountains below.

Chapter 26
Traditions

Clark's oversized parachute slowed his descent, and I soon caught up with them. Soaring through the crisp, early afternoon air, and the sensation of descending to the earth beneath a billowing canopy was one of the most exhilarating and peaceful experiences I'd ever known.

I glanced over to see Norikova's body hanging limply in front of Clark's. His hands were perched above his head, grasping the toggles to control the chute, but hers draped lifelessly. I pointed toward Norikova and then flashed the signal asking if she was okay. He peeked over her shoulder, and then back at me, and turned both palms skyward in the universal I-don't-know signal.

If she was unconscious, the landing could be disastrous for her. Clark would find a way to protect her as much as possible, but he wouldn't sacrifice his safety for hers.

The rugged terrain below was rapidly ascending. The DPVs landed with a cloud of brown sand billowing up in all directions and made an excellent windsock, allowing us to gauge the wind speed and direction accurately. The equipment pallet landed on a downslope and tumbled end over end, tangling the parachute rigging and coming to rest upside down on the edge of a ravine. Mongo was next to land, and he stirred up almost as much dust as the DPVs. Snake and Smoke touched down like ballerinas and gathered their chutes before they hit the ground. I was next, and I turned into the wind to slow both my forward motion as well as my descent rate. Just above the rocky terrain, I pulled the toggles to my knees, causing the outside cells of my ram-air parachute to curl downward, essentially acting as brakes. My landing wasn't as graceful as the others, but I stayed on my feet and managed to wrangle my chute under control before it sent me tumbling down the slope like the equipment pallet. As the chaos of the landing gave way to silence, I thought I heard a choir. I looked up to see Singer drifting to earth, serenading us with his rendition of "Amazing Grace," that to me sounded a lot like "House of the Rising Sun," and that was just wrong. He landed as gracefully as the others and immediately broke into "I'll Fly Away," and that somehow seemed appropriate.

Clark and Norikova were approaching from the northeast with her body still lifeless in front of him. I watched him shake her several times and even reach around and force her head up once. She showed no reaction, and I could see the frustration building on his face. Her height, coupled with the orientation of the harnesses, left Norikova's feet dangling at least a foot below Clark's. Landing like that would fold her legs between his and send both of them careening into the dirt face-first.

Regardless of the outcome, it was going to be an interesting show. The rest of the operators had noticed the predicament as well, and were all looking skyward with great anticipation. Singer bowed his head either to pray or simply to avoid watching the inevitable train wreck that was about to occur.

I watched Clark squirm and twist until both of his legs were pressed firmly behind Norikova's. He flexed his legs twice as practice for what he was about to attempt. A few feet above the rocky, ragged ground, Clark pulled the toggles downward with all of his strength and raised his legs simultaneously. Norikova's legs rode atop Clark's and lifted into the air in front of them. Clark winced as his butt hit the ground, and the two slid across a surface no one wants to slide across.

The cloud of dust they stirred up soon dissipated, and I heard Clark say, "You're really turning into a pain in my ass, lady."

Weak and taken by her fever, Norikova tried to look up. "I am sorry," she said.

"Yeah, well, it's like I tell College Boy. Don't be sorry. Be better."

Singer helped disconnect the harnesses and lifted Norikova to her feet. Snake and Smoke were unstrapping the DPVs from their pallets and stowing the parachutes. Singer stayed with Norikova. In addition to being one of the best long-range snipers on the planet, he'd also been to the combat medic's course at Fort Sam Houston. That made him the logical choice to guard her and keep her alive as long as possible.

The engines of the two DPVs fired up, and Snake and Smoke pulled the combat dune buggies onto a relatively level spot where we could load Norikova. Clark, Singer, Smoke, and Norikova mounted vehicle number one. I climbed in with Snake, and we headed for the overturned equipment pallet. When we arrived, Mongo was bracing off between an enormous rock and the pallet. I had planned to pull the pallet upright with one of the DPVs, but Mongo clearly had the situation under control. He grunted, and I watched as the pallet stood upright and then fell perfectly positioned as if the hand of God had placed it there.

We dismounted the vehicles and loaded our equipment aboard.

"The Russian border is less than ten clicks to the north," Smoke said. "I didn't see any living thing between us and the border on the jump. Did any of you?"

Everyone shook their heads, and we were soon headed north, leaving a huge trail of dust and sand in our wake.

Snake was at the wheel, and Mongo was in the front because he couldn't fit anywhere else. That left the back seat for me. As we descended toward the border, the terrain changed dramatically. The rocky, arid earth gave way to vegetation that I imagined would be lush and green in July. We came to the edge of a slow-moving river, and both vehicles stopped.

"I'm just wondering…"—Snake placed his hand on the dash and turned around—"is this going to be the first illegal Russian border crossing for anyone?"

The Brinkwater team laughed and shook their heads.

Clark scoffed. "This won't even be our first illegal Russian border crossing this week."

Norikova's voice cracked. "It will be first time for me."

Everyone froze in silence, unsure what to make of her involvement in the banter. And then she chuckled.

Smoke shook his finger at her. "Oh, now that's funny, Miss Spy Lady. That's funny."

"You're not going to make her do it, are you?" Singer asked.

"Do what?" Norikova said, her voice still weak.

None of the operators would look at her, but I was just as curious as she was.

Snake chimed in. "You've heard of the navy's shellback ceremony for when a sailor crosses the equator for the first time, right?"

I had heard of the ridiculous antics in the age-old maritime tradition, but I couldn't imagine what that had to do with this.

"Well, it's kinda the same the first time you illegally cross the Russian border. You're supposed to do it with your pants around your ankles."

Uncomfortable laughter rolled across the group, ending in awkward silence, which Clark broke up. "Okay, enough. Let's get across. We've got too much to do to be playing silly games."

We found a shallow spot in the narrow waterway and wasted no time making the crossing. The DPVs were incredibly capable and fast. Snake, Mongo, and I were in the first vehicle across, and we made it without getting wet. We watched the second impressive vehicle bounce across the rocky, shallow stream, and it made it look like a Sunday drive, but Singer had his hands pressed over his eyes, and his face was as red as a fire engine. I had to know what was happening in the back seat of that buggy. We pulled alongside to see Norikova struggling to pull her pants back up.

She locked eyes with me. "I am Russian, and tradition is important to Russian people."

I wanted so badly to hate her, but it was becoming more difficult every day.

The operators—everyone except Singer—found her performance hilarious.

"Okay, now that we're here," I said, "I need to make a phone call." I climbed from the DPV for a little privacy and dialed Skipper.

"Hey, it looks like you made it back to the Mother Land," she said.

"Yeah, we're on the ground. We're six plus one, and the one is pretty sick. She's got a nasty fever."

Skipper showed no sympathy. "Yeah, I'll bet Anya's pretty miserable in that prison, too."

Way to point out the obvious and get my mind straight.

"Okay," she said. "Here's what's happening. Just like you predicted, they bought your ploy, and they're not willing to risk getting her snatched out of the Black Dolphin. They've added extra security around the prison, and they'll be moving Anya tomorrow morning for the ten o'clock train out of Sol-Iletsk. I can't be sure where they're taking her, but that train runs west toward Moscow. Our best guess is that they'll be taking her to another prison where she'll be interrogated about the plan to break her out of the Dolphin."

"I'm sure that's their plan, but it won't be Anya they're interrogating. Did you get us a truck?"

"I did. Well, Ginger did. I had no idea how to procure a truck in a Russian town I've never heard of, but I know how to do it now."

"Excellent. Where, and what is it?"

"It's a two-ton millwright truck with dual rear wheels and four-wheel-drive. It weighs about fifteen thousand pounds. Is that heavy enough?"

"It sounds perfect. Where will I find it?"

"There's a sheep farm one mile east of the town on the south side of the P239. You'll see two large white barns, and you'll find your trucks in the southernmost one. That's also where you'll spend the night."

"You said *trucks*…plural. There's more than one?"

"Yeah, there's another one in the barn that's yours if you need it, but it's a light truck. I can't remember what it's called."

"Whatever did I do to deserve you, Skipper?"

"Oh, don't you worry. You'll be getting my bill as soon as you get home."

"And you'll be getting a big tip if this all plays out like we planned. I'll call you from the barn."

I briefed the team, and we headed northeast, determined to avoid being seen. We couldn't afford a run-in with anyone—especially not the military or local police.

The sheep farm was where Skipper said it was, and the barn was unlocked. The DPVs fit nicely, and there was even a wood stove and several cots. Mongo checked out the truck and declared it to be "close to perfect."

The second truck was a LuAZ 969 M, commonly referred to as the Russian Land Rover. It wasn't pretty, but it certainly looked rugged. I knew what to do with the LuAZ.

We split up into three teams. Clark took Singer in the LuAZ to scout for an overwatch position while I took the rest of the team, minus Mongo, to find the perfect place to hit the prison convoy on its way to the train station. Mongo would stay behind with Norikova. I didn't need that beast of a man stumbling around downtown and sticking out like Goliath at a kiddie park.

Clark found a nice little nest for Singer, high atop an abandoned industrial building with a beautiful view of both the Black Dolphin Prison and the park where we'd hit the transport. Five blocks north of the prison, the *Ulitsa Sovetskaya* met the *Orskaya Ulitsa* in a blind intersection with abandoned buildings on all four corners. The northwest corner was open just enough to allow for the scuffle I needed to pull off my little shell game.

An hour later, we were back in the barn, warming by the wood stove and putting the finishing touches on the plan for the next morning. Singer prayed before we ate and asked God for all sorts of things I never would've been brave enough to ask for out loud, and for some reason, having him on the team made me feel better. I think my father would have liked him. I envied his faith, and I quietly asked God to take care of my team. As much as I wanted to believe we had the skill to pull it off, the coming morning would be the perfect time for a little Divine intervention.

Chapter 27
Tent Revival

Dawn broke with the sun at our backs and everyone in position. Singer was nestled on the rooftop one block northeast of the prison and four blocks south of me. Smoke, who everyone agreed was the best driver on the team, was behind the wheel of the millwright truck one block east of the intersection that would soon be center stage for the wildest show that little town had ever seen. He had the engine running and a folded, inflatable air mattress between his chest and the steering wheel. Staged nearby was the LuAZ, poised to play the most crucial role in the entire mission.

Norikova, who had taken half a dozen Tylenol and antibiotics through the night, was shivering in the corner behind Mongo. She was handcuffed to a pipe that even Mongo couldn't pull from the wall, so I was confident she wouldn't make a break for it. The enormous man knelt with his M4 rifle perched across his thigh, making the weapon look like a child's toy. I was a dozen feet in front of him, nestled behind a stack of empty store shelves, with a clear line of sight down Ulitsa Sovetskaya and to the gates of the Black Dolphin Prison. Snake and Clark were across the street inside an abandoned, one-story building that had, apparently, once been a feed store. There were old bags of rotten livestock feed and fertilizer still scattered about the space.

I anticipated the transport carrying Anya would be no more than two vehicles: one van with heavy steel caging, and possibly an armored escort vehicle with a mounted, large-caliber machine gun. Singer would take care of the machine gunner if it became necessary, but I hoped we could complete the mission without sending bullets through any brains.

The morning was eerily quiet; so much so, that I could hear my own heart beating. That may have been more a function of my energy than of the lack of outside sounds, but either way, I would've much preferred hearing Singer belt out a stanza or two of "The Old Rugged Cross."

In the midst of the silence, while trying to ignore the cadence of my heartbeat, I thought I heard Norikova say my name. I wasn't sure if I'd actually heard her voice or if I was replaying our previous conversation. But she said it again, and this time she wasn't as quiet.

I glanced over my shoulder to see her staring at me. I took another long look down the street and then shuffled my way to her, trying to stay low enough to avoid being seen through the windows of the storefront.

"What is it?" I asked quietly.

"Why are you doing this?"

"What do you mean?"

"Why are you risking your life, and why are these men willing to risk theirs to take my sister to freedom? She is only simple Russian woman."

I didn't have to think about her question. The answer came to me as if it had been imprinted on my brain. "A man who I loved like a father, and who loved me like his son, once loved your mother more deeply than you or I could ever understand. Your sister is the result of that love. That man devoted his life to the pursuit of one single thing: freedom. He couldn't give that gift to your mother, Katerina Burinkova, but I can give it to his daughter on his behalf. I owe that to him, and to Anya, because she was once willing to give her life to save mine."

She cast her eyes to the cold concrete floor and whispered, "I hope to know such love before I die."

My earpiece crackled, and Singer's voice filled my head. "They're out of the sally port. It's a single-vehicle. One hardened van. I see two armed guards plus the driver. He has a sidearm, but no rifle. The prisoner is…"—he paused long enough for me to believe my earpiece had failed—"My God! She's identical to Norikova."

I keyed my mic. "Roger. Call the intersections. Verify you copy, Smoke."

"Smoke copies."

"Roger. Call the crossings," Singer said.

Clark's voice filled my ear. "Two is ready."

In slow, steady succession, Singer called out the cross streets as the van passed each.

"Ural'skaya."

Fifteen seconds…

"Tsvillinga."

Thirteen seconds…

"Volodarskogo."

Fifteen seconds…

"Ordzhohnikidze."

Eleven seconds…

"Kraznoarmeyskaya."

I keyed my mic and ordered, "Roll, Smoke!"

The world slowed as I watched the van carrying Anastasia Burinkova drive away from the most infamous prison on Earth, and toward me. The heavy truck accelerated from the east with Smoke at the wheel, and the two vehicles closed on each other as if drawn together by some invisible alien force. The timing was perfect.

The truck roared by the window in front of me at the same instant the van entered the intersection, and the resulting collision was explosive and chaotic. The rear of the truck left the ground and climbed upward until gravity declared its hold and forced the bed back down. The van spun wildly through two hundred and seventy degrees, rolling onto its side, and becoming twisted and warped almost beyond recognition.

Clark and Snake stormed from the northwest corner with M4 rifles held across their chests and ready to engage any resistance with blinding speed. Smoke leapt from the truck, having been protected by his field-expedient airbag, and thundered toward the van.

"Let's go, Mongo!" I yelled as I thrust the door open in front of me. I'd taken only four strides when Mongo's enormous frame passed me as if I were standing still. The speed of the big man was remarkable.

Snake had a sledgehammer bouncing off the windshield as the driver lay motionless with blood pouring from his skull. Clark rounded the van and approached from the back with his rifle tucked tightly against his shoulder and both eyes recording everything that moved in the intersection. He grabbed the door handle and pulled with all his weight, but it wouldn't surrender.

Clark yelled into his mic. "Blow the door, Singer!"

Half a second later, a fifty-caliber round impacted dead center of the locking mechanism, and the door buckled from the shock of the projectile.

Mongo grabbed what remained of the door and threw it into the street as I leapt into the overturned van. One guard was pinned forward, his head and neck twisted at an impossible angle. The second guard was still alive, but badly injured and completely disoriented. He pointed his radio at me as if it were a pistol, and yelled something I couldn't understand. I landed the heel of my boot beneath his chin and ended his delirious rambling.

And there she was—the woman I'd once loved. Her face, although gaunt from hunger and neglect, was still beautiful and impossible to forget. Long blonde hair fell in tangles against the steel bars of the window, and her hands were cuffed to a steel ring once welded to the floor but now hanging loosely at the end of her chain. Unlike the strong woman I had known a year before, her body was thin, and her skin was drawn and pale, but the beauty she inherited from her mother was still there, still undeniable, and still irresistible.

I threw myself to the twisted pile of metal and felt for her pulse. Her skin was dry and warm, but the blood coursing through my hand, driven so brutally by my pounding heart, made it impossible to distinguish her pulse from mine. I held her face in my hands and placed my ear to her lips, hoping…praying…to hear her breathing. I tried to calm my breathing enough to hear hers, and finally, as if from the lips of an angel, I heard, "My Chasechka. You have come for me."

I forced my arms beneath her body and tried to stand, but she was bound. Her feet were trapped beneath a tangled web of iron that had folded and encased her lower legs in what was nothing less than a bear trap.

I pulled at the railing, grunting and kicking to find purchase on the metal walls of the van. "Mongo!"

The big man climbed over me and buried his hands in the twisted steel. His thick chest filled with a long breath, and the veins in his neck bulged as he cried out like an Olympic weightlifter deadlifting for the world record. The iron creaked and groaned under the strain of his force until I saw daylight between Anya's feet and the bars.

I pulled her legs free and lifted her body into my arms. It may have been the adrenaline that made her body feel so light in my arms, or perhaps she'd been starved to near death in the hell she'd endured behind the walls of that prison, but carrying her seemed to consume none of my strength. I leapt from the van and ran back for the building, where Norikova lay cuffed to the pipe.

I dropped Anya by her sister's side and began pulling her black-and-white prison-issued clothing from her frail body. Terror and shock filled her deep eyes as she stared into the face of the sister she'd never seen and never knew existed. Norikova returned the look of disbelief, even though she had read her sister's file, examined hundreds of photographs, and spent hours trying to perfect her sister's mannerisms. The shock of seeing Anya for the first time shone on her face as if she'd seen a ghost.

Clark came through the door and slid to a stop beside me. "We've got thirty seconds. No more!"

He unlocked the handcuffs from Anya's wrists, and I freed Norikova. The weak and fevered Russian spy began tearing off her clothes and threw them to the ground beside her sister. She took the black-and-white uniform I'd removed from Anya and slid it onto her body. Anya watched with a look of awe and utter disbelief on her face, as her sister, Captain Ekaterina Norikova, held out her hands, awaiting the cuffs that had bound Anya's wrists only seconds before.

I slid the cuffs in place and squeezed them against her skin. She made no effort to resist or run. Instead, she knelt by her sister and stroked her hair with the back of her cuffed hand. "Freedom is yours, my sister. Our mother would have wanted nothing more for you." Norikova leaned toward Anya and kissed her on both cheeks.

She turned to me, and I expected to hear words I would never forget. I thought she would charge me with protecting her sister, or threaten to find and kill me, but the words never came. She bowed her head and began the slow march of the condemned toward the door. Clark caught Norikova's arm and hurried her to the van, and I helped Anya into her sister's clothes.

"It's not over yet," I said. "They'll be coming, but I have a way out. Can you walk?"

She nodded and took my hand. I led her through the back of the building and into the park where the LuAZ idled beneath a statue of Mikhail Gorbachev. I glanced back down the street where Captain Ekaterina Gregorovna Norikova lay inside the mangled remains of the prison transport van. Anya watched as if she were trying to understand the last few minutes of her life—a thousand questions churning through her mind.

"Get in the car!" I said, holding the door for her. She obeyed and slid inside the LuAZ, and I climbed behind the wheel. "Stay down."

I drove one block north to our rendezvous point and then slowed as Snake, Smoke, Clark, and finally, Mongo squeezed into the back of the car. I headed one block east and then turned south where a smiling Singer was running toward me with his rifle slung over his back. As he continued past the car and tried to wedge his way into the back, I heard him singing "When the Roll Is Called up Yonder." In some kind of unavoidable, post-mission euphoria, as if we were at an old-time tent revival, we all sang along. Anya sat in silence, gazing into the first sunrise she'd seen in months, and making no effort to hide the tears falling from her eyes.

* * *

Back at the sheep farm, the elation continued, and Singer examined Anya. He believed that other than malnutrition, some bruises, maybe a broken rib from the crash, and of course the absence of the little toe on her right foot, she was going to be just fine.

I sat with Anya. With a Pelican case at my feet, I handed her a small, tattered, cardboard box.

"These are letters from my mother to my father, yes?"

One by one she pulled the envelopes from the box, holding each of them to her nose, just as she'd done in Dr. Richter's hangar the day that seemed so distant in our past—the day he'd seen his daughter for the first time, and the day she obviously wanted so desperately to relive.

"Your father is dead, Anya. He died of heart failure. But he knew the truth. You are, without question, his daughter, and he is forever your father. Those letters are the story of the love your parents shared, and you are all that remains of that love. You are now free to live the life they both would have died to give you."

She squeezed her lips together in a tight, thin line, and let the tears come. She placed her head on my shoulder, and I wrapped my arms around her. Her golden hair fell across my face, and her trembling hands grasped at my sides.

She finally lifted her head and met my eyes. "I have nothing, my Chasechka. What am I to do?"

I opened the Pelican case and pulled out an envelope. I placed it in her hands and laid her old passport on top.

When she opened the passport, I watched her lips form the name "Ana R. Fulton." She pulled at the flap of the envelope and removed the stacks of Russian and American bills and a black credit card from the Bank of the Caymans with the same name etched on the bottom.

She looked at me questioningly and then back at the items in her hands.

I said, "Your father amassed some money throughout his life, and it's now yours. There's a little over two million dollars in the Cayman account and about a hundred thousand there in cash."

I handed her my holstered Makarov. She placed the money back inside the Pelican case and slid the pistol inside her waistband.

"The money is yours, Anya. The pistol is yours. And the car is yours. The Kazakh border is fifteen miles south, and freedom is now yours."

She took my hands in hers. "But you are not mine. You are now for someone else. Someone who is not spy, yes?"

I sighed. "That's right."

"I am no more Anya," she said. "I am Ana. I have American passport. Would you like to see?"

I hugged her and brushed her hair behind her ear for the last time. "I wish it hadn't all been a lie."

She closed her eyes and placed her hand on my chest. "I lied to you about many things, my Chasechka, but never when I said I loved you."

Chapter 28
Chase Fulton?

Perhaps I should've anticipated a yearning to have Anya back in my arms, back aboard my boat, back in my bed, but those feelings never came. Perhaps I should've felt some measure of guilt for delivering Ekaterina Norikova into the hands of the Russian Prison system in Anya's place, but that guilt also never came.

What did come was a newfound respect for a group of men who fought alongside me to accomplish a mission that wasn't theirs. They followed me as if I were Spartacus or John Wayne. They were brave men, honorable men who believed in freedom in every form. I paid them well, but financial rewards were not the things that fueled men of such valor and spirit. Belief in freedom and liberty is the force behind the fearlessness of such men. I envied their experience and courage, and I would forever treasure the newfound friendships and camaraderie we'd formed.

That's not all I felt. I ached to hold Penny Thomas in my arms and feel her body against mine. I longed to feel the sense of home that she brought to my life, and I prayed I'd learn to be the kind of man she deserved. And perhaps most of all, I wanted something I'd never truly known: I wanted to experience "normal." Maybe it was a house that didn't float, a picket fence, and a boy and a girl and a black lab. Maybe I'd go back to school, and maybe I'd teach psychology to twenty-year-olds who thought they knew how the world worked. Maybe for me there would never be normal.

We landed at Dover Air Force Base in Delaware and stepped off the plane. The cold north wind stung like a thousand bees, but the flag flying above the passenger services terminal wasn't discouraged. She snapped and waved as she had for over two hundred years, and I thought I could almost hear her whispering, "Thank you," as if she were expressing her gratitude for the men and women who served beneath her, making the necessary sacrifices to keep her flying, and occasionally adding stars. I was proud to walk and serve beneath that flag, and I was proud to do so at the side of Clark Johnson, the bravest warrior I would ever know.

I paid Clark before we parted because I doubted the people for whom we worked would be writing him a check for the mission. In fact, I suspected both he and I would have a great many questions to answer in the near future—possibly even in front of Congress. I was confident that our answers to those questions would be nearly identical. Although our backgrounds were quite different, inside our chests beat the same heart that pounded in the chests of the men who threw a few tons of tea into Boston Harbor and dared the British to stop them. The same heart that beat inside the men who charged up San Juan Hill with Roosevelt in the name of freedom. The same heart that beat inside every man and woman who had ever stood in the face of tyranny and were willing to give their last drop of blood defending their home and the home of those they loved. We weren't elite; we were just chosen to guard the gates and give freedom a place to pour itself out on anyone who wanted it… anyone who needed it. And underneath everything else, there may be nothing any of us needs more than our freedom.

* * *

It was November seventh when I walked back onto the floating dock at the marina on the Matanzas River in historic St. Augustine, Florida. The warm, subtropical breeze blew from the southwest and tasted like salt and home. The sun smiled down, dancing off the rippling water, and seagulls cried overhead. A calico cat raced down the dock beside me in pursuit of a lizard scurrying across the boards. I secretly rooted for the lizard, although I knew the cat had to eat. The eleven-week-old black lab puppy in my arms turned into a twisting, squirming tornado and leapt to the dock in an instinctual pursuit of both the cat and lizard, but he had no idea why.

The chase ended with the lizard diving into the river in a desperate, last-ditch effort to save his hide. It worked, only because the cat hated the thought of getting wet worse than he hated being hungry. The clumsy, lumbering puppy had no clue the chase was over and plowed into the cat with a galloping thud that sent the cat tumbling awkwardly into the river with the lizard. For a second, I thought the dog was going to do what black labs had done for generations: dive into the water and retrieve his prize—a sopping wet cat. But fate intervened, and the most beautiful woman I'd ever seen stepped from the stern of my boat and reached down for the frolicking puppy, who was all too happy to jump into her arms and lick every inch of her exposed skin. Interestingly, I had the same desire.

With the exuberant lab in her arms, Penny ran to me, her bare feet slapping at the dock, and tears streaming from her flawless eyes.

"Oh, Chase. He's perfect. I love him, and I love you. I'm so glad you're home."

I held her in my arms and kissed her until the puppy almost licked both of us to death. I stepped back and took in every beautiful inch of the woman who was my home and who deserved more than I could ever be. I got down on one knee and took her hand in mine. "Penny Thomas—"

"Chase Fulton?"

A resounding, baritone voice full of authority rang out from behind me. I could feel the pounding of the approaching footsteps on the dock sending waves of dread through the trembling knee on which I knelt in front of the woman I loved.

"Chase Fulton, you're under arrest for the murder of Salvatore D'Angelo."

About the Author

Cap Daniels

Cap Daniels is a former sailing charter captain, scuba and sailing instructor, pilot, Air Force combat veteran, and civil servant of the U.S. Department of Defense. Raised far from the ocean in rural East Tennessee, his early infatuation with salt water was sparked by the fascinating, and sometimes true, sea stories told by his father, a retired Navy Chief Petty Officer. Those stories of adventure on the high seas sent Cap in search of adventure of his own, which eventually landed him on Florida's Gulf Coast where he spends as much time as possible on, in, and under the waters of the Emerald Coast.

With a headful of larger-than-life characters and their thrilling exploits, Cap pours his love of adventure and passion for the ocean onto the pages of The Chase Fulton Novels series.

Visit www.CapDaniels.com to join the mailing list to receive newsletter and release updates.

Connect with Cap Daniels

Facebook: www.Facebook.com/WriterCapDaniels
Instagram: https://www.instagram.com/authorcapdaniels/
BookBub: https://www.bookbub.com/profile/cap-daniels

Made in the USA
Coppell, TX
28 February 2024

29555110R00142